More Than Friends

A Novel

DENISE HUNTER

THOMAS NELSON
Since 1798

More Than Friends

Published in Nashville, Tennessee, by Thomas Nelson. Thomas Nelson is a registered trademark of HarperCollins Christian Publishing, Inc.

Thomas Nelson titles may be purchased in bulk for educational, business, fundraising, or sales promotional use. For information, please e-mail SpecialMarkets@ThomasNelson.com.

HarperCollins Publishers, Macken House, 39/40 Mayor Street Upper, Dublin 1, D01 C9W8, Ireland (https://www.harpercollins.com)

ISBN 978-1-4003-4875-6 (epub)
ISBN 978-1-4003-4874-9 (HC)
ISBN 978-1-4003-4873-2 (TP)
ISBN 978-1-4003-4876-3 (audio download)

Library of Congress Cataloging-in-Publication Data

Printed in the United States of America

26 27 28 29 30 LBC 5 4 3 2 1

Chapter 1

When Jenna Greene's boyfriend got down on bended knee in the middle of their favorite upscale restaurant, she frowned in confusion. "*Jason* . . ." Wow, so many ways to finish that sentence.

Didn't we talk about this?

Please don't do this.

Everyone is watching.

Because yes, as luck would have it, every table at The Bradley was full. The ambient noise of muted chatter and clanking silverware was outdone only by Frank Sinatra, who crooned "Fly Me to the Moon." Which incidentally sounded like a lovely idea right now.

The clamor hushed as their audience caught on to the moment. Jason gazed up at Jenna, his hazel eyes gleaming behind clear-framed glasses. "Jenna, when you first walked in the door at Fleming Orthodontics I knew you were the one—and not just for the office position."

Jenna's heart threatened to burst from her chest. As he continued talking, her thoughts spun like a top. She should've seen this coming! It was the second anniversary of their first date. It was Valentine's Day. And hadn't he just brought up marriage (again) last week?

But why was he proposing when she'd told him (again) she wasn't ready for that? Well, maybe not *told*, but certainly intimated! She was in no hurry. She was only twenty-seven. They had the rest of their lives to take the next step.

Jason continued regaling her with what she could only assume were romantic sentiments. Her smile felt plastic as her gaze darted around the room. Yep, every eye was locked on them, hopeful anticipation animating each face. Women were practically swooning over the grand gesture. Jenna was practically swooning too, if you went by the literal definition.

She put her fingers to her spinning head. She *had* to say yes, didn't she? It was pretty much a prerequisite of a public proposal. Besides which, friends of his family were likely present. Alexandria, Virginia, wasn't exactly a metropolis, and the Flemings were well-known since his mother was the mayor.

If Jenna said no, word would spread quickly and Jason would be humiliated. His family would hate her. There would be no way for him to save face if she rejected him so publicly.

Maybe that was the whole point.

She shook away the unproductive thought as the rich scent of hot fudge wafted to her nose. The double-chocolate brownie now sat in her stomach like a lead brick. Her cloth dinner napkin slipped from the table, and the room was so quiet she actually heard it hit the wooden floor.

Then Jason reached into his pocket and produced a ring: a shiny gold band set with a flashy oval diamond. So very lovely—if not exactly her style. But what did one expect when one avoided ring shopping with one's boyfriend?

He bought a ring.

She definitely had to say yes. Then once they were alone, she'd gently walk back her answer. It was the kind thing to do—wasn't it?

Or maybe she'd just go along with it. Sure, she'd wanted to wait awhile longer. Till she was ready. But she loved Jason. And it *had* been two years. Maybe she should just bite the bullet.

She winced at the unromantic thought. But really, she did love the guy. He was a kind man. Great with kids. Handsome in that John Krasinski way. She loved everything about him. Except that he rooted for the Nationals. And, okay, the way he didn't quite *hear* her sometimes. (Case in point.) Also, that teensy problem with his holding grudges. But nobody was perfect!

So she would say yes. Maybe she wouldn't even take it back later. Or maybe she would. She'd have to postpone that decision because Jason was taking a breath, the anticipated question hovering on his lips, and there was nothing she could do to stop it.

"Jenna Mae Greene . . . will you marry me?" Jason's sparkling eyes cheered her on. His lips curved in that about-to-win smirk she saw regularly just before his final checkmate.

It was her turn to talk. But the abrupt silence was like a black hole. A vacuum sucking every thought from her head. Literally everything she'd been thinking . . . gone. Lost. Vanished.

Say something!

How about yes!

Just say yes!

She opened her mouth. But her thick tongue was cemented to the roof of her mouth.

Jason gave a nervous chuckle. "Jenna?"

"I—" she croaked. Then her throat constricted as if she'd suddenly developed a severe allergy to chocolate—or to sudden, unwanted proposals.

Say yes, dummy! Then joy would transform his expression, and he'd slip that ring on her finger and kiss her like she'd just made him the happiest man alive. The entire restaurant would explode with approval, the server would offer their best bottle of champagne, and they would toast to the rest of their lives.

But.

A yes would also be the biggest, meanest lie she ever told. Because the cold fingers of dread clamping around her heart told her everything she needed to know.

"Jenna . . . ?" His eyes searched hers, the sparkle extinguishing even as the smile wilted from his lips.

Robbed of her ability to speak, she gave her head a miniscule shake.

His neck mottled with color as his eyes turned hard. Harder than she'd ever seen them. "Are you serious right now?" he whispered. Or maybe it was a hiss.

She opened her mouth, then closed it.

His nostrils flared and a shadow flickered in his jaw as it clenched.

The jewelry box's loud, sharp *snap* made her jump.

He shot to his feet, dug out his wallet, and flung some bills onto the table. Without another glance he strode away from her and disappeared around the corner.

She had to go after him. Explain. Comfort him.

The room had somehow gotten even quieter, all eyeballs fixed on her like hot lasers. The palpable hatred spurred her into action.

She stood and grabbed her purse from the chair, but it caught. Her hands trembled as she freed it. Then she followed in Jason's wake, not quite impervious to the glares aimed her way.

When she exited the restaurant she spotted him under a streetlight, heading toward his car. "Jason!" Oh, sure, now her voice worked. "Jason, wait." She quickened her steps, wobbly in her four-inch heels.

He slowed but only because he neared his car. The lights flashed as he unlocked the door with his key fob.

She caught up to him as he reached for the handle. "Please, Jason, let's go somewhere and talk."

"Oh, now you want to talk."

The scene in the restaurant flashed in her brain and she winced. "I'm so sorry. I meant to say yes."

"You *meant* to say yes? What's that supposed to mean?"

She grimaced. "Well, what did you expect? You caught me off guard. You put me on the spot. We just talked about this. You knew I wasn't ready."

He waved away her words. "You always say that."

"Because that's how I feel! I like things the way they are. Why did you have to do that—ask me like that in front of everyone?"

"I thought you could use a little push."

A little *push*? As if she were a child who didn't know her own mind? "What I could *use* is a little more time."

He gave a bitter laugh. "It's been two years, Jenna. How much time do you need?" His frosty gaze never left her as he shook his head, the moment lengthening. "What was I thinking? You'll never settle down."

That wasn't true. Was it? "You're wrong."

"Really? You're twenty-seven, and this isn't exactly your first serious relationship. In case you haven't noticed, they all seem to end the same way—just like this one."

End? This one? Her chest tightened as she took his hand. "Jason. Come on. Just because I don't want to get married today doesn't mean I don't want to be with you. I love you. I see a future with you. This doesn't have to change anything."

His expression tightened as he withdrew his hand. "It changes everything. I'm not wasting any more time with someone who's not interested in a commitment."

"I am committed to you!"

"I want marriage, Jenna. And kids. I'm tired of waiting around for you to be *ready*." He sneered the word.

He was breaking up with her? But things had been fine! Why did he have to go and ruin everything?

A shiver swept over her. The sleeveless dress was no match for the February chill, and she'd left her wrap inside—where it would stay because no way was she going back in there.

"And thank you for the public humiliation. That was a real treat. I'm sure you can manage an Uber." He reached for the handle and yanked open the door.

She jumped from harm's way. He was leaving her here? She tried to process his atypical behavior even while her head swam with tonight's chain of events.

He turned just before he slipped into the car and aimed an icy stare her way. "Oh, and you're fired."

With that his door shut, then he started the car and pulled from the curb, leaving her alone on the sidewalk.

Chapter 2

Almost three months later

The unread email sat at the top of Jenna's inbox like a beacon of hope. She perched on a barstool at her kitchen island, forgetting her intention to make lunch, and homed in on the subject: *Office Manager Position*. The line didn't divulge the answer she sought.

She'd been waiting almost a week for this response. The owners of Renew Physical Therapy were new to town, so they didn't know Mayor Fleming and certainly hadn't heard about Jason's untimely proposal back in February. Nor did they know Jenna had become persona non grata citywide. In fact, she'd hit it off with the husband-and-wife owners and had been waiting breathlessly for this very email.

Her fingers hovered over her laptop's tracking pad.

Jenna's BA in business qualified her for many positions, and she'd applied at a variety of local places, including the offices of a CPA, a chiropractor, a dentist, a veterinarian, you name it. But with her recent, ahem, notoriety she'd struggled to land interviews, even though most positions would've been a pay cut. But hey, beggars and choosers.

She'd garnered only three interviews but hadn't been called back or hired. And she knew exactly why: good ol' Jason. She hadn't listed him as a reference, but as her most recent employer, they'd probably contacted him anyway. And she highly doubted he'd had anything positive to say. He'd fired her after all. For rejecting his proposal.

She could sue him for wrongful termination, but to what end? She couldn't work in his office anymore and she'd probably done enough damage to his heart.

She pushed away the disturbing thought and stared at the new email. She felt good about this. That terrific interview, their connection over their love for the Braves. They even shared the same alma mater. *I mean, come on!* Bolstered, she clicked on the email.

Dear Ms. Greene,

Thank you for interviewing for the office manager position at Renew. We appreciate your interest in joining our company, and we're pleased that you invested time and effort in applying for one of our positions. Unfortunately, we've decided to move forward with another candidate for this position . . .

A weight sank like an anchor in her stomach. The letter went on but she couldn't bear to read another word. She practically had these form letters memorized anyway. Unable to see those words on her screen for another second, she closed the laptop.

This company had truly been her best shot. If anything, she'd been overqualified even though she'd only held two professional jobs. She'd gotten an internship at Dolman Wellness during her senior year, which had led to her first grown-up job. When the place went belly-up three years later, she'd gotten the office manager position at Fleming.

She'd have to go back to the drawing board. Put in more applications. She was all right financially. She had Grandma's trust fund she could fall back on, though she'd hate to use that money on bills. She wanted to utilize it for something special. Perhaps to start her own business.

Her phone buzzed in her pocket and a quick peek at the screen made her smile. Tyson Parker beamed from an old photo she'd taken at his graduation from the fire academy. They'd grown up across the street from each other, and his large, rowdy family had become like her own. Though she'd always been closest to Tyson since he was her age. She accepted the call. "Told ya you should've worn your lucky hat."

"Again, Greene, that only works on home games."

Because yes, the Braves had lost last night to the Giants in a 9–8 heartbreaker. "It can't hurt though, right? I mean, you could at least do your part."

"I was on a call anyway. I missed the last inning."

The mention of his volunteer position made worry tug at her stomach. She tried not to think about her best friend's dangerous role. "Anything serious?"

"Just Mrs. Ledbetter and her smoke alarms—also her cat. I swear that woman will be the death of us all."

Despite his irritation, warmth filled Jenna at the thought of her community on Chincoteague, a barrier island along the coast of Virginia. She'd been blessed to grow up in a place where neighbors looked out for one another. "And how is little Luna?"

"She's a menace, that's what. But she's safe for the time being. How's the job hunting?"

"Less successful than your rescue mission, I'm afraid. I just got a rejection from that interview I thought went so well."

"Oh, man. I'm sorry. You'll find something soon."

"Hope so. It's getting a little discouraging."

"It's just a matter of time. You'll see. You've got a lot to offer. I'll bet it's your idiot boyfriend's fault."

"Ex-boyfriend."

"Maybe I should come up there and give him a little talking-to."

His tone made it clear the convincing wouldn't be verbal. It reminded her fondly of the time he'd slugged Robbie Brown for slapping her on the butt when they were fourteen. They'd both served detention for their actions. "Appreciate the thought, but I really don't want to have to bail you out of jail."

"It would make my day. Have you heard from him?"

"Not a single word. And I don't care to, honestly." It was pretty horrible what he'd done. And his departure had relieved her of a pressure she hadn't realized she'd been feeling while they were together. "I should probably thank him for ending things. He wasn't right for me."

"You're definitely better off without him."

She didn't even miss him that much. And what did that say about their relationship? She glanced at the email on the screen. Her primary feeling right now was frustration that he was likely blockading her employment opportunities. "Maybe I should extend my job search to DC." Alexandria was a suburb of the city, after all.

"You've never been one for big cities. And there's the infamous traffic."

"Fair point. I guess I could put out some feelers back home." She'd only ended up in Alexandria because of job opportunities, and those seem to have dried up. Along with most of her friendships, which seemed to have gone with Jason in the split.

"Now there's an idea I could get behind. I'll keep my ear to the ground and let you know if I hear of anything."

"Thanks. How's your family? I saw the king suite renovation on Instagram. It turned out great." Once their three boys had left the nest, the Parkers turned their large home into a bed-and-breakfast. Tyson worked there full-time when he wasn't volunteering for the Chincoteague Fire Company.

"Thanks. I'm glad to have it done in time for summer. Hey, uh, have you talked to your mom since she returned from the cruise?"

"No, but she checked in via Messenger a couple times from the Caribbean. Seemed to be having a great time. Did she come back with a nice tan?"

"Um, yeah . . . but that's not all she came back with. I was over there mowing this morning when she got home. I didn't think she was returning till tomorrow. A man was with her—and he had a suitcase."

"*What?* What man? Who was he?"

"Someone she met on the cruise, apparently. Gordon Smith? Does that ring a bell?"

"No . . ." A thread of anxiety wormed through her. "She's only known him for a matter of days and he's staying overnight? Are you sure?" That didn't sound like her mom.

"She didn't say so directly, but he was unloading his suitcase and hers, and they seemed kind of chummy."

"Oh no." Though Jenna's wonderful dad had passed when she was twelve, her mom hadn't started dating until Jenna left for college. And only then had she discovered just how naive her mom was where men and dating were concerned.

"Thought you might want to know."

"Yeah, thanks." The thought of some strange man staying there tonight alone with her mother—what could she be thinking? A quick call would answer some questions, but her mom was independent and—as Jenna had found out the hard way—not too fond of her daughter's interference. "I should come home for the weekend."

"I was hoping you'd say that." His tone was heavy with relief. "She'd be glad to see you. I'm more than happy to check in on her, but it might be best if she wasn't alone tonight."

"I could just say I was depressed about my job situation"—hardly a lie—"and I am missing her."

"There you go. He's probably just spending the night on his way home or something."

Way too risky for Jenna's liking. "Thanks again for the heads-up. I'll give my mom a call, pack a few things, and be there by suppertime."

Chapter 3

The wild ponies grunted as Tyson and his best friend, Luke, coaxed them toward the horse trailer. Two rangers from US Fish & Wildlife assisted them in the rescue.

Riptide, a chestnut stallion, reared, kicking up dust. He was wild and beautiful with a flaxen mane, a white blaze, and four white boots. He was also among the most spirited of the 150 feral ponies living on Virginia's barrier island Assateague, a wildlife refuge.

Bridge traffic was blocked and the line of cars extended as far as the eye could see. The bridge to Assateague was well traveled during the warmer months. Tourists crossed the channel to see the wild ponies grazing on marsh grass. But today they'd ended up getting quite the show.

Ten minutes later the sun was low in the sky when the men ushered the stallion into the trailer. The mare, Summer, followed docilely. Tyson shut the trailer doors and turned to the rangers. "How'd they get loose?" The ponies had managed to get clear across the long bridge connecting the barrier islands—a feat that had happened only twice before to Tyson's knowledge.

"Best we could tell, some tourists accidentally blocked their escape route. Me and Greg chased 'em on foot half a mile and across the bridge. Thankfully they found some nice grass here and stopped for a spell, or they might've been halfway to the mainland by now."

Or been tragically hit by a car. The rangers had set up a portable corral to contain the ponies until members of the volunteer fire company could come get them. Though the US government owned Assateague Island, the Virginian herd was tended by the Chincoteague Fire Company, who leased grazing rights from them.

"Thanks for your help." Luke's wavy hair gleamed copper under the late-afternoon sunlight, contrasting with his pale blue eyes.

Tyson gave a nod. "We'll get them back home."

Once the pair returned to the truck, Tyson started it and turned toward the bridge, careful of his load. People waved and honked their horns, no doubt grateful for both the show and its end. "We'll need to find the break in the fence and fix it. Otherwise we'll be doing this all over again."

"Sure didn't expect all this when I rolled out of bed this morning."

"Riptide likes to keep the grapevine buzzing. Today's little jaunt will be one for the record books."

"He's a pistol, that one."

Luke had been Tyson's best friend since high school, and they'd also graduated from the academy together. Though Tyson was a fourth-generation firefighter, Luke was the first in his family to join the company. He was a hard worker and had earned the respect of their fellow firefighters.

The bridge to Assateague was empty of cars, the traffic having been blocked on the other side as well. Though they were barely into May, the season was getting underway. His home island of Chincoteague was only ten square miles and home to about three thousand residents. But that number swelled during the summer, culminating in as many as forty thousand in late July for the Pony Penning Days, all coordinated by the volunteer fire company.

Luke adjusted the air-conditioning. "How's that other matter going?"

"What matter?"

"Come on, Ty. Maybe I haven't been through it yet, but it has to be hard, losing someone."

The image of that seventeen-year-old kid, brown eyes full of fear, flashed in his head for the millionth time. He shook it away. "Part of the job."

"Sure it is. But that doesn't make it easy."

Tyson didn't want to talk about the incident from four weeks ago, a car accident—vehicle versus tree. He'd give anything to go back and do things differently.

"You've hardly missed a call since then."

"I don't have a wife and kid like most of the others." And Ty just wanted to erase that night from his memory.

"It wasn't your fault, man."

He gripped the steering wheel. "I know that."

"We've been friends a long time. I can tell it's eating at you."

"Don't want to talk about it." He felt Luke's eyes on him.

"Maybe not, but you shouldn't let it fester."

It wasn't festering. Okay, maybe it was. But at least he'd learned something valuable from that terrible night. He'd been burning the candle at both ends since his divorce last fall. Dating had become an Olympic sport, and he made the mistake of getting tangled up with Marissa Moran, one of the two paramedics who operated out of the firehouse.

Stupid.

His idea of casual and hers hadn't been the same apparently. The dustup had created tension at the station, and there wasn't a single volunteer unaware of it.

"At least Marissa seems to have settled down," Luke said. "Not that she had any right to get up in your face like that."

"Maybe I wasn't clear enough with her."

"You'd only been on two dates, for crying out loud. And everyone on the island knows you've been sowing your wild oats the past six months."

Tyson rolled his eyes. A bit of an exaggeration. But yeah, the divorce had made him a little unstable. He could see that now. He'd been on a mission of some kind. But that was over now. He'd learned his lesson.

"Trinity Evans was eyeing you the other night at Chatties," Luke said. "She broke up with her boyfriend a while back. You should ask her out."

Trinity was the sweetest server at the seafood restaurant. "Why don't you ask her out? Seems more your type." Plus, he was pretty sure Luke had a good crush going.

"Beautiful and brunette?" A mottled flush—curse of the redheads, Luke called it—worked its way up from the collar of his tee.

"Sweet and smart. Bet she'd say yes."

"Aw, she was looking at you, not me."

"I don't think so. Anyway, I'm officially on a dating moratorium, and I'm sure she'd warm up to you if you could squeeze two words past those lovelorn lips of yours."

"Dating moratorium? Since when?"

"Since now." Tyson had sought distraction after the divorce and he'd gotten one. Or twenty. Time to focus on other things. Like his work at The Sand and Saddle, his parents' bed-and-breakfast. Now that summer was gearing up, the place was starting to fill up again.

More tourists on the island meant more calls. Scooter accidents, water rescues, runaway campfires. Then in late July, Pony Penning Days.

There'd be plenty to keep his mind off the divorce he'd never wanted.

For now he just had to get these ponies back to the refuge. Once they were settled with their band, he and Luke would repair the fence, then Ty would go check on Jenna. She'd surely arrived at her mom's by now—and who knew how that would turn out?

Chapter 4

As Jenna crossed the causeway separating the mainland from Chincoteague Island, the familiar sight of sea and salt marshes spread out like a welcome mat. The last of the day's sun sparkled on the sound.

Home.

Peace stirred inside and a warm healing response spread through her limbs, relaxing muscles that held three months of tension. It wasn't easy being spurned by half of one's city. She was relieved to escape Alexandria for the weekend.

She breathed in the present and exhaled the past. Sure, she still had her mom's situation ahead of her. But she was home. This was a place where she was known and loved. A place where family and tradition flowed like lifeblood through the community. She'd come to help her mother, but Jenna needed this island. She hadn't realized how much until now.

She'd left the island with big dreams. She wanted an education and a career. She wanted to experience new things—things that couldn't be found on the small island where she'd grown up.

The scholarship to Georgetown had been her ticket to the future. Leaving the island—everything and everyone she knew—hadn't been easy. It also felt as if she was leaving her dad behind. And that might've been the hardest thing of all. But she persevered with the knowledge that he would've been so proud of her for having the courage to step out on her own.

She eventually made it through four years of college. After that her goal was to build her résumé and eventually open her own business—once she discovered her passion.

She should've known after her internship that the medical world wasn't her thing. But she'd lost the job suddenly and felt anxious about being without work. The job at Fleming had been kind of a rebound position.

But then she became involved with Jason, and she'd let the relationship distract her from her goals. Why else would she have stayed so long in a field that didn't excite her?

Summer traffic had arrived early on the island, so she took a few shortcuts to reach her mom's house. Everything along Ridge Road was the same as when she'd visited in January, except summer had driven away winter's cold breath.

The sweetgum and sassafras trees were cheerful green, and beach roses and goldenrod brightened the landscape. The smell of freshly mown grass traveled through her air vents, reminding her of sweaty summers playing football and tag in Tyson's spacious backyard.

She spotted the Mitchells' seashell stand by the side of the road and the Davises' split-rail fence that she and the Parker boys used to jump when they accessed the Wallaces' swimming pool.

And there was her childhood home on the left, its short drive shaded by towering loblolly pines. The butter-yellow Cape Cod sported blue shutters, a welcoming porch, and a matching detached garage, which was too full of boxed-up memories to house an actual car.

Seashell bits popped under her tires as she pulled into the drive. Moments later she exited her Camry and drew in a deep breath of sea and salt before she opened the rear door to grab her bag.

The familiar slap of the screen door preceded her mother's voice. "Jenna! What a nice surprise."

Jenna hip-checked the car door and watched her petite fifty-three-year-old mom rush toward her. Her fresh Caribbean tan set off pale blue eyes, and her dishwater-blonde hair gleamed in the waning sunlight. Everyone said Mom was a dead ringer for Cameron Diaz, and they weren't wrong.

Alas, Jenna, with her chestnut hair and brown eyes, had taken after her father in appearance. "Didn't you get my message? I left a voicemail and texted you." Jenna's five-foot-seven-inch frame seemed to swallow her mom as they hugged.

"My phone's been charging all afternoon, and I've been so busy I haven't thought twice about it. But I'm so happy to see you. What brings you home?"

"Just thought I'd get away for the weekend. You know."

Mom pulled back and palmed Jenna's cheek, her eyes softening. "Oh, honey. Of course. You've had such a rough time of it, haven't you? You need your home and your mama. I'll take good care of you this weekend. Some home cooking and TLC is just what the doctor ordered."

"You just got home yourself. You must be tired from all that traveling."

"I'm always ready to take care of my baby girl. And your timing couldn't be better. There's someone I want you to—"

"Dee, honey, I can't seem to figure out your washer." At the sight of them, the older man came to a dead stop on the porch. His headful of gray hair was tousled, but somehow neither that nor his weathered skin detracted from his appearance. A pair of khaki shorts hung almost to his knees and a navy tee showed off a lean torso. Jenna put him around sixty.

"Gordon, come meet my daughter. She's staying for the weekend."

He offered Jenna a friendly smile as he took the porch steps, his blue eyes twinkling. "Well, how wonderful. I'm pleased to meet you, Jenna. I've heard so much about you."

That made one of them. She offered a smile as they shook hands. "Hi there."

"I have so much to tell you," Mom said. "But let's get out of the heat. I can only offer water since we haven't made it to the grocery store yet."

We?

Jenna's mind whirled as Mom ushered her into the house. Sure didn't sound as if the man was only here for a night.

"Let me take your bag." Before Jenna could protest, Gordon took the bag and headed straight up the stairs like a man already familiar with the layout. And quite at home.

Mom got Jenna a water bottle from the pantry, then she and Jenna sat at the kitchen table. "You must be wondering what in the world's going on. Gordon and I met day one of the cruise as the girls and I were checking in. They asked for my passport, and I couldn't find the silly thing! I checked my purse, my pockets. I was getting pretty frantic, wondering if I'd lost it along the way or in that big warehouse they herded us through. Then this fine-looking gentleman appeared with my passport in hand. Turns out he found it on the ground and recognized my picture. He brought it right over and saved the day!"

Jenna manufactured a smile. "Well, isn't that something."

"It was meant to be. He hung out with us the rest of the cruise—

can you believe he came by himself? Shore excursions, beach bumming, mealtimes . . . we had the best fun! Pam and Ellen just adore him."

"Wow, Mom. You didn't say anything in your messages."

"It was too much to write with the little bit of internet we had. Besides, I figured I'd just tell you when we got home."

We.

Jenna wanted to say more. A lot more. She had plenty of questions. But the sound of footsteps on the stairs held her tongue.

Chapter 5

Jenna consulted the grocery list as she pushed the buggy through the produce section of Island Foods. *Bananas?* Her mom hated bananas. She stopped by the fruit stand and picked up a bunch.

Five bananas. Would Gordon be staying long enough to eat a whole bunch of bananas? The niggle of discomfort told her she already knew the answer. But she pushed the thought from her head and wheeled on. She had to get Mom alone tonight and ask some questions.

Jenna worked quickly through the produce and meat sections, moving on to the interior of the store, where she picked up bread, pasta, and cereal. She was looking for the oatmeal her mom preferred when she heard a familiar voice.

"Jenna Greene, is that you, honey?" Her former boss beamed as she headed Jenna's way.

"Miss Molly! It's so good to see you." They exchanged a hug. The woman was Jenna's height and she still had the same wiry strength she'd always possessed. She wore the same black glasses, but her oval face had collected a few new wrinkles, and her short hair was now fully gray.

"Are you back home now?"

Islanders always assumed that when she visited. It sometimes frustrated her because she'd been so determined to make something of herself. But it hit a little differently this time since her plans seemed to have gone up in smoke. "Just for the weekend, I'm afraid."

"Oh, pooh. I've missed you. Why did you have to go away and educate yourself?"

Jenna chuckled. Miss Molly ran the island's premier kayak touring company. Jenna had been a guide every summer since she turned sixteen and until she left for Georgetown University. "Not all of us can build a business with nothing more than four kayaks and sweat equity."

"And look where it's got me! I'm sixty-eight and trying to wrangle eighteen high schoolers and a packed summer schedule. They think if they memorize the spiel that's good enough. I'll tell you, today's youth just don't have the passion for this island's history. If only I could've cloned you. Some days I think I should just sell the business and be done with it."

"Like you'll ever hang up those paddles."

"It's a lot of aggravation these days, that's what it is."

"Well, I know for a fact you can get those youngsters in line. You were always quite capable of inspiring me."

"That's because you're smart and ambitious and had a care about this island. Well, enough about me. How's life in Alexandria and that boyfriend of yours?"

Jenna winced. "Oh, you haven't heard. We're not seeing each other anymore."

"Good." Miss Molly gave a sharp nod. "Never liked him."

Jenna laughed. "You only met him one time."

"And I didn't like him. Seemed arrogant and like he didn't know what he had in you. You're better off without him."

"Well, thank you, Miss Molly. I appreciate that."

"And how's that Tyson doing? I was so upset to hear about Britt up and leaving him last year. He's such a nice young man."

"Don't you worry—he's doing just fine without her. It'll be good to spend some time with him."

"You two always were thick as thieves."

"He's a good friend. And how is Mr. Paul doing? Still fishing every second he can?"

"Same as always. We did a little traveling to see the grandbabies during the winter, and that was wonderful. They're growing up too fast. How's your mama? I saw her at bingo a few months ago and wondered why she never seems to age. Maybe you can find out her secret and pass it on to me."

"You're as gorgeous as ever. And for what it's worth, I think Mom's just got good genes."

"Lucky you then."

"Here's hoping. Did you know she just returned from a Caribbean cruise with Pam and Ellen? I'm restocking her pantry as we speak."

"Oh, I'll bet that was a hoot." She gave her glasses a push. "Well, I'd better scoot. Paul's mint chip ice cream is melting. You tell your mama hi for me."

"Sure thing, Miss Molly. Tell Mr. Paul I said hello."

After they parted ways, Jenna finished up the list and paid using her mom's credit card. It was dark as she returned to the house. It felt odd knowing a strange man would be staying overnight. To her knowledge a man hadn't spent the night since her dad passed away.

He must be rolling over in his grave right now. He'd been gone fifteen years. When Jenna had turned twenty-four, the birthday hit her like a two-by-four. She'd officially lived as many years without him as she had with him. She'd been a daddy's girl through and through, and losing him had been the kind of trauma no twelve-year-old should have to face.

Jenna shook away the sad thought as she approached the house. She had to figure out what was going on with this Gordon guy. He was attractive for his age and seemed congenial enough. But anyone could put on a good face for one measly week. What kind of man moved this quickly? And what was wrong with her mom that she trusted so easily? Hadn't she learned to be more cautious?

Apparently not.

Jenna had no more stopped the car than Gordon was scurrying down the porch steps and insisting on carrying the groceries. She was happy to accommodate as this might give her a few minutes alone with her mother.

Jenna found Mom in the laundry room, transferring a load from the washer to the dryer. "Oh good, you're back. Thanks for running to the grocery store, honey."

"Happy to help."

Gordon's footsteps sounded as he entered the house, then grocery bags rattled as he set them down in the kitchen.

"I ran into Miss Molly at the store. She's as sassy as ever."

"She's something else. She stays in such good shape. I bet you'll be the same way."

Jenna had always been the active and outdoorsy type. But she'd gotten away from that recently. Her office job kept her indoors and Jason hadn't really been very sporty. He'd been more interested in art and culture.

The sound of Gordon's retreating footsteps reached her ears, followed by the slap of the screen door.

"So how did Gordon end up coming here instead of flying home?"

"Oh, you know how it is. We just weren't ready to part ways, and it was easy enough for him to change his flight."

Jenna bit her lip as she carefully considered her response. "And you feel you know him well enough to have him here at the house?"

"Of course. You'd be surprised how well you can know someone after all the time we spent together. I feel like I've known him all my life." She shoved the last of the load into the dryer.

"It's just . . . this isn't really like you, Mom. You don't bring home strange men. I've never known you to bring home a man at all."

"You needn't be concerned. Gordon's harmless. And he's staying in the garage apartment, for heaven's sake. It's all perfectly proper."

Well, Jenna was glad of that at least. Her mom had renovated the apartment over the winter with hopes of renting it out. "I thought it wasn't finished just yet."

"It only lacks a few pieces of furniture and all the extra touches. But he's a man—give him a bed and a shower and he's good to go. After that tiny ship cabin, he's living large."

When the slap of the screen indicated Gordon's return, Jenna lowered her voice. "Do you know how long he'll be staying?"

Mom gave her a look intended to convey that Jenna was treading on thin ice. "We haven't exactly set a deadline. We're just playing it by ear."

"He doesn't have a job to return to?"

"Jenna, *enough*. He's retired. And I'm well beyond the age of being interrogated about my love life." Mom shut the dryer door and started the cycle. "Now, I'm going to help Gordon put away the groceries and get supper started. Did you already have something to eat?"

"I had a burger on the way."

"All right then." Mom squeezed her arm and offered a warm smile. "It's good to have you home, honey."

"Good to be home, Mom."

Except *home* now seemed to come with a strange man who had no immediate plans to leave and unspecified intentions toward her mother.

The familiar creak of the porch swing soothed Jenna's nerves. It had been hanging out here as long as she could remember and bore so many coats of white paint that the slats sported rounded edges.

She'd spent many summer evenings out here with Dad, listening to the night sounds, smelling the lilac bushes and scent of the ocean. She'd gotten her love of the outdoors from him. Mom didn't mind a walk in the woods or a day at the beach. But she preferred the indoors to the heat of summer and all the mosquitoes and flies that came with it.

Across the street The Sand and Saddle B and B glowed. The white clapboard farmhouse boasted black shutters and a front porch wide enough for an entire family. An American flag angled from a post, fluttering in the breeze. A porch light illuminated the broad stairs leading to a welcoming entryway. How many times had she run up those steps and knocked on that door?

She'd always been welcomed into the Parkers' happy, chaotic home. The couple and their three sons had moved in as she was starting sixth grade. She formed a tentative friendship with the boys—especially Tyson. He was in her grade at school, but they'd never known each other well. Like most elementary kids, Jenna hung with her girlfriends and Ty with his guy group.

Then, several months after the Parkers moved in across the street, her dad had died unexpectedly, and her whole world turned upside down. The shock of loss was as cruel as it was confusing. The pain of missing him was a deep-down ache no one could even touch, much less fix. Though her mom tried. But she was grieving too, and that seemed like one more pain than Jenna could bear.

She navigated the days afterward in some kind of trance. Learned that most people didn't know what to say or do, so they said and did nothing.

Except the Parkers.

They wrapped their arms around Jenna and her mom, literally and metaphorically. They brought meals and shopped for groceries and picked Jenna up from softball practice when Mom worked second shift at the clinic. That led to suppers at their house most nights. They made Jenna feel like part of their family.

Alex, Seth, and Tyson were the siblings she'd always wanted and never had. Okay, she'd always wanted sisters, but she learned boys could also be fun. They knew how to play football and basketball, and over the years their size and strength made her a tougher competitor.

A truck rumbled down the road, slowing when it neared. As she recognized Ty's Silverado, relief swept over her. Finally someone she could talk to about this situation with her mom.

After parking at the house he crossed the street, heading toward her. His long legs ate up the distance between them, and by the time he was loping up the porch steps, she was on her feet, ready with a hug.

Ty's arms swallowed her up and that feeling of relief swelled. She'd somehow forgotten the comfort of his embrace. He was so big and strong. Felt so different in her arms than Jason with his lean five-foot-ten frame. Ty smelled pleasantly of sunshine and the outdoors. She hung on an extra beat as he set his head on top of hers.

"Don't wait so long next time," he said softly.

"I won't."

They parted and settled on the swing. His shoulders were so wide, their arms were flush. He looked every inch the firefighter with his muscular build and stoic expression. The porch light did nice things for his patrician nose and high cheekbones. Its golden light shimmered in his dark hair.

"What's that mess on your jaw?" she asked.

A smile played around his mouth as he stroked the stubbly growth. "A beard in the making."

"You've always been an optimist."

"It's only been a week." Growing facial hair was the one thing Ty couldn't do as well as his brothers—and they loved giving him a hard time about it. He lowered his voice, his green eyes almost black in the shadows. "So what's the deal with this guy and your mom?"

She shrugged. "According to her they spent a lot of time together on the cruise. She feels like she's known him all her life, and now he's staying with her indefinitely."

His head jerked back. *"Indefinitely?"*

"That's what she says. He's up in the garage apartment. I guess we can be thankful for that much. For the record, I don't trust him. He's too nicey-nice. Acted like he was so happy to have me here, carried my bag to my room, couldn't unload the groceries for me fast enough. And he's in there right now slicing vegetables for supper."

"Sounds like a real jerk."

She elbowed him in the stomach. But the flesh didn't give so much as an inch. "Nobody's that nice."

"Doesn't he have a home to get back to?"

"All I could get out of her is that he's retired and apparently doesn't have any pressing obligations."

"I hope that's not because he's a con artist who makes his living off lonely widows."

Lonely widow. Guilt gave a good, hard jab. Was Mom lonely? Jenna used to visit every month or two. But the past couple of years she'd slacked off with her visits *and* phone calls. Work kept her busy and she used weekends to decompress. And now that she thought about it, Jason was never eager to make the trip. He didn't mind Jenna going home without him, but she didn't want to leave him. After they broke up she should've come for a visit right away—without an ulterior motive.

"She say anything else?"

"Not really. And I had to be careful. Ever since the Douglas Debacle she's been pretty adamant that I butt out of her love life." Mom had met Douglas online and, despite Jenna's advice, allowed him to pick her up at her house. The date didn't go well, but that didn't stop Douglas from stopping by and making a regular nuisance of himself.

"It doesn't matter that you were right?" Ty said.

"Nope."

"So you're just supposed to be okay with some strange guy living on your mom's property?"

"Apparently. But obviously I can't leave her here alone with him."

"You said he was staying indefinitely."

"I suspect this will end, probably in disaster, sooner rather than later. I mean, she's known him one week. Eventually he'll show his true colors. I'll just have to stick around until that happens."

He tilted a smile at her. "I don't hate the sound of that."

She bumped his shoulder. "Aw, you've gone soft on me, Parker."

"Nah. Just a little more in touch with my feelings these days."

Jenna sobered at the reminder of his broken heart. Britt had left Ty suddenly last year, and it took a while for him to discover she'd been cheating on him for months. Understandably, he took it pretty hard. "Have you seen her yet?"

"Not this year." Her family was from Annapolis and owned a summer home on the island, which Britt visited sometimes.

"She was never good enough for you, you know."

"I could say the same about what's his name."

"You wouldn't be the first. Know what? We should set each other up. I'll bet I could find a woman worthy of you."

"You'll have to put that on hold as I've sworn off women altogether for the time being."

Jenna gave a mock startled look. "What? I think I heard wrong. Did the new poster boy for 'dating around' just say he's sworn off women?"

"I need a break, that's all."

"But will the women of Chincoteague Island survive now that Tyson Parker is out of play?"

"They'll survive just fine." His expression sobered. "I was out of control, Jen. I never should have asked Marissa out. That was stupid."

"She's the paramedic?" He'd brushed over the situation on the phone.

"Yeah. It's still pretty uncomfortable at the station. A few of the guys have taken her side and the rest are upset that I brought all that tension into the house. They're not wrong."

"Have you apologized to them?"

"Of course. And I've tried to rectify things with Marissa, but she's still angry. One of the guys said she'd had a crush on me since she was hired. If I'd known that, I never would've gone down that path."

"So you made it clear you weren't looking for a relationship, but she hoped to change your mind, then got mad when you didn't?"

"That's how it seems. I never meant to hurt her."

"Things will settle down. You'll see. Broken hearts take time to mend."

His gaze darted her way. "Speaking of which, how's yours doing? It's only been a few months."

"I'm doing surprisingly well." She frowned thoughtfully. "I've been doing a lot of thinking about all that. I thought I was in love with Jason—and maybe I was a little. Can you be a little in love with someone? I do miss him sometimes. Or maybe I just miss having weekend plans, having the closeness of a relationship. Yeah, I don't think I miss him any more than I miss that stupid job."

"I thought you liked your job."

"Ty, if I ever have to smell eugenol again, it'll be too soon. And the sound of a drill grinding away at teeth? Never again. Also, paperwork? So not my thing. I'm starting to wonder why I stayed so long doing something I didn't enjoy." Jason. Jason was why. But if she wasn't head over heels for him, why had she stuck around?

"You used to prefer working outdoors. A park ranger, wasn't it?"

"I was fourteen. I also wanted to be an Olympian and an astronaut. But you're right—I do like working outdoors. If there's anything I've learned, it's that I don't want to ride a desk forty hours a week."

"That's good information to know. You don't have to rush into anything. Be picky. Look for the position that excites you. You deserve that."

"Thanks. I'll rev up my job search online and look for opportunities more suitable to my actual desires, though that's not necessarily where my experience lies."

"I mean, you have a degree from Georgetown—and in business, that's pretty versatile."

"It is." She turned a grateful smile his way. He'd always been a good sounding board. "Thanks, Ty."

"What for?"

"For helping me sort out what I really want." She glanced at the house. "And also for alerting me to what's going on here." Whatever that was.

"That'll work itself out too."

She sure hoped so. And she hoped her mom wouldn't get hurt in the process.

Chapter 6

As Tyson slipped inside his parents' fenced pasture, the mares trotted toward him. Penny led the way, her reddish-brown coat almost black under the starry skies. She slowed and nickered as she reached him.

Ty stroked her neck. "Hey, girl. Been good today?"

Patches, not to be outdone, edged in beside Penny and whinnied.

Tyson spread his affection between the two. "There's room for both of you."

The mares got along great, but Patches wanted whatever Penny had, be it an apple, a carrot, or a little affection. They were like a couple of preschool sisters sometimes.

Shortly after his parents opened the bed-and-breakfast, they'd bought the pair at the pony auction. Because the land lease for the Chincoteague ponies only allowed for 150 ponies, each year most of the foals had to be auctioned off. The proceeds from the auction completely sustained the island's fire company plus allowed for a few extras like student scholarships. People came from around the country to see the festivities leading up to the pony auction: the pony penning, beach walk, Pony Swim, and carnival.

Tourists visited the island year-round just to see the ponies on the refuge, so having two from the wild herd right at the B and B was a boon. They were tame and saddle broke now and enjoyed giving rides to the kids. Basically living their best life in this large, grassy pasture.

Ty pulled a twig from Penny's black mane as his thoughts returned to Jenna. She seemed to think Mama Dee and Gordon's relationship would self-implode quickly. And she might be right. But Jenna's mother, as sweet and smart as she was, seemed to lack awareness when it came to men—with the exception of her late husband, Allen.

A few years ago Tyson had discovered the man Dee was dating was a known womanizer. Breaking that news hadn't been fun. He'd had to pull Jenna in on that one. Then there was The Sand and Saddle guest who, Dad discovered, had a wife and three kids back home. Jerry and Dee had already been out on several dates. Then there was Douglas . . . and now there was Gordon.

If Jenna didn't want to leave them alone, she might be here for longer than she anticipated. A pleasant thought. He hadn't realized how much he'd missed her until he got his arms around her tonight. She'd lived away so long, he sometimes forgot she was all grown up.

She'd grown into her wide smile and doe-brown eyes that danced when she laughed. Was it strange to admit his tomboy neighbor had turned into a gorgeous creature?

Gorgeous? *Whoa.*

Maybe true, but definitely weird to think about. Although he was human. He had eyes. How could he not see how attractive she'd become? Especially because his recent dating habits had apparently instilled a routine of noticing women.

But that shouldn't include your best friend, pal.

He gave his head a shake. "I'm losing it."

Penny blew air through her nostrils, a sign of affection, and Patches followed suit.

"Aw, love you too, ladies."

A few minutes later Tyson entered the B and B's back door, keeping the noise down. It was almost ten and his parents had a full house. He found his dad in the kitchen, loading the dishwasher.

Rick Parker had married his mom when Ty was four, so he didn't remember not having him in his life. Rick was a lifelong member of the volunteer fire company and had been chief for eight years before retiring to run the bed-and-breakfast with Mom. His steady influence and passion for the job had obviously rubbed off on Ty.

At fifty-five Dad was still lean and strong with a thick head of black hair, though the color had faded a bit over time. He had blue eyes and a kind smile, both of which could flatten in a way that made a teenage boy's heart crumble with regret when he was in trouble. But once Dad had made his point and delivered an appropriate consequence, he was quick to forgive and forget.

"Hey, Dad. Sorry that took so long."

Dad closed and started the dishwasher. "No worries. Mom and I had things covered around here. Get the ponies back on the sanctuary?"

"Yeah, and the fence mended. Riptide was pretty agitated."

"He'll settle down now that he's back where he belongs." His attention dropped to Ty's chin. "Forget to shave this morning?"

"Funny. Jenna's back home."

He hiked his eyebrows. "For good?"

"No, just for a while. Her mom returned from the cruise with a man in tow." Ty expounded on the situation, ending with Jenna's decision to stick around as long as necessary.

"I understand she's worried about her mom, but Dee's a grown woman and a pretty independent one at that."

"It won't hurt Jenna to hang around. She's between jobs anyway."

"That's right. We should have them over for supper one night."

"That would be good."

Dad's gaze sharpened on him. He was worried about Tyson, about the fallout after losing that kid. He'd already brought it up several times and probably didn't want to address it again. At least, not this late at night.

"I should let you get to bed," Ty said.

"Sure. Unless there's something else you wanted to talk about . . ."

Ty glanced at the clock. Since that call a few weeks ago, sleep had been fraught with nightmares. It had gotten to the point where he dreaded falling asleep. Tried to put it off as long as possible. "No, I'm good. Just thought I'd stop by since I was across the street. Anything you need for tomorrow?"

"No, we're all set."

Ty moved toward the back door. "See you in the morning then."

"Good night."

A few minutes later Tyson pulled from the drive and headed toward his house, where he'd inevitably search for reasons to stay awake.

Chapter 7

Jenna didn't get it. She frowned as Mom and Gordon got into her mom's Mazda—Gordon in the driver's seat—and took off for the beach. The pair had been together all weekend, and now they were halfway into the next week and nothing had changed.

Unless her mom was working, they were on the go: the pony museum, the village shops, one of the local restaurants. On Sunday they'd driven up to Ocean City for the day. What had happened to her homebody mother?

They always invited Jenna to go along. On Saturday night she'd joined them for supper at Captain Zack's, where she'd tried to casually extract information from Gordon while the singer of a local band belted out song after song. He was friendly and cooperative, though decidedly vague in his answers.

But having a man in the house who wasn't her dad felt weird. Jarring. Jenna tried to seem friendly and accepting, but she didn't like having this stranger in her mom's house, sitting in her dad's seat at the table, watching Mom's TV, and washing his clothes in her laundry room.

Now as Mom's car pulled from the drive, Jenna stepped away from the window and wandered back to the kitchen, where they'd just enjoyed a cozy breakfast for three. When Jenna had entered the kitchen this morning, she'd caught Gordon and Mom in a lip-lock over a griddle of pancakes.

She wrung the image from her brain and pulled out her phone.

They're off to the beach now.

Seconds later Tyson replied.

You can hang out over here if you want. We can put you to work. Dishes, toilets, grout work, whatever your pleasure.

I assure you, none of those things are my pleasure.

I tried.

She was feeling stir-crazy. And what her soul really craved was the ocean, some quiet outdoor time to soothe her worries and process her thoughts. Most of all she longed to see Jenna's Dream again. It had been too long since she'd visited her beautiful girl. She'd missed that special connection she always felt with her dad when she watched the mare grazing on the refuge.

Jenna's old kayak was still in the garage, but there was no chance it would fit in her car. She had another idea, however.

Coastal Currents Kayak Tours was just minutes down the road on the Assateague Channel. Fond memories washed over Jenna as she pulled into the full lot. At sixteen she'd been so proud to get her first job here. Though she'd known Miss Molly all her life, the woman still insisted on a proper interview.

The job didn't feel like work at all. Each day she got to breathe in the ocean's fragrance and share her passion for the island's history and the wild ponies. And while most of the tour guides stuck to the script, Jenna enjoyed using her own words. She loved seeing children's eyes light up when they spotted their first pony, usually grazing in the saltwater marshes lining the channel.

Back then she'd known all 150 ponies by name, but in the years since she'd left, some had died and new foals had been added to the herd.

She pulled into the one empty parking space and exited the vehicle. It was a beautiful morning with pure blue skies and a balmy breeze coming off the water. The turquoise-blue building stood like a bright seashell on the channel's shoreline.

Orange and red kayaks lined the small marina, and at least a dozen people gathered around the dock area. Some were removing life vests while others waited for their tours. From inside the grass tiki hut, Miss Molly offered the customers a strained smile as she gathered signed forms.

Tina Birchfield, Miss Molly's right hand for as long as Jenna could remember, exited the building, said something to Miss Molly, then shrugged. The older woman closed her eyes for a brief second, then nodded. Tina returned to the building.

Jenna had picked the wrong day to rent a kayak. She stopped the owner as the woman headed toward the building. "Everything okay, Miss Molly?"

"Oh, Jenna, thank God. Honey, can you help me out?"

"Of course. What do you need?"

"A retirement plan and a prescription for Xanax! But I'll settle for a tour guide. I'm short-staffed by two this morning. Are you game?"

"Uh, sure. I have nothing but time today."

The woman's slim shoulders practically drooped with relief. "God bless you. Grab a life vest and take the Jacksons—pony tour, family of four. They're suited up and ready to go."

"Got it."

Jenna sluiced her paddle through the calm waters of the channel, the Jacksons trailing her like ducklings: Skylar and Jaden and their teenagers Mila and Carson. All of them had kayaked before, so instructions had been minimal.

Beyond the introductions and small talk, most of the information would wait until they reached Assateague's shore where, she could already see, a band of ponies currently grazed.

"There they are!" Mila called.

Carson, already man-sized though he looked to be about sixteen, had caught up with Jenna. "They're not very big."

Not to be outdone, Mila came along Jenna's other side as they paddled toward the marshy shoreline.

"They average only twelve to thirteen hands," Jenna said. "Do you know what that means?"

"That they're shorties like Mila."

"Don't be dumb. Horses are measured in hands."

"You're right, Mila. Since medieval times we've measured horses by the distance between your thumb and outstretched fingers—about four inches. And we only measure from the ground to the horse's shoulder." Jenna stopped talking to catch her breath—something she didn't used to have to do. Her arms were also getting fatigued. Boy, was she out of shape.

Mr. and Mrs. Jackson glided up, flanking their kids, eyes glued to the ponies.

"They're so pretty," Mila said. "Their fur's kind of shaggy. I like the spotted ones."

"Those are pintos. You'll notice the ponies' legs are short compared to horses. That helps them navigate the boggy terrain. From left to right, we have Sky Dancer, Wendy's Carolina Girl, and Pennies from Heaven."

"They have names?" Carson asked.

Mila sliced her paddle through the water. "I thought they were wild."

"They are. I'll explain how they got their names in a minute. But first, do you know how they got here to begin with?"

"I heard they were left here by farmers," Mr. Jackson said.

Jenna was glad they were nearly to the shoreline. She lifted her paddle from the water and the others followed suit. They slowly drifted into the marsh and came to a stop.

"There are some who say that's where they came from. Early settlers did let their animals forage here. What we know for sure is that the Chincoteague ponies have been here for hundreds of years. Evidence suggests they're survivors of a Spanish shipwreck that occurred near the coastline and that the ponies swam ashore."

"What evidence?" Mrs. Jackson asked.

"Well, before modern navigation there were a remarkable number of shipwrecks on the mid-Atlantic coastline. There've been hundreds of shipwrecks along Assateague Island, and it was common in the day for those ships to transport horses to the colonies."

"I like the shipwreck story best," Mr. Jackson said, "but I'm still not convinced they weren't just left behind by farmers."

Jenna grinned at the teens. "I saved the best for last. In 2022 a Spanish horse tooth was found in an old colony in the Caribbean. And a DNA study showed that the closest genetic match existing today was the Chincoteague pony."

Mila beamed. "That's so cool."

"It's hard to argue with genetics. What we have here is a very unique and hardy breed." Jenna used her paddle to shift the wind-blown kayak. She let them take pictures and talk among themselves for a few minutes.

"Who owns the island?" Mrs. Jackson asked.

Jenna explained how the land lease worked and how the Chincoteague Fire Company took care of the ponies.

"But how do they keep the herd to one hundred fifty ponies?" Carson asked. "Don't they have babies?"

"They sure do. Since they have to keep the herd number limited, that means they can't keep all the new foals. So each year in July those foals are auctioned off during our Pony Penning Days."

"I heard about the Pony Swim," Mrs. Jackson said. "Is that the same thing?"

Mila shifted in the kayak. "We saw pictures of it in one of the stores."

"As many as forty thousand people come to the island the last week in July to see the ponies swim across the channel from Assateague to Chincoteague for the auction. But before that can happen, the ponies on the refuge have to be rounded up. We call the people who do this the saltwater cowboys. Many of them are from the fire company, and it's considered a privilege to participate in the penning and Pony Swim. They have to earn the right."

"Are they on horseback?" Carson asked.

"Yep. And they're expert horse people. They not only have to round up the ponies, but they also have to get them safely across the channel to Chincoteague, where the auction takes place. We're talking a hundred fifty ponies plus sixty to seventy foals."

"Sounds like a lot of chaos," Mr. Jackson said.

"Oh, it's something else. My friend Tyson is a saltwater cowboy—fourth generation, in fact. They have to get all those ponies through marsh and mud, and it's extremely stressful. The cowboys worry about the ponies getting injured or killed—stallions can be a real handful. He's told me when they finally get the ponies to the swim site, right over there"—she pointed toward the narrowest part of the channel—"and all the ponies are safe and accounted for, the relief is immense."

"Do the ponies really swim?" Mila asked.

"They sure do. Even the foals can swim. In fact, the first foal to swim ashore each year is dubbed King or Queen Neptune and is raffled off to a lucky winner later that day."

Mila gave her parents a beseeching look. "Aw, can we come back in July?"

"Unfortunately not," Mrs. Jackson said. "But it does sound pretty amazing."

"You said you'd tell us how the ponies got their names," Carson said.

"After the ponies swim ashore on Chincoteague, they're led through town and end up at the carnival grounds, and that's where the foals are auctioned off. The average auction price is around four thousand. But . . ." She paused dramatically. "Since the herd needs to be replenished, some of the foals are auctioned with the stipulation that they'll return to Assateague Island with the rest of the herd.

These are called buyback ponies. And those who purchased those ponies get naming rights."

"But they don't get to keep them?" Carson asked.

"Nope, those foals get to go home with their mamas."

Mila grinned. "Aw, I like that."

"So do I—as do a lot of other folks. That's why our buyback ponies fetch the highest price at auction, averaging sixteen thousand. But we've had them go as high as fifty."

Mrs. Jackson's eyes widened. "What do they do with the proceeds?"

"They use some of it for veterinary care of the ponies and some to keep the fire company running. It helps pay for the trucks, equipment, even the building. And some of it goes toward community scholarships."

"That seems like a great business model," Mr. Jackson said.

"It is. But to the fire company and even the islanders, the ponies are much more than business assets. We have an emotional bond with them and a strong desire to take care of them and make sure they're around for many more generations."

"I want to purchase a buyback pony," Mila said.

Mr. Jackson grinned at his daughter. "If you find sixteen grand lying around, it's going into your college fund, young lady."

Mila rolled her eyes. "Oh, Dad."

Chapter 8

Jenna was going to feel this tomorrow. Her quads strained from the weight as she pulled the last kayak from the water. She'd done four tours today. But sore muscles aside, she was joyful and energized by the conversations and physical activity.

This sure hadn't turned out to be the day she'd expected. She hadn't had time alone and she hadn't spied Dream among the grazing bands of ponies. Jenna was tired, but it was the good kind of tired. The kind she hadn't experienced in a while.

The afternoon tours were still out, leaving the dock empty and quiet. She found Miss Molly inside the building, hanging life jackets to dry. Jenna joined her, grabbing vests and hooking them on the pegs.

"How was your last tour? They seemed like a lively group."

"They were fun. A girls' trip, Pennsylvanians who take a short vacation without their kids and husbands every May. One of their grandmas had read *Misty of Chincoteague* to her when she was a child, and she'd always wanted to see our wild ponies. She talked her friends into it." The book by Marguerite Henry, published in the forties, had made the ponies famous.

"I had a friend group like that back in the day. We still keep in touch, but everyone's moved away."

"It's good that you stay connected, though." Jenna had kept in touch with a few girlfriends from high school, but most of them had moved off island except Sofia. Since this trip was turning into quite a bit more than a weekend, Jenna should reach out and see if they could get together.

It had been five days and Jenna still couldn't figure Gordon out. His life back home sounded rather boring. He was retired from a career in forensic accounting with an insurance company. He'd been married twice. The first wife divorced him after seventeen years, and the second wife passed away unexpectedly after two years. He'd been single for a few years and had gone on the cruise because he'd always wanted to and neither wife had enjoyed traveling.

He seemed like the perfect gentleman, pulling out Mom's chair and helping around the house. Mom was eating it up, gazing at him with sparkling eyes, lighting up when he entered the room. It all seemed too fast and a little too good to be true.

Miss Molly hung the last vest, then turned her way. "The boy who didn't show up to work wouldn't answer my calls all morning. Then this afternoon he quit via text after working for me for only two weeks."

"Sheesh."

"Don't suppose you'd like to fill in till I can find a replacement? I'd take the tours, but there really have to be two of us working the office and dock."

Jenna hadn't imagined working on Chincoteague during this break, but then, she hadn't known this would turn into an extended stay. With Gordon showing no signs of leaving and with him and Mom gallivanting all over the island, Jenna might as well stay busy. She shrugged. "I guess I could fill in for a bit. I really enjoyed the tours today, but I'm not sure how long I'll be on the island."

"I'll take whatever I can get. Thank you. You're a godsend. I'll get right on finding a replacement."

"It'll be nice to have a purpose while I'm here." Other than making sure her mom was safe. Though unfortunately there was no way to protect her heart.

Miss Molly gave her a side hug. "It'll be like old times."

Jenna dropped her clothes into the washer and added detergent. She needed to make a trip back home for more of her things. The little bits she'd brought weren't going to cut it. After starting the load she was grabbing two used fabric softeners off the floor when she saw a piece of folded paper next to the dryer.

It was a piece of her mom's lined stationery. Before tossing it, Jenna opened it to see a list written in small, fine print.

Wildlife Refuge $10.00
AmaRin Coffee $17.23
Mister Whippy $9.52
Ropewalk $62.48

The list went on. Since the handwriting wasn't Mom's, she could only presume it was Gordon's.

Jenna frowned as she entered the living room where her mom was eating a bowl of cereal for her evening snack. Gordon had already turned in, saying he hadn't slept well the night before.

"Is this yours, Mom?" She handed over the paper.

Mom took the sheet and gave an indulgent smile. "It's Gordon's.

He's so cute. He's keeping track of what I spend so he can pay me back."

A red flag waved, bold and foreboding. "Pay you back?"

"He didn't bring enough cash for an extended time away, so I'm covering for him. He uses a local bank." She smiled adoringly at the list. "Right down to the penny. It's such an accountant thing to do."

Even if Gordon did bank locally, what about credit cards? And surely the bank gave him access to ATM machines. She wanted to ask more questions but risked alienating her mom.

"Thanks, honey." Mom set down the list and returned to her cereal and the reality TV show featuring newly married couples.

Taking that as a dismissal, Jenna went out to the porch and settled on the swing. Maybe the rhythmic motion would soothe her nerves. She glanced up at the garage attic where the one window was darkened. Who was this guy who'd followed her mom home from a cruise, stayed at her place for free, and mooched off her day after day?

An itemized list didn't prove he intended to pay her back.

Movement across the street caught her eye. A family was returning to the Parkers' B and B, their laughter carrying across the yard. She spied Tyson's truck in the lot and opened her phone.

Guess what? I got a job.

He'd assume she meant back home, of course.

He responded seconds later.

That's great! Where at?

Coastal Currents.

She smiled as she sent the text.

Her phone buzzed as a call came in. "I'm confused," Tyson said in lieu of a greeting.

"That makes two of us."

"Are you staying for good then?"

"No, the job's only temporary." She told him about her unexpected day and Miss Molly's predicament.

"That's really nice of you to help out. I'm sure she appreciates it."

"It's hardly a chore. I enjoyed my day. I miss working outside—you were right about that."

"I'm sorry, what did you say?"

She rolled her eyes. "I'm not saying it again."

"That's okay, I heard you the first time. So are you thinking you'll be here awhile?"

Jenna sighed and told him about finding the list and what her mom had said. "I don't understand how he wouldn't even have a credit card."

"That doesn't make sense. You have to use a credit card to open an account on a cruise, don't you?"

"Maybe they can work around that," Jenna said. "But really, who doesn't have a credit card these days?"

"Or access to a cash machine."

"Exactly. I might question Mom about it later. But she seems so enamored with him. I'm afraid he's just using her and she's going to wind up hurt."

"Hurt *and* ripped off," Ty said. "But if he managed to pay for a cruise, he can't be dirt poor."

"Unless he does that kind of thing to find single women to take advantage of. Don't forget, he went on that cruise alone."

"That does seem kind of strange."

"Not if you're looking for an affluent woman to support you. Not that Mom's well-to-do, but she's certainly comfortable. And probably lonely. Her girlfriends are busy with their kids and grandkids. Other than that cruise, she mostly just works and hangs out at the house."

"She's always been more of a homebody. But she probably misses being in a relationship. It's been a long time, and the one she had with your dad was obviously fulfilling."

Jenna gave a wistful smile. "They were great together. So in love and easy with each other. I wish you could've known my dad better."

"I feel like I knew him pretty well just from all the stories. He's got a great reputation at the firehouse."

"We were both blessed in the dad department." Ty's dad was actually his stepdad, though neither he nor his brothers viewed Rick that way. According to Ty, their biological father left when Ronda was pregnant with Alex and never looked back. Years ago he'd confessed the whole thing had left him feeling rejected. She couldn't even imagine feeling unwanted by a parent.

"Has your mom done any baking since she got home?" Ty asked.

"That's a random question."

"I'm craving something sweet."

"Lucky for you she's got a fresh batch of brownies in the kitchen."

"I'll be right over."

Chapter 9

Tyson glanced at Jenna in the passenger seat of his truck. She'd worn her chestnut hair up, highlighting her long, graceful neck. Her skin was sun-kissed from the last few days at her new job, adding a touch of pink to her cheeks. Or was that makeup? Or maybe it was just the lighting of the golden hour. Whatever it was, she looked really pretty.

"What?" she asked.

He jerked his attention back to the road. "Nothing."

"Do I have chocolate on my face or something?" She flipped down the visor. "This thing with Gordon had me stress-eating Oreos this afternoon."

Why had he been staring at Jenna? Noticing the way the light looked on her skin?

Weirdo.

He gave his head a shake as Jenna flipped the visor back up. They were headed to Chatties for seafood and a favorite local band playing there tonight. "Seth and Alex said they might stop by."

"Oh good. It's been like two years since I've seen your brothers."

"What? Really?"

"We keep missing each other. What have they been up to lately?"

"Alex still works for the bank, and Seth has been building his marketing business. He's handling The Sand and Saddle's account and doing a great job. Business has increased by 28 percent."

"Wow, that's great. Your parents must be thrilled. Is he still the consummate bachelor?"

"Some things never change." The middle Parker brother had gotten their dad's good looks—black hair, blue eyes, chiseled jaw. Seth had always been popular with the women, and his affable charm and salesman personality assured he never lacked for company.

Tyson maneuvered carefully around a boy on a scooter. Church Street was coming up on the left. Ty gripped the steering wheel even as his palms turned sweaty. Andre Wallace had been conscious briefly when the team arrived on scene. Just long enough for Ty to memorize the fear and shock in his liquid brown eyes. The image haunted Ty every night.

"Hey, you missed your turn."

His pulse was thrumming like crazy. "It's okay. I'll take Maddox."

"You might be better off turning around." She was right. This time of the evening Maddox would be backed up with traffic.

But Church Street was no longer an option. "That's okay." He continued along Ridge Road until they came to Maddox, where he turned.

"Mom sent me the article about the accident. Sounded like it was a bad one. Were you on the scene that night?"

He shouldn't be surprised she'd put it together so quickly. "Yeah."

"I'm sorry. I'm not sure how you guys deal with all that stuff. It must be a heavy load to carry sometimes."

Usually he just talked to the other guys about it, blew off steam in the weight room or on the court. This time was different, though. He couldn't play enough basketball or lift enough weights to rid himself of this. The guilt was eating at him and he didn't know how to shed it.

"He was so young. That must make it even harder."

"Seventeen. Just getting started in life." A lump swelled in his throat. Andre had been on Chincoteague vacationing with his family. His parents had gone home to plan a funeral for their son—all because Tyson had been too distracted to think straight.

Tyson still hadn't escaped the dark cloud when they got a table at Chatties almost an hour later. Summer, with the arrival of tourists, made most restaurants overcrowded. But this establishment, being upstairs with discreet signage, was lesser known by tourists. The clamor of chatter and clattering silverware filled the dimmed space. Muted TVs offered baseball and trivia games. Onstage, a band set up and readied to perform.

He and Jenna ordered their favorite seafood platters, and while they waited for their food they talked with each other and their neighbors. When the food came, they dug in. By unspoken agreement, Jenna forked his hush puppies and he stole her oysters. Chincoteague oysters were renowned worldwide for their unique salty flavor, but Jenna wasn't a fan of oysters in general. Twenty minutes later they were making good use of the lemon-scented towelette when Alex and Seth ascended the stairs.

Seth beamed. "Jenna!"

She popped up from her seat and Seth engulfed her in a hug. She laughed when he lifted her clean off her feet. "It's been too long."

Seth's hands looked big, one splayed across her sun-kissed shoulder and the other planted in the small of her back.

When he set her down again, she embraced Alex, whose hugs were, like the man himself, much more reserved. His light brown hair had an enviable wave on top, and he wore a couple days of stubble, which practically amounted to a beard.

Ty greeted his brothers.

"Sit down, you guys," Jenna said with the ease of someone who'd spent half her childhood playing *Super Mario* on Wii with them. "We've already eaten, but go ahead and order some dinner. It's on me."

Seth grabbed a seat to one side of her while Alex grabbed the other.

"No way," Seth said. "I never let the ladies pay."

"Jenna's not a lady," Alex said. "She's family."

"Gee, I'm not sure if I should be insulted or flattered."

"Dude, your game needs some work." Seth turned a smile on Jenna. "Thanks for the offer, but unfortunately, we can't stay long anyway."

"We're helping a buddy set up a new TV system," Alex said. "Well, I'm helping him. Seth will mostly just stand there and look pretty."

Seth smirked. "I *am* the good-looking one after all."

Tyson couldn't let that go. "You're the charming one. *I'm* the good-looking one."

"Hey, what am I?" Alex said.

"The smart one," the other three said in unison, then laughed when Alex scowled.

Jenna patted Alex's arm. "You're good-looking too. You're all too handsome for your own good."

Trinity came to take Alex's and Seth's drink orders. They chatted amiably for a moment, then she glanced shyly at Tyson. "Is Luke coming tonight?" Though her tone was casual, the hope in her eyes gave her away.

"I don't think so. But I'll let him know you asked about him."

"Oh, you don't have to do that. I'll be right back with your drinks." She dashed off toward the bar.

Grinning, Tyson pulled out his phone and texted Luke.

I'm at Chatties and Trinity just asked about you. You should come down.

His text came in seconds later.

Really? What'd she say?

Just wanted to know if you were coming tonight. She was all flustered and blushing.

No, she wasn't.

I'm telling you.

I wish I could come but I'm babysitting my nephew, and my sister won't be home till late.

Can't say I didn't try.

"Are you seeing anyone these days, Alex?" Jenna's question pulled Tyson back to the present.

"He's head over heels with Suni Moore," Seth said.

Alex shot his brother a disgruntled look. "We've only been dating a few months."

"Oh, I remember her," Jenna said. "I always liked her. She used to work at the bakery."

"She still does." Tyson thought they made a good couple. Suni was outgoing and expressive, a perfect foil for his more introverted brother. "We're not sure how she puts up with him."

Alex rolled his eyes, then addressed Jenna. "You've been scarce lately. I can't even remember the last time I saw you."

"Oh, you know me. I've been busy rejecting marriage proposals and getting fired."

Seth grinned at her. "You don't seem too sad about either. You were too good for that loser anyway."

"She's working for Miss Molly now," Ty offered.

"Seriously?" Alex undid the top of his button-up. "You moving back to the island?"

"It's just temporary. Kayak tours don't pay much more than they used to, and I've still got to make a living."

Seth nudged her. "You could do that here as well as anywhere. You've always had a great head for business." He winked affably. "All that and good looks too. Ty didn't mention you got so gorgeous. You keeping her all to yourself, bro?"

Heat flared in Ty's cheeks. But he just sat there like an idiot because he couldn't seem to get his tongue and brain on the same page. Thankfully, the lead singer grabbed the mic and introduced the band, capturing their attention.

As the band kicked off the first song, Jenna chatted with his brothers, but Ty was too far away to catch what they were saying. He texted Luke a bit more about Trinity and also sent a text to a recent B and B guest who'd left her designer sunglasses behind.

A few songs into the set, Alex wandered off to talk to a friend from work while Jenna headed to the restroom. Seth watched her weave through the tables on the way to the far corner. Ty didn't care for the gleam of interest in his brother's eyes.

And he liked it even less when Seth turned to him and said, "Is Jenna seeing anyone these days?"

"She just came out of a serious relationship, remember? Why do you ask?" Ty's tone all but dared him to declare a personal interest.

He lifted a shoulder. "Just curious."

Tyson frowned. Seth was the last thing she needed right now. "She's practically our sister, Seth."

Seth's blue eyes twinkled. "Speak for yourself."

Tyson pressed his lips together even as he squirmed at his own statement. Because he'd once put his lips on Jenna in a very unbrotherly way.

Chapter 10

Ten years earlier

He's not coming.

The words formed in Jenna's mind even as her heart shriveled in her chest. The text from her best friend, Sofia, blurred as Jenna's eyes filled with tears.

> I just heard from Taylor. She said Evan is coming with Amanda Doherty! I'm so sorry!

Jenna sank onto the edge of her bed, the tight dress squeezing her hips. Amanda Doherty? She was petite, outgoing, and well liked—definitely a couple rungs above Evan Sanders on the social ladder. And though Evan was fairly attractive, his placement on the chess team and in the debate club hadn't exactly rendered him Mr. Popularity. As far as Jenna was concerned, that had been part of his appeal.

The tears pressed against her eyes, threatening to ruin the makeup she'd spent so much time applying. A phone call vibrated her phone. It was Sofia. But Evan's rejection had hit her hard, and Jenna couldn't bear to talk about it just yet. Swallowing against the lump in her throat, she denied the call and texted instead.

It's okay! I'm fine. Have a good time with Jack! Call me tomorrow. I want all the details. ☺

At least Jenna's mom was downstairs and unable to witness her heartbreak. A month ago when Evan had asked her to prom, Jenna jumped at the chance. She wanted to go and though she wasn't unpopular herself, as a girl athlete, she was mostly viewed by her male peers as one of the guys. Boys didn't date girls who'd beaten them at arm wrestling or humiliated them on the basketball court.

At seventeen she'd been on a total of two dates and had yet to even experience her first kiss. She'd hoped tonight might be the night it actually happened. Not that Evan had been especially attentive since he'd invited her. Well, that wasn't true. He was attentive for a few weeks. But over the past few days he'd distanced himself. He hadn't called. She'd hardly seen him at school. She'd written it off as busy work and school schedules.

But she now saw it was something much more. He'd changed his mind about her, decided he didn't like her after all. Or maybe Amanda had asked him to prom and he couldn't refuse.

He could've at least had the decency to tell Jenna. All her friends knew she was going with Evan, and now they'd see him there with Amanda instead. On Monday morning, if not before then, she'd have to face all the questions. The thought of the coming humiliation bottomed out her stomach.

Just as quickly a wave of anger swelled inside. Evan was the one who'd wronged her. She hadn't done anything to deserve this treatment. She should go to prom by herself, show him he hadn't gotten the best of her. She didn't need him to attend her own prom or have a good time!

The thought lifted the cloud of humiliation for a few minutes. But soon reality sank in. Who was she kidding? Going to prom alone?

She'd have a miserable time, and she didn't have the emotional bandwidth to fake it all night long.

She glanced in the mirror where only moments ago she'd been admiring the way her brown hair fell in waves past her bare shoulders. For once in her life she felt like she looked feminine and pretty. And since Evan was a very lanky six feet, she'd splurged on new four-inch heels that made her legs look longer than ever.

Her gaze slipped down to the satiny red dress, modest but for the slit at the thigh. She never wore dresses, much less bold red ones. But when she'd tried it on a few weeks ago, her mother's eyes had misted. *"Oh, honey. You look so grown up. So beautiful."* She'd insisted the dress was made for Jenna, despite the exorbitant price tag.

Jenna wiped the tears from her face and glanced at the closed door. Not only had Mom wasted a lot of money on this dress, but she'd taken the night off work to take pictures and see Jenna and Evan off. Now Jenna would have to go downstairs and tell her Evan wasn't coming at all.

Somehow, facing Mom's sympathy seemed even worse than Evan's rejection. Jenna had been mourning that her dad was missing yet another milestone, but now she was glad he wouldn't have to witness her humiliation.

She wasn't sure how long she'd been sitting there wallowing in misery when Mom called from downstairs. "Jenna, wasn't he supposed to come at six?"

With a weary sigh Jenna stood, smoothing the pretty satin material. She was opening her mouth to call, "Be right down!" when the doorbell rang.

Grateful for a minute's reprieve, Jenna leaned into the mirror and dabbed her face with a tissue, fixing the visible evidence of her distress. She would play it off as a last-minute change. No big deal. She hadn't really cared about going anyway. Now Jenna could stay home with Mom and . . . have a movie night.

"Jenna . . . your date's here?" Mom called.

Jenna frowned. *My date?* What was going on? Had Sofia somehow gotten faulty information? She must've. And now Jenna had just spent all this time crying over nothing. She was going to kill her best friend!

"Coming!" Jenna quickly touched up her makeup and hoped the glassy sheen of her eyes looked less like the remnants of a crying jag and more like prom-night excitement. She stuffed her feet into the red heels, fluffed her hair, and left the room. She had to walk carefully down the stairs as she wasn't used to wearing heels, much less the spiky things she'd bought.

She was barely cognizant of her efforts as the bottom edge of the foyer came into view. A pair of shiny black dress shoes appeared, then black pants, a suit coat and crisp white shirt, and . . .

She blinked at the unexpected face. *"Ty?"*

His eyes flared at the sight of her and he beamed. "Wow, Jenna. You look amazing."

Jenna glanced around and, not seeing her mother, lowered her voice. "What are you doing here?"

"Sofia called and told me what happened." He shrugged adorably.

And he'd decided to step in last minute? Jenna's heart squeezed tight at the generous gesture. "You don't even want to go to prom. You said it was a stupid tradition."

"That was before I had such an awesome date. You'll increase my street cred tenfold."

She scrunched up her face in a mock scowl. "You don't have to do this, Ty. My ego will survive the rejection."

"I want to help." He stood back and held out his arms in a "look at me" way. "Now are you going to tell me how handsome I look or what? It took me almost five whole minutes to get ready and you haven't even complimented me."

Something deep inside brightened at Ty's kindness. A light that shone into some darkened corner of her heart. "Thank you, Tyson. Really. And you do look very handsome."

"Why thank you." He lowered his voice. "I told your mom there was a last-minute change. She didn't really question it."

Jenna wasn't surprised. Her mom had always thought she and Tyson should be together. An idea that had always made Jenna roll her eyes.

Rushed footsteps sounded from the other room. "Wait, wait, wait." Mom dashed into the foyer carrying a plastic boutonniere box. Her face fell when she saw Jenna. "Oh, shoot! I wanted to get a video of you coming down the stairs."

"Not a problem." Ty grabbed Jenna by the shoulders and turned her around. "Get back up there, Greene. This calls for a do-over!"

"Fine." Jenna sighed and began climbing the stairs, taking careful steps.

"Mama Dee, be sure and catch my expression as I set eyes on my gorgeous date for the first time."

"Oh, don't you worry. I won't miss a thing."

Jenna tossed Ty a mock scowl over her shoulder, even though his words warmed her through. She couldn't believe he was doing this. When she reached the top of the staircase, she pivoted. "Ready for me, Mom?"

"Just a second . . . Gotta turn on the camera. Go slow so I don't miss anything. Okay, I'm ready."

"Are you sure? I don't know how many times I can make it down the steps in these heels. I was lucky I made it the first time."

"I tried to warn you . . ."

"You're not going to flake out on me, are you?" Tyson called. "I mean, *my* shoes aren't exactly comfortable, but I have every intention of dancing the night away."

"Are you coming?"

Jenna rolled her eyes though no one could see. "Yes, Mother." Jenna grabbed the handrail and took the first step, feeling suddenly lighter. The weight she'd felt only moments before seemed to have fallen right off—and just like that she was looking forward to the evening ahead.

Four hours later Jenna couldn't even believe she'd been sitting in her room crying over stupid Evan Sanders earlier. She was having a blast! She'd forgotten what a great dancer Tyson was. She'd slipped off her shoes only a few songs into the night, and they'd boogied the night away.

She was so busy being spun around the floor, she hardly even spared a glance at Evan and Amanda. Though Jenna had to admit the girl was a knockout in her formfitting dress. She was petite and curvy in all the right places, the ice-pink gown setting off her long blonde hair and sun-kissed skin.

But it was easy to forget the other couple since Tyson was the perfect date, fetching her drinks, making her laugh, and ensuring she was having a good time.

They hung out mostly with Sofia and Jack, but Tyson's friends also included them in their group. Early in the night some of them had done a double take upon seeing Jenna. It served as a much-needed ego bolster on a night when her self-esteem had taken a hard hit. Maybe she shouldn't be so reluctant to dress up and fix her hair now and then. Just because she was athletic didn't mean she was condemned to sweats and jeans for the rest of her life.

Late in the night they were taking a break by the drink station with Sofia and Jack when the band began the melodic strains of a slow song. Sofia tugged a groaning Jack onto the dance floor. He lacked rhythm and refused to fast-dance, so he'd promised Sofia he'd dance every slow song to make it up to her. Her friend looked gorgeous tonight, the gold gown making the most of her warm olive skin tone. Jack's golden-blond hair and lightly freckled skin made him the perfect counterpart for Sofia.

Jenna smiled at Jack's reticence to dance, then chuckled a moment later when he began shuffling in a circle, his movements as stiff as a flagpole.

"You gotta hand it to him," Ty said as he watched the couple. "He's keeping his word."

"And see how happy she looks?"

"They make a good couple. How long have they been dating?"

"A few months, I guess. They bonded over their love of math."

He made a face. "Really?"

"Yeah, it's not something she and I have in common. But she did manage to get me through trig, so there's that."

"Where was she when I was in trig?"

She slid Ty a coy look. "Probably watching you date Danielle Collins." Who was known more for her bra size than her IQ.

"That class wreaked havoc on my GPA. Maybe I should be more strategic about who I go out with."

Jenna caught sight of Evan and Amanda dancing so closely that you couldn't fit a feather between them. The sight triggered her earlier feelings of rejection. What had happened between him and Jenna? They'd spent many hours on the phone and texting over those few weeks. Had she bored him to death? Or had he just decided the cute, curvaceous Amanda was more to his liking?

Tyson tugged her hand. "Hey, let's dance, Greene. I like this song."

She'd never known him to like country ballads, but she let him lead her to the dance floor anyway. When he turned and took her into his arms, she put her hands on his shoulders. They seemed so broad even without the suit coat he'd ditched long ago. The white shirt stretched over his muscular arms and looked crisp against his tanned neck.

They hadn't slow-danced all night, so she hadn't really gotten a close-up look at him since the foyer. His angled jawline had a bit of stubble in uneven patches. When he'd gotten that call from Sofia, he must not have had time to shave. Had been in too big a hurry to come to her rescue. She was a modern girl—she was perfectly capable of saving herself. But it was nice having a friend who came through when needed. The thought curved her lips into a smile.

"What?" he called over the music, fingering his jaw. "Admiring my beard?"

She laughed. "That is not a beard, buddy."

"Well, not yet, but it will be someday."

"Whatever you say." She gave his shoulder a placating pat. "I'm just grateful you rescued me tonight. I thought it was going to be an awful night, and instead I've had a lot of fun. You're not a bad date, Parker."

"You're pretty fun yourself, Greene. Got yourself some sweet moves even." The corner of his mouth ticked up.

Tyson had nice lips—the bottom one slightly fuller than the top. She'd never noticed before. Oh, she knew he was good-looking. He got his share of attention from their female classmates, and she knew of at least three girls who would've given anything to be his prom date. But his on-and-off relationship with Danielle had ended on a sour note, complicating things for him at school, and he'd decided to refrain from dating the rest of the school year.

The band segued into the chorus, and Tyson spun her out dramatically, then pulled her back into his arms, making her laugh. He'd been delighting her all night long with silly dance moves and humorous anecdotes.

She was blessed to have such a loyal friend. Their similar interests—mainly sports and the outdoors—had drawn them together. And his extroverted disposition complemented her more introspective personality. They'd always made a great team, and she could see them being friends well beyond high school. She hoped so. A woman would be lucky to have someone like Tyson in her corner. Not to mention his whole family.

She pressed a little closer and linked her hands behind his neck. Without her heels the top of her head only reached his chin. His height and muscular build made her feel small and feminine, a rarity. She might enjoy feeling strong and powerful on the ball diamond and the volleyball court. But it was also nice to feel dainty and pretty sometimes. Beneath the ponytail and athletic wear, she was still a girl.

As the music ramped up she caught sight of Evan and Amanda again just to her left. They were still wrapped up like a burrito, one of Evan's hands against the small of her back, the other scandalously low. When his gaze landed on Jenna, she jerked her attention back to Tyson's chest.

Was she somehow lacking whatever it was that boys liked in girls? Was that why no one asked her out? Maybe it had nothing to do with her athleticism and everything to do with her personality. Maybe she was too dull to hold a boy's interest.

Tyson tilted her chin upward, his eyes taking in her features and probably seeing the hurt and self-doubt that plagued her.

"Want to make him sorry he ever stood you up?"

What did Ty mean? It didn't even matter. Of course she wanted to put Evan in his place. "How?"

A smile flickered in Tyson's eyes before he leaned down and brushed his lips across hers. The touch of his lips should've felt foreign and awkward. But his mouth was warm and inviting. His pace slow and reverent. She sank into the kiss even as her heart stuttered.

He pulled back, then pressed her head to his chest, allowing her a moment to recover.

She'd always feared her first kiss would be unskilled and embarrassing. But it had been neither of those things. It had felt like the most natural thing in the world. But at the same time it had also made her breath hitch and her knees wobble.

The biggest surprise—it hadn't felt like a friend's kiss. Whenever her mother had teased her about Tyson, Jenna had always recoiled a little, thinking of him like that. Of them, together.

But the kiss hadn't grossed her out at all. Not by a long shot. Maybe that's the way kisses were with anyone. How would she know any different? Or maybe he'd had so much experience kissing Danielle Collins that he was just that good. Strangely, the thought pricked Jenna with jealousy.

Tyson leaned down and whispered into her ear, "Mission accomplished."

Chapter 11

The day after she hung out at Chatties with Ty and his brothers, Jenna had a few kayak tours. A sunny Saturday was sure to bring out all the tourists. Earlier her muscles had protested loudly as she got out of bed, but by afternoon she'd worked out the tightness and felt energized again.

She was currently crossing the channel as she guided a private tour—Cameron and Maya, a pair of honeymooners from Tennessee. Maya had read about the wild ponies years ago and always wanted to visit Assateague Island. Her groom had surprised her with a honeymoon on Chincoteague. They were in their mid-twenties, wearing matching Titans caps, and so obviously in love. They frequently traded infatuated gazes and were hardly able to keep their hands off each other, even as they paddled separate kayaks.

As the couple's laughter carried across the water, a prick of jealousy stabbed Jenna in the heart. She wanted that kind of love and intimacy for herself. Wanted a lifelong commitment with a partner she could grow old with. Who didn't?

That could've been you, if only you'd said yes.

Even as she chastised herself, she gave her head a shake. That wasn't really true, was it? She hadn't gazed at Jason the way Maya stared at Cameron. And Jason never would've planned a honeymoon to some tiny island just so she could fulfill a youthful fantasy. He'd always wanted to go to Italy on his honeymoon and talked about their eventual trip there often. At the time she'd been amenable to the idea. It was Italy after all.

But she'd always imagined a mountain-lodge honeymoon, just the two of them, a fire crackling in the fireplace while falling snow spread a white blanket over the landscape. She'd never really stated her wishes, though. So she could hardly blame him for assuming she wanted Italy too.

"Look, there's a pony!" A huge smile spread across Maya's face.

Jenna jerked her thoughts to the present and told them the stallion's name, then pointed out two mares hiding among the scrub. "They're part of the same band—that's what we call groups of ponies that hang together, kind of like a family."

The trio continued paddling until they reached the marshy shoreline. Although Maya already knew a lot about the ponies, she wanted Cameron to hear the full spiel, so Jenna happily complied. The couple listened attentively, frequently taking photos.

"Why does the fire company manage the ponies?" Cameron asked. "That seems kind of random."

"It all started back in the 1920s after two devastating fires destroyed large sections of the island of Chincoteague. The villagers realized they didn't have the equipment they needed to protect the town. So they authorized the company to hold a carnival to raise funds during Pony Penning Days—by then pony penning was already an ancient tradition. That year more than fifteen colts were auctioned off, and the carnival was hugely successful.

"Word got around and by 1937 crowds were estimated at twenty-five thousand. The revenue from the carnival and auction afforded the fire company the modern equipment and facilities they needed. Then in 1943 the Chincoteague National Wildlife Refuge was established on Assateague to protect migratory birds, and the fire company was eventually able to secure grazing rights for one hundred fifty ponies."

Maya pitched in. "Then *Misty of Chincoteague* was published and word about the ponies spread even farther."

"Which brings us to today, when we can hopefully continue preserving this wild herd for future generations to enjoy."

Before moving on toward the lighthouse, Jenna took a few shots of the couple with the ponies in the background. Next she took them around the bay where a few more ponies grazed.

Her heart gave a soft squeeze as she caught sight of Dream. Her white coat gleamed in the afternoon sunshine. *There you are. I've missed you, girl.*

Seeing the mare brought back so many fond memories. Dad, being a captain with the fire company and a saltwater cowboy, had engendered her love for the ponies from a young age. For as long as Jenna could remember, she'd wanted to purchase a buyback pony.

Finally, when she was eight, Dad had encouraged her to save her money for an entire year so they could afford a buyback. Of course she was much older by the time she realized her savings had been a drop in the bucket. Dad had gotten a promotion that year, and he and Mom invested their hard-earned money to fulfill Jenna's dream. He just wanted her to have some skin in the game.

The auction was so exciting. Jenna had had her eye on the white foal because she was beautiful, and that day she took one look in the pony's eyes and knew she was the one. The bidding was competitive, though, and Dad had to go a little beyond what they'd anticipated. She'd hugged him so hard when their final bid held.

Her eyes stung at the memory. *Look, Daddy. She's still here. Still so beautiful.*

Just then Dream lifted her head and seemed to stare straight at Jenna. She felt it right in the middle of her chest. Could hardly breathe for a few seconds.

"Ooh, that one's all white," Maya said. "She's so pretty."

Jenna swallowed against the lump in her throat. "That's Dream. She's eighteen so she's getting up in years. The average life span of the ponies is twenty to thirty years, slightly less than domestic horses. But because of the fire company's care, they live longer in the harsh environment than they otherwise would."

"She's so unique."

"She is." And then, because Jenna felt comfortable with the couple, she added, "But Dream is extra special to me because my dad and I bought her seventeen years ago as a buyback."

Maya beamed. "Aw, and you got to name her."

"Her full name is Jenna's Dream, but mostly she just goes by Dream. She's actually a descendant of Misty."

"That's very cool," Cameron said.

Jenna didn't mention that her dad had passed. She didn't want pity marring the poignant moment. While the couple occupied themselves taking photos of the grazing ponies, Jenna just rested in her kayak, the warm breeze skating over her skin, watching Dream and remembering her dad.

Chapter 12

Tyson stowed his turnout gear in his locker, his heart still racing from the call. It had only been a grill fire, but the grill had been near the overhang of the house, making it a threat to the structure and other nearby homes. As a captain he assumed leadership at the scene, oversaw the other firefighters, and made critical decisions.

Luke put his boots in the locker next to Ty's. The other firefighters did the same, talking among themselves, the noise echoing through the large apparatus bay. The building was new and modern, and the firefighters took pride in keeping it and the fire trucks pristine.

Luke glanced at Ty as he shoved his coat into the red mesh locker. "You all right?"

"Sure." Adrenaline from the action kept him a little hyped, but the call had gone well. No one was hurt and the only loss was the grill—a pretty old one at that.

"You seemed a little intense back there."

"Well, the house could've caught fire."

"Sure, but we would've put that out quickly enough." Luke made an effort to tame his hat hair. "Think you were a little rough on Wheeler back there?"

"He's got a lot to learn."

"He's a probie but he's coming along all right."

Ty turned to Luke and gave him a pointed look. “Is there something you’re trying to say?”

Luke met his gaze quietly for a long moment.

The pause gave Ty a chance to reflect on his words and tone. “Sorry. Guess I am a little amped up.”

“What’s going on?”

Ty paused as the other firefighters said good-bye to them. Walker and Drury barely glanced Tyson’s way. They were still miffed about the whole Marissa deal. Ty had hoped things would’ve returned to normal by now, but there was still tension at the station.

He turned his attention back to Luke. “I’m just feeling a lot of pressure, I guess. And I’m tired.” Also he was scared to death of losing someone else. Scared of screwing up and being to blame. The guilt he already carried was heavy enough. But the nightmares were keeping him from getting a good night’s sleep, and that wasn’t good either.

“Stay out late with Jenna last night?”

“Yeah,” Ty said, even though he’d made it home long before midnight. The outing at Chatties had been fun. Lots of laughter and dancing. Felt like old times. Even though Seth’s misplaced interest in Jenna still rattled him. “Alex and Seth joined us for a while.”

“Sounds like fun.” Luke straightened his boots. “Did Trinity say anything else to you?”

“You mean about you? Just call the woman and ask her out already.”

“I don’t have her number.”

“Well, you know where she works. Put the both of you out of your misery.”

Luke slid Ty a pained look. “She’s out of my league, man. She’s gorgeous and she's going to law school, so she's also way smarter than me."

"You're plenty smart. And she's obviously interested or she wouldn't have gotten all flustered just asking about you."

"We probably don't have anything in common."

"Well, gee, how will you ever figure that out?"

"All right, all right. Point taken."

"You're a good guy, Luke, and you've got a lot to offer. You should go for it."

Luke's shoulders raised on a breath and lowered on an exhale. "You're right. I'll head over to Chatties tonight for a drink, and if she seems receptive I'll ask her out."

"How do you know she's working tonight?"

Luke shifted and mumbled something.

Ty's lips twitched. "You have her schedule memorized."

"No, I don't." But the flush in Luke's cheeks told a different story.

Ty let out a bark of laughter as they headed toward the exit.

Luke gave him a shove. "Shut up."

"I'll meet you at Chatties. No way I'm going to miss this."

"Golly gee, thanks. How can I turn down that kind of support?"

Ty clapped him on the back. "Always there for you, buddy." The grin fell from Ty's face as he spotted Wheeler waiting by the back door, expression tight, shoulders rigid. He was young and small for a firefighter—maybe five seven and pretty lean. But he made up for his size with effort and determination.

"Need a ride?" Luke said to Wheeler.

"No, my girlfriend's coming."

Tyson paused by the door as Luke exited. "See you at Chatties—six o'clock?"

"Sure." Luke glanced between Ty and Wheeler. "See you guys later."

The door fell shut and quiet prevailed for a drawn-out moment. He owed the guy an apology for earlier. Part of being a leader was being able to admit when you were wrong. "Hey, sorry for being so rough on you today. It was no reflection on your work. You're doing great."

"I've made some mistakes."

"Everybody makes mistakes when they're learning. You've got what it takes to do the job."

Wheeler's eyes lit with hope. "Think so?"

"I've seen a lot of men and women come and go. Keep doing what you're doing and you'll be fine."

Wheeler's face relaxed in a smile. "Thanks, Captain. I really appreciate it." His attention turned toward the door. "Allie's here. See you later."

"Have a good one." After Wheeler left, Ty started to push through the door but paused yet again. He needed to get back to the B and B, but his successful apology to Wheeler gave him hope that he could rectify things with Marissa too.

He turned back toward the bay where the two paramedics on staff, Marissa and O'Neil, were mopping the far side of the bay. As usual Marissa wore her brunette hair in a neat bun for work.

"Hey, guys."

Marissa glanced his way. "Hey."

The thirtysomething man barely gave Ty a nod.

Ty turned his attention toward Marissa. "I was wondering if I could have a word with you? In private?"

They both glanced at O'Neil, who kept mopping, seemingly reluctant to leave them alone.

As if Ty posed some kind of threat to Marissa. Ty frowned at him.

Marissa leaned her mop against the bay door and headed toward the break room, obviously expecting Ty to follow, which he did.

Once inside the room she turned, crossing her arms over her chest. She seemed young with her fine features and wide green eyes. But then, she *was* young at only twenty-two. Probably too young for him.

She hiked her arched brows, waiting.

"Listen, I know I screwed up. I was really in no place emotionally to be dating at all, and mixing business with pleasure was a terrible idea. I didn't mean to hurt you, but I know I did, so I'm really sorry."

Her green eyes flashed. "You embarrassed me in front of my friends."

He winced. A bit harsh, but he could see her point. "I'm sorry. I didn't mean to do that."

"You showed up in public with another woman when I thought our relationship was going somewhere. Do you have any idea how hurtful that was?"

He scratched his neck. He'd told her he wasn't looking for a relationship. They'd barely even kissed. But he was here to put things right, not upset her even more. "I didn't realize that. I thought we were on the same—"

The emergency alarm sounded throughout the speaker system. The paramedics were being called to a scene.

"I have to go." Marissa didn't so much as glance his way as she tore from the room.

Releasing a heavy sigh, Ty watched her leave. He'd thought they just might be able to put this conflict in the past. Oh well. One for two wasn't bad.

Chapter 13

The sun beat down relentlessly as Jenna carried the flat of annuals to her mom. She seemed completely out of her element, squatting over the mulch bed, wearing a pair of rubber dish gloves. "I don't think I've ever seen you garden, Mom."

"I'm not gardening. I'm just planting a few flowers. Aren't they pretty? They'll be a nice splash of color, and I chose flowers that don't need a lot of care—I know my limitations."

They'd already planted three flats, and the bright purple and yellow did look nice against the house.

Mom sat back on her haunches. "How's your job search going?"

"I've put some résumés in at various places, but I haven't heard back yet. There's a Parks and Recreation position that might be interesting."

"That seems right up your alley."

Jenna set down the flat. "It sounds fun."

"Or . . . you could apply for a few jobs on the island, see what turns up." Mom's voice lilted up at the end. "It would be great to have you close by again—not that I'm trying to pressure you into anything."

It wasn't as if Jenna hadn't considered the idea. Nothing was holding her in Alexandria anymore. "I'm not averse to the idea. I love Chincoteague, and it would be great if we didn't live over three hours from each other. But there isn't much opportunity here." Most of the jobs were retail work, catering to tourists—not the best use of her degree. And a lot of them didn't pay a living wage. In recent years real estate on the island had shot up as people from away purchased vacation homes. "I wouldn't be able to afford a house."

"You're welcome to stay here as long as you want, honey."

"Thanks, Mom, but I'm heading toward thirty—way too old to be sleeping in my childhood bedroom." She waited for Mom to say something about the apartment above the garage. Something to indicate it would soon be vacant and available.

"You could always use Gram's trust fund to help you along. I think she would've been happy to see you return to the island."

"I don't want to spend that money just making ends meet. I want to invest it in something special. Something that would've made Gram proud."

Mom offered a smile. "It's your money to do with as you wish. Gram was already proud of you."

"I know that."

A frown pinched Mom's brows. "If I hadn't let go of her house, you could've moved right in."

"You can't foretell the future, Mom. You did what you thought was best at the time. That's all we can do."

"Well, I'll keep my ear to the ground for an open position. Maybe something interesting will turn up."

"Thanks, Mom." Jenna rose to her feet and dragged a hand over her sweaty brow. "I'm going to grab a water. Want one?"

"Could you get me one of those raspberry teas?"

The drink Gordon had introduced Mom to was quickly becoming her favorite. "Sure."

The cool air-conditioning swept over Jenna's skin as she entered the house. The effect Gordon was having on her mom was so weird.

She was *gardening* now? What next—bird-watching? Jujitsu? Flame-throwing?

She reined in her sarcasm. It was *good* that Mom was trying new things and getting out of the house more. It just . . . wasn't really *her*. Or not the mom she'd known all her life.

Jenna was reaching for the fridge door when she heard a voice. Gordon. The sound trickled in from the backyard through the patio door, which was slightly ajar.

"I'm not sure . . . Yeah, it's going well . . ."

As a pause drew out, Jenna crept closer to the door. His voice was low and tender. He was obviously talking to someone with whom he was close.

"It's beautiful here. Who knew Maine was so nice this time of year?"

Maine? Jenna frowned. Why was he lying about where he was? The potential answers stirred up a hornet's nest in her gut. She feared he wasn't the man he portrayed himself to be. He was probably using her mom for financial reasons. Meanwhile she was falling head over heels for him and would wind up heartbroken.

Jenna pressed her fingers to her temple. Maybe she should confront him. Tell him she'd heard what he said. But what if he simply claimed she'd misunderstood? What if she stirred up trouble and Mom took his side?

"I'm glad to hear it," Gordon said softly. "Okay . . . I miss you too."

The call was winding down, and he would soon enter the house. What should Jenna do? She didn't have actual proof. All she had was hearsay, and her mother was so besotted with him, she feared Mom might believe she'd simply heard wrong.

Making a quick decision, she grabbed the drinks and scooted

from the room. But not before she heard Gordon's quiet parting words: "All right. Love you too."

"Are you sure that's what he said?" Tyson asked Jenna thirty minutes later.

Jenna had hunted him down at his house the first chance she got. His small home was predictably tidy, and he'd recently invested in some nice leather furniture and gray paint. It now looked less early American dorm room and more responsible adult male.

They sat at his well-lit island over glasses of water because that was the only beverage he had on hand.

"I heard every word," Jenna said. "Do you think he's got another woman stashed away somewhere?"

"There's a limited number of people you say 'I love you' to."

"It could be his son or daughter, I guess. From his tone, it seemed he was speaking with a woman. But it still could've been a female relative."

Ty frowned. "But why would he lie to a relative about where he was?"

"Good question." For that very reason Jenna didn't believe it had been a relative at all.

Ty stood and retrieved his laptop from the coffee table. "I think it's time we did a little research on this guy."

She followed him to the sofa. "He's not on social media. I already checked."

"There are other ways of investigating people."

"Oh, you've stalked someone before, then?"

He clacked away at the keyboard. "We're not stalking. We're just digging a little."

"Potatoes, po-tah-toes. Oh, put in Washington, DC. That's where he's from."

A screen opened up with a list of Gordon Smiths living in DC. Her hopes sank. "There are fifty-two of them?"

He pointed to the screen. "Yeah, but the listings include the ages. Do you know how old he is?"

"Around sixty, I'd say."

He began clicking on all the Gordons ranging from fifty-five to sixty-five. The complete listings included people related to each Gordon as well as associated phone numbers and addresses.

Jenna soon became overwhelmed by all the information. "That didn't narrow it down much."

"We need more information so we can refine the search. You said he was twice divorced, right?"

"Once divorced and once widowed. Or widowered? But who knows if it's the truth. We don't even know for sure that's his real name. I mean, *Smith.* Really?"

"He would've had to provide proof of identity for the cruise. Surely your mom saw his key card, which would've had his name on it."

"True. That's something, I guess. We'll assume it's his real name for now."

"He has two grown kids and he was an accountant?" Ty asked.

"As far as I know. I haven't learned very much about him. He really doesn't talk about himself much, so I have to ask questions."

"And it's hard not to sound like you're suspicious."

"I *am* suspicious."

Ty nodded. "Me too. I don't like that he's letting your mom pay for everything. That's odd."

"And then there's the mysterious person on the other end of his 'I love you.'"

"If you could find out his address or his exact age, we could narrow this down a lot."

"That's true." Jenna sagged against the sofa. This was so frustrating, knowing the man might be taking advantage of her mother and feeling so helpless to fix it. Her mom had already been hurt so badly when Dad died. It was a rough few years for both of them. The last thing Mom deserved was some con man scamming her.

Jenna's heart pinched at the thought of the pain this would cause.

Ty touched her arm. "Hey, you okay? Having second thoughts about this?"

"No, I just . . . I don't want to see Mom get hurt again." She pressed a palm to the pinch in her chest. Funny how you could love someone so much that you could actually feel their pain as your own. "She's already falling for him, Ty. You should see the way she looks at him. It reminds me of . . ."

"What?"

"The way she used to look at my dad. I can't believe this has progressed so quickly, and I can't help but think it's because Gordon's manipulating her."

His eyes softened. "I'll do whatever I can to help. You know that, right?"

"Thanks. You're always there when I need you."

He bumped her shoulder. "That goes both ways."

He'd been so supportive when she and Jason parted ways. Ty had always been supportive. Back when she'd left for college and was missing home, he stayed in close contact. When she'd struggled with her statistics class, he even came up several times to study with her. He was a true-blue friend. It meant a lot, especially after the way she'd lost most of her Alexandria "friends" when she and Jason broke up.

The reminder of Jason stirred some thoughts she'd been struggling with lately. Thoughts about their relationship and her own part in what had happened.

Tyson's gaze sharpened on her. "There something else bothering you?"

Should she share the concerns she'd been having lately? She took in Ty's warm and caring expression. If not with Ty, then with who? "I've been thinking about my relationship with Jason and processing what went wrong."

Ty gave a droll smile. "Ah, the postmortem. I'm familiar. And as I recall, I did a fair amount of that processing with you."

He'd had plenty to sort out when Britt left him for another man. "Right. I just can't help but think . . . that maybe I didn't love Jason the way I was supposed to. I mean, I got over him so quickly. So that can't be love, right? I thought I was in love, but there must've been some reason I was putting off marriage. Some reason I couldn't say yes when he proposed. Maybe he was right about that after all."

"Why do you think you stayed with him so long, if not for love?"

She'd wondered this dozens of times over the past few months. Her sigh seemed to come from her toes. "I don't know. When I first met him I looked up to him. Maybe I just wanted to be with someone. Wanted that connection, that intimacy." She leaned into the warmth radiating from Ty's expression and spoke the truth. "I don't think I've ever been in love, Ty. Not really."

"Well, that's okay. It can take time to find the right person."

"Yeah, but . . ." She clamped her lips shut over the words threatening to escape. They seemed to pile up in her throat, forming a big lump.

"But what?"

Her heart was thudding so hard that it felt like it might burst from her chest. "I think there might be something wrong with me."

"Ah, Jen." He wrapped an arm around her and pulled her in. "There's nothing wrong with you."

Tears pressed against her eyes as she dropped her head to his shoulder. "Then why did I stay with him so long? I led him on."

"Not intentionally. Maybe you wanted it to work so badly that you let yourself believe it was true. It sounds like you admired him a lot."

She snorted. "That's a far cry from being in love, isn't it?"

"If you've never been in love, how can you know for sure what it feels like? Don't be so hard on yourself. Remember how I second-guessed everything with Britt? Maybe I wasn't a good husband. Maybe I didn't meet her needs. Maybe I wasn't enough."

Jenna pressed away and gave him a stern look. "You *are* enough. And her cheating was *not* your fault."

"Maybe not. But that didn't stop me from wondering." He cupped her cheek as his gaze homed in on her. "There is nothing wrong with you. You are a very loving person, and when you find the right man, you'll fall in love."

She huffed. "You have to say that. You're my best friend." But the way his touch warmed her skin, the way his gaze burned through her, seemed to challenge that claim. Her heart did a strange little wobble. The pause lengthened between them.

His gaze held hers.

Her pulse skittered to a halt. Seeking his touch, she leaned ever so slightly into his palm.

His gaze softened on her. His lips parted.

What would his mouth feel like on hers? She already knew the answer. Once upon a time he'd kissed her. It was over so fast, but not before she realized Tyson was a masterful kisser. The soft, reverent touch was a memory she'd carried for years, judging each first kiss by it—and often finding they fell far short.

And though she'd tried to put it from her mind all these years, there'd been a while after that kiss when she'd caught feelings for her best friend. But before she could even process those feelings, Ty got back with Danielle Collins and ended any fantasy Jenna might've had about being more than friends.

She'd never told a soul about those feelings—especially not Ty. She felt too vulnerable. Too embarrassed that it was so obviously one-sided. And eventually, as the summer wore on, she decided it was for the best. Romantic relationships came and went. But her friendship with Tyson was steady and strong. Nothing was worth the risk of losing it.

But now those same thoughts and feelings seemed to be resurfacing.

Tyson cleared his throat, jerking Jenna to the present. He gave her shoulder a quick squeeze before he released her altogether.

She shook the strange thoughts and feelings away. *Seriously, what is wrong with you? You cannot have romantic feelings for Tyson.*

And now he was putting space between them, probably completely perplexed by her behavior.

Jenna popped to her feet. "I should probably go. Maybe I'll just, uh, talk to Mom. Tell her what I overheard." That would eliminate the need for Tyson and her to do more research together. She apparently needed some space to get her head on straight. And after that awkward moment, he probably wanted that space even more than she did.

Ty followed her to the door. "But the few times you questioned her about Gordon, she was resistant. If you tell her about the phone call, she'll just assume it was his daughter—and think you misheard the part about Maine."

The last thing Jenna wanted was to drive a wedge between herself and Mom.

"If she's invested in this relationship," he said, "you might need actual proof."

"You're probably right." At the door she turned to him. "But I don't have to drag you into this. I can figure it out on my own. This isn't your problem."

"You're not dragging me. I offered." A twinkle entered his eyes. "Besides, I'm better at this stuff than you are."

"You stalker, you."

He elbowed her.

Relief swelled now that they were back in familiar territory. And also because he didn't seem put off or act like he wanted space. "You sure? I know summers are busy for you."

He gave a steady grin. "I'm sure."

"Have it your way. I'll be in touch."

"Address and age," he called as she headed toward her car.

She waved. "I'll let you know."

Chapter 14

Coffee at AmaRin was one of the things Jenna had missed most about living off island. The shop, famous for its rich java and flaky pastries, had run out of the latter by the time she and Sofia met up at four o'clock on Monday. A shame, since their chocolate croissant was the stuff of legends.

After greeting each other, Sofia and Jenna settled into one of the back wooden booths. The place was almost quiet compared to the busy mornings at the shop, and Jenna was eager for some uninterrupted girl time.

She took the first sip of her caramel macchiato and felt her world tip upright. "Ah . . . all is right with the world again."

Sofia arched a brow, her brown eyes sparkling. "Should I leave you two alone?"

Jenna cradled her white mug. "You might feel the same about yours if it had a little flavoring."

"I'll take mine strong and cold, thank you very much. You know it's ninety degrees outside, right?"

Sofia had always teased her about drinking hot coffee year-round. "Coffee should not be served cold. I'll go to the grave defending that opinion."

"Except for coffee ice cream?"

"That's a food, not a drink."

Sofia held up her cold brew. "Well, here's to caffeine, in whatever form."

Jenna tapped her glass. "Hear, hear." Then she took another sip. "How's the practice going?" Sofia was a clinical psychologist who counseled online, which gave her a flexible schedule.

"It's been very busy. I hired an assistant to help with scheduling and she's a dream. Sara Blevins. Do you know her?"

"I don't think so."

"She's new to the island. Single mom, super nice with two cute kiddos."

"I'm glad she's working out well for you. And how's Jack doing? You two still seem like quite the lovebirds." Sofia posted regularly on Instagram.

"When it's meant to be, it's meant to be. Not that there's no work involved, of course. But he's a good man." Sofia offered a coy smile. "I guess I'll keep him."

Jenna sighed. "You're so blessed to have found each other so early in life. You saved yourself a lot of dating nightmares. Single life is for the birds."

"I'm sorry things didn't work out with Jason. How are you doing with that?"

"I've been trying to process it all." She caught her friend up on some of the thoughts she'd shared with Ty yesterday, omitting the part where she was questioning her own capacity for love.

"When you turned down his proposal you trusted your instincts. And it sounds as if he didn't respond very well."

"Because he fired me on the spot?" Jenna joked.

"And left you standing on the sidewalk, the jerk. You know,

sometimes it just takes a while to find your person. There's nothing wrong with that."

"That's what Ty said."

Sofia's lips tilted upward. "How is Tyson? I haven't seen him in months. I feel like I've had my face in front of the computer screen all winter."

"He's the same old Ty. Still working for his parents and volunteering for the fire company." He was, in fact, one of the steadiest men she'd ever known.

"Is he still pining after Britt? I always thought he could do better, and I don't think anyone except Tyson was too sad when she moved back home."

"I'm happy to say he seems to have gotten beyond all that. It was hard to see him struggling. But he's doing much better these days. He's trying to help me figure out who Mom's new boyfriend is." Jenna had already filled Sofia in on her suspicions.

"How's he doing that?"

"We're gathering information and digging around online."

A pause ensued as Sofia took a sip of her cold brew. "Have you tried talking to your mom about your concerns?"

"Have you met my mom?"

Sofia's laugh was infectious. "Okay, okay, point taken. But she might not be too thrilled when she finds out you've been investigating her new love interest behind her back."

"Probably not, but that beats letting her heart get broken because I stood around doing nothing."

"Hey, guys." Tyson strode their way, wearing a warm smile and a white Sand and Saddle polo that showed off his tan. They stood and greeted him, Sofia going in for a big hug.

The two caught up for a quick minute, then Jenna invited him to sit down.

"Thanks, but I can't stay. I'm on a coffee run for Mom and Dad. Any luck with that intel?"

Jenna cut him a *really?* look. "It's been less than twenty-four hours."

"What can I say, Greene? I had high expectations of you."

She gave him a gentle shove. "There are high expectations, and then there are miracles."

"Wouldn't be the first time you pulled off one of those."

As a shortstop Jenna had been known to snag line drives that were seemingly impossible to reach. "Sadly, I'm less spectacular on the field of life."

"Stop it." Ty softened the rebuke with a grin. "You're as impressive as ever."

"Parker!" one of the baristas called.

"I should take off while the coffee's hot. Mom'll be disappointed they're out of chocolate croissants."

"I feel her pain," Jenna said.

They said their good-byes, then Ty retrieved the drinks and gave a final wave before he slipped out the door.

Jenna took another sip of her drink as she scanned the local artwork on the wall.

"Okay . . . what was that?" Sofia said.

"What was what?"

"That. The two of you just now."

"I don't know what you mean." But the heat rolling into her cheeks belied the statement.

"You guys were flirting with each other." Sofia's tone was infused with delight.

"No . . ."

"Yes."

Jenna thought back to the conversation. Had they been flirting? Maybe just a little. If so, that was new.

"What is going on? There's something you're not telling me—you're biting your lip."

Jenna released it. "Nothing. There's nothing going on. But we did have kind of a weird thing yesterday." Jenna tried to explain the tense moment that had passed between them, but she ended up feeling stupid—as nothing had actually happened.

"It sounds as if you experienced a fresh awareness of Tyson."

"I'm perfectly aware of Tyson."

Sofia gave a droll grin. "Don't be obtuse. You saw him in a new way. As a *man*. And maybe he saw you in a new way too."

Jenna squirmed. "I don't think so. He cleared his throat and that was that."

"Well, if he cleared his throat then."

"He was putting an end to the . . . the . . . whatever it was!"

"Moment of heightened awareness. If your friendship's moving in a different direction, that's a delicate matter. And if he ended the moment, it might've been because he was just as confused as you. But I'd also like to point out once again that he was flirting with you just now, so . . ."

"He was just teasing me, his good ol' buddy."

Sofia offered a saucy grin. "Somebody's in deep denial."

Jenna sent her a mock scowl. But was her friend right? Were Tyson's feelings for Jenna evolving? Did she want them to? Something took flight inside her at the thought. She sure hadn't minded the flirting. And those fluttery feelings he'd stirred yesterday had been rather pleasant.

"Do you think your feelings for him are shifting? There's nothing wrong with that, you know. Tyson's a great guy."

"I have no business thinking about *any* man right now. I just ended a long-term relationship." She had to figure out if something was wrong with her before she plunged headlong into another relationship.

"I hear what you're saying, and that's certainly a valid point. But just for the record"—Sofia cocked a brow—"you didn't answer my question."

Chapter 15

Tyson frowned as Mama Dee cozied up to Gordon on the patio love seat. Ty's parents had invited the couple and Jenna for supper. They'd also invited Ty and his brothers, but Alex and Seth had other plans.

Now the group was settled in the outdoor oasis they'd created two summers ago. Ty laid the brick pavers, forming the sweeping curves of the free-form patio. Dad made and set the firepit. Mom hung the overhead lights, picked out the furniture, and added all the finishing touches. The guests loved it.

As sparks shot up into the darkened sky and conversation carried around the pit, Ty could see why. A warm breeze rustled the treetops. Out in the darkened paddock Penny nickered. Patches' answer followed soon after.

"And then one of those monkeys jumped right on top of my head!" Mama Dee said.

Gordon peered down at her. "She squealed like a little schoolgirl."

"Then another one jumped on my shoulder and on my lap, and those men just kept throwing seeds right at me. And the more seeds they threw, the more monkeys piled on."

"She must've had eight monkeys on her at once. Show 'em the pictures, honey."

Honey? It had been all of two and a half weeks since they'd first met. Ty traded a glance with Jenna as Mama Dee showed off the photos.

Mom laughed, her gray hair gleaming in the firelight. "I think the little guys are kind of cute. Though I'm not sure I'd want them crawling all over me. You look terrified, Dee."

"I *was* terrified!"

"Seconds after this photo she jumped up and left the enclosure."

"One of those cute little creatures peed on my shoulder!"

Gordon wrapped his arm around her. "After that she couldn't get back to the cabin quick enough."

"Well, I can't blame you there," Dad said.

Ty could tell Jenna was trying to laugh along, but her smile was tight and didn't quite reach her eyes. He didn't like seeing her upset. He wanted to help her figure out this Gordon guy. She'd put her intel task on hold when she found out about this supper. They both figured his parents would naturally quiz Gordon about himself, relieving her of the job. But so far they'd spent most of the time regaling each other with stories. Plus, with a houseful of guests, there had been interruptions throughout the meal.

His attention returned to Jenna. She'd worn a sleeveless white shirt that glowed in the dimness and revealed her nice shoulders and toned arms. She looked pretty with the firelight flickering off the highlights in her hair, casting a warm glow over her face.

He jerked his attention from her. Why was he thinking about Jenna's appearance again?

He'd given a lot of thought to their relationship since that moment of connection they'd shared five days ago at his place. He was definitely catching feelings for his best friend.

It was a scary thought—though not entirely unpleasant. But no, he'd sworn off women for the time being. He needed to focus on his job, on his firefighting. Distractions led to mistakes, and women were the greatest distraction of all.

But . . . Jenna wasn't just any woman. He already knew her inside and out.

Besides, idiot, she probably has no idea how you're feeling.

She'd probably been baffled by the moment they'd shared. By his reaction. Although she'd seemed normal enough when he'd run into her at the coffee shop the next day. She'd even been kind of playful.

"I'm trying to talk him into another one," Mom said.

Ty jerked his attention back to the present.

"We should at least get Tyson's opinion on that." Dad turned his way.

Ty had no idea what they were talking about. "Uh, what was that?"

"Mom thinks we need another pony, but since you're the one who takes care of them . . ."

Ty shrugged. "I wouldn't mind another. Penny would probably like another friend to boss around."

"One of Patches' siblings will be up for auction," Mom said. "Wouldn't that be nice for her?"

"I see your point, sweetheart. Let's talk about it later." Dad regarded her affectionately before shifting his attention to Gordon. "Where's home for you, Gordon?"

"DC, born and raised."

"How lovely," Mom said. "And so close to where Jenna lives. What area of DC?"

"I have a row house in a nice residential neighborhood. I'm hoping to take Dee for a visit sometime soon." He smiled into her eyes. "You'll love it. I have a rooftop view of the city. It's a beautiful sight."

"I can't wait," Dee said.

"Do you have any children?" Dad asked.

"Yes, two of them."

"A son and a daughter," Mama Dee added. "His daughter lives in DC also, and his son lives in Detroit."

Mom stirred the logs in the firepit. "We love going to DC for the cherry blossoms in the spring. And I'm not much of an urban girl, but I can appreciate the museums and monuments."

"We went ice-skating there one winter," Dad said, "and Alex sprained his ankle."

Mom nodded. "That's also where Tyson decided he wanted to be a professional hockey player when he grew up."

Ty gave a wry grin. "That didn't work out so well, I'm afraid."

"Lucky for us," Mom said. "We couldn't run this place without you."

"It's a labor of love."

"Oh, shoot." Mom set down the stick. "That nice elderly couple in the Seashell Room wanted turndown service and I completely forgot."

"I'll get it, Mom." She'd been on duty since seven this morning.

"I'll come help," Jenna said as Ty stood.

"Well, thanks, kids."

Jenna probably wanted to talk about what they'd gleaned about Gordon. She followed Ty across the pavers and through the back door. The house was quiet as they traipsed through the kitchen and dining room. Most of the guests were out enjoying the Friday night.

He grabbed the room's key from under the check-in desk as they passed. The Seashell Room was a main-floor suite they saved for people with mobility issues. He opened the door, let Jenna in.

"She called him *honey*," Jenna said as soon as he closed the door behind them. "And they're so affectionate with each other. You can't tell me things aren't moving too fast."

"It's pretty fast." Tyson went to work on the summer-weight duvet.

Jenna scanned the room. "What can I do?"

"Tidy up. Grab any used towels."

Jenna slipped into the bathroom. "Don't you think he was a little vague about where he lives? Your mom asked which area he lives in and he avoided answering. Just said something about a row house."

"Your mom also ended up elaborating about his kids."

"I noticed that. His answers were as brief as possible."

"Like he's hiding something," Ty said.

"Exactly. But since we now know where his kids live, maybe that could help us find the right listing."

"It would help even more if we knew their names."

Jenna entered the bedroom clutching a bundle of towels. "Even if we do find the right listing, that'll only offer basic information. How will that help us figure out if he's up to no good?"

"We could run a background check, see if he has a criminal record, see his employment history and previous residences."

"That's public information?"

"For the right price. Didn't you ever look up people before you hired them?"

"Never." She dumped the towels by the door and began tidying up the room. "Even if he doesn't have a criminal record, we can see if the other information lines up with what he's told us."

"Exactly." Ty pulled the duvet taut and turned down a corner.

Jenna pulled the other side and together they straightened the fold. Her top dipped low as she bent over the bed, exposing golden-bronze skin.

Ty jerked his gaze away and went to adjust the throw pillows on the sofa. "Can you grab a couple mints from the hall closet? And clean towels?"

"Sure thing." Jenna returned a minute later with the towels and placed mints on the pillows. "And just like that I know how to turn down a room."

He tipped a grin her way. "You're hired."

Chapter 16

Jenna pumped her fist as the Braves put up another run against the Nationals, bringing the score to eight to three in the fifth inning. She gave Ty a high five. "Your lucky hat is working."

Across Ty's living room, Seth scowled. "He looked out to me."

Ty laughed. "What are you talking about? He was safe by a mile."

Feeling parched, Jenna got up for another soda. "I have to agree with Ty—and the umpire."

"Yeah, well," Alex said. "This one's in the can, I'm afraid."

"Have you talked to Mom and Dad lately?" Ty asked as a commercial came on.

"Just texting mostly," Alex said. "But I have an advertising campaign I want to go over with them soon."

Ty turned down the commercial. "Mom's wanting another pony. I can't tell if Dad's going to cave or not."

"Oh, he'll cave," Seth said. "Mom only has to bat her eyelashes his direction."

"Yeah," Alex said, "but Dad watches the finances, and ponies aren't cheap to maintain."

Seth regarded his brother. "But their profits are up, and the guests love the ponies. It's good business."

"I don't see it happening," Alex said.

"I'll bet it does," Seth said.

"Bet it doesn't."

Ty quirked a brow. "What are you willing to bet?"

Jenna shook her head at their antics. "You guys."

"Well, I *have* been eyeing your new kayak," Alex told Seth.

"I'm not betting my new kayak! You know how much that thing set me back?"

Alex gave a smug look. "Must not be too sure of yourself."

"I don't need a kayak," Ty said. "But I wouldn't turn down a big-screen TV. Let's just bet cold, hard cash. A hundred bucks."

"I'd rather have the kayak."

"A hundred dollars," Seth said.

"All right, fine." Alex turned to Ty. "Who are you putting your money on?"

"Mom, of course."

"Darn right." Seth turned to Jenna. "You want in?"

"No way. This'll be more fun as a spectator."

"Suit yourself." Ty turned up the TV as the game resumed.

Seth checked his watch. "I've got to get home. Seems like I won't be missing much anyway."

Alex stood. "Yeah, I should get going too."

"What's your hurry?" Ty said as his brothers headed toward the door. "It's only nine thirty."

"I might stay if you had decent snacks," Seth said. "But your cupboards are practically empty, dude."

"I've been busy."

"Our company isn't reason enough to stay?" Jenna teased as she saw them to the door.

Seth's blue eyes sparkled down at her. "If anyone's was, it would be yours, gorgeous. But I have to be up at the crack of dawn."

Jenna shook her head. "I'm not falling for your charm, buddy, but you can have a good-bye hug." She gave him a quick embrace, then offered one to Alex. "When are you going to bring your new girlfriend around? I'm dying to see the two of you together."

"It's *new*," Alex insisted for about the hundredth time that night as he opened the door.

Seth whispered loudly, "Totally smitten."

Alex smacked the back of his head. "You wouldn't know the meaning of the word."

"See you guys later," Ty said from the sofa.

"See you!" they both called as they headed out the door.

"And for the record, I've been smitten plenty of times."

"Oh yeah, when?" The door closed but the brothers' verbal sparring carried through the door, growing quieter as they headed down the porch steps.

"You're not leaving yet, are you?" Ty asked Jenna.

"You kidding? I want to see every moment of this blowout. Want a drink?"

"What's left?"

"Diet Coke and tap water. You really do need groceries."

"Between the B and B and the calls, I haven't had time. I'll take water, please."

Jenna snagged the last Diet Coke, filled a glass with water, and joined him on the sofa.

"Thanks."

"You don't have to go on every call, you know. You're a *volunteer*."

He tipped his head back dramatically. "*That's* why I haven't received a paycheck."

"Funny. You shouldn't run yourself ragged. There are plenty of other firefighters." But being captain, Ty felt responsible. Still, he'd been looking a little run-down since she'd gotten home. Which made her feel guilty about pulling him into this Gordon situation.

As the game broke for another commercial, Jenna propped her feet on the large ottoman beside Ty's.

"Have you had a chance to look up Gordon again?" he asked as if reading her mind.

"No, I went to church with Mom and Gordon this morning and worked all afternoon."

"We could do it now."

Jenna wanted answers, but the thought of getting into all that tonight felt heavy and depressing. She rolled her head his way. "Mind if we just watch the game? I kind of just want to chill."

"I could use some downtime too."

They watched a couple commercials in silence, then Jenna asked, "How goes it at the station? Are things with Marissa any better?"

"Not really. I tried to apologize again last week, but we got interrupted."

"Maybe you can pick up the conversation later."

"It wasn't going very well anyway."

"She might just need more time."

The game came back on and they got wrapped up in the inning. The Braves shut down the Nationals with a strikeout and two caught balls, then they were up at bat again. They got two on base and were heading to the top of the lineup.

"Load 'em up, baby." She aimed a smile Ty's way.

But his eyes were closed and he was breathing deeply. The lamplight glowed on his features, highlighting his cheekbones and the curve of his jaw. The dark fringe of his lashes cast shadows under his eyes.

He really was burning the candle at both ends. But he'd always had a great work ethic. There was a reason they'd made him captain. Maybe she should go home and let him get to bed.

But then, he was getting some sleep right now, and she was in no hurry to head home, where Mom and Gordon would likely be curled up on the sofa watching the game. At home Jenna had to either pretend she approved of him or avoid him altogether. She didn't love either option.

She got up to flip off the overhead light, then turned her attention back to the game. Ty would want a recap when he woke up.

It was the bottom of the seventh when some quiet snoring drew her attention. She glanced at him, lips twitching. She couldn't wait to tease him about that. His brothers claimed he snored and Ty always denied it. She was an eyewitness now. Ear witness?

Her gaze skated over his face, so peaceful, his lips parted in sleep. He'd apparently given up on the patchy beard—his chin was shaved smooth now. She didn't mind a beard on a man, but Ty looked better without the facial hair. Honestly, there was no good reason to hide those lips.

She ripped her gaze away and gave her head a shake.

Sofia was right, apparently. These were not thoughts she'd ever had about Tyson before. Why was she suddenly thinking of him this way? Why did the sight of him now make her stomach flutter? And why now, when she felt so messed up inside?

She thought of the months after the prom kiss and how she'd carried a torch for him. But those feelings had faded eventually as she put their friendship first. And in the light of his relationship with Danielle. Were they coming back?

The crack of the bat drew her attention back to the screen where a line drive loaded the bases. The Braves' cleanup hitter was next up to bat, so there was a chance of a grand slam. Should she wake Ty?

She glanced his way.

Nah. Seemed like he could use the rest, and it wasn't as if the game was tied. If Olson cleared the bases, Ty could always watch the replay online.

A minute later the batter entered the box. *Come on, Olson.* If he hit the ball over the fence, it would be the Braves' first grand slam of the season—a cherry on top of this series against the Nationals.

A low moan had her glancing Ty's way. His brows pulled together, and his eyelids flickered. He wasn't snoring now. His leg jerked in sleep and he moaned again, the sound quiet and mournful.

Must be having a bad dream. When he moaned again she quietly called his name. But he didn't stir.

His breaths came more quickly. His heartbeat pulsed quickly in his neck.

She scooted closer and touched his shoulder. "Hey, Ty? You okay?"

He slept on, the grooves between his brows deepening. He mumbled something, tossed his head.

She gave his shoulders a little shake and found them rigid. "Wake up, Ty. You're having a bad dream."

His eyes popped open and he sucked in a big breath as if just surfacing from a deep dive. His gaze tracked to her, his expression dazed.

"It's okay. You're okay. I think you were having a nightmare."

Tyson blinked, his vision clearing in the space of a few heartbeats. His thoughts not so much. That stupid dream lingered like a heavy fog, leaving him disoriented and grappling for reality. He met Jenna's concerned gaze, then pushed himself up. "Sorry. Didn't mean to fall asleep on you."

"Are you okay?"

He ran his hand through his hair. "Yeah, I'm fine."

"You don't seem fine. You seem kind of shaken."

That was because he *was* shaken. Seeing the fear in that kid's eyes rattled him every time. He wished he could scour the image from his brain. But memories didn't work like that, did they?

She placed her hand on his arm. "Hey."

The touch soothed him somehow. Grounded him. He sought her gaze and locked in. He was glad she was here. Waking in the middle of the night, alone and distressed, made him feel empty and lonely.

"Want to talk about it?" she asked gently. "What was it about?"

He took a few seconds to regulate his breathing, get his heart rate down. Sometimes it felt like he was about to hyperventilate. "The accident on Church Street," he managed a minute later.

Jenna was quiet a moment. "The one with the seventeen-year-old kid?"

He nodded, his throat too thick to say anything more.

"What happened in your dream?"

The image replayed in his mind. He cleared his throat. Swallowed hard. "Pretty much what happened on the scene. He hit a tree and was pinned. A limb came through the window and nicked his jugular. We got there just in time to see him bleed out."

"Oh, Ty, how awful."

"I always see his eyes in my dreams. He was so scared. So young. Just a kid."

"I'm sorry. Have you had this nightmare a lot?"

He hadn't admitted that to anyone and didn't really want to admit it to Jenna. It made him feel weak and vulnerable. He was a tough firefighter. A captain. This was part of the job.

Except this time he'd messed up.

Jenna set her hand on his chest. "You have, haven't you? That's why you've seemed so worn-out lately."

He tore his gaze from her. "I see his eyes every time I go to sleep. So . . . I've been avoiding it, I guess."

"Avoiding sleep? Oh, Ty. That's not good. You can't function without proper rest."

"I don't know what else to do. I've been jogging and working out more, trying to exhaust myself so I can sleep better. Nothing works."

Jenna's stare burned into his face. "This isn't your first loss. What is it about this one that's so hard? His age? It must be really hard to lose someone so young."

His lips pressed together. He didn't want to think about this anymore. Didn't want anyone else to know his part in what happened. Not even Jenna.

"Ty?"

"I don't want to say."

His heart was like a battering ram against his ribs. His mouth suddenly so dry.

She took his hand. "Maybe you need to tell someone. Get it off your chest. And who better than me, huh? Something's gotta give. You can't go on like this."

She was right. He'd almost fallen asleep at work last week. And he needed his wits when he was on a call. Another tragedy could happen on his watch, and God help him if he was responsible. Still, the guilt made it hard. No one liked admitting failure.

She leaned in. "It's me, Ty. You can tell me anything. You know that."

He stared into her familiar brown eyes. She'd been a part of him since they were twelve. She wouldn't think less of him. Would she?

He swallowed hard and dredged up the courage to admit the truth. "The night of the call I was at The Pearl with a woman named Gretchen. I'd met her at the beach that week. It was just a first date. We were having a nice quiet dinner—until Marissa walked in with a friend.

"She spotted me on the way to her table, stormed over, and confronted me. I was confused because I thought we'd had an understanding. I thought I'd made it clear I wasn't looking for a relationship. That we were completely casual. But she acted like we were engaged or something. I tried to keep the conversation low-key, but she kept getting louder. It escalated. I tried to take the conversation someplace private, but she resisted. Gretchen finally threw her hands up and left, wanting no part of the drama. I couldn't blame her. I was actually relieved when the town siren went off." The moment replayed in his head and he wished so badly he could go back and do it over.

"Go on." Jenna's eyes were soft and filled with compassion.

He drew a deep breath. "I read the text. Saw there'd been an accident on Church Street. I paid the bill and rushed out to my truck and . . . headed straight to the station." He could barely look at her.

When he didn't continue she shook her head. "And then what?"

"Jen, I was at *The Pearl.* I had to pass right by Church Street to get to the station. Any other time I would've gone directly to the scene. But my head was so full of Marissa and what happened at the restaurant that I totally spaced it. Don't you see? If I'd stopped there instead of heading to the station, Andre Wallace would be alive today."

"Oh, Ty. You can't know that."

"He was bleeding out. I could've applied pressure, staunched the blood flow. That ten minutes would've made all the difference. It was *my* fault. I was distracted by a woman and that's on me. I got divorced and had to go and make dating an Olympic event."

"You were hurt."

"And seeking distraction—that's just what I got. And while the distraction might've helped me cope for a while, it cost the life of an innocent young man. And I have to live with that."

"It's always easy to see things in retrospect. But we don't have that kind of foresight as we move through life. We have to make decisions based on what we know now. On what we're feeling now." She set her hand on his jaw. "A kid drank a few beers and got in his car to drive home. He was impaired and he crashed his car. That's not your fault."

"But he didn't deserve to die."

"No, he didn't. And you don't deserve a life sentence of guilt. He was a kid who made a mistake. You're a first responder who made a mistake. We're all human. Who can know why these things happen? But you can't let guilt weigh you down for the rest of your life. What good will that do? You have to let it go."

His throat swelled like a balloon. "I don't know how."

Their gazes connected over the mere inches that separated them. "I don't know if you remember, but I had nightmares after my dad died. Terrible ones. I'd wake up in a cold sweat and be so afraid and panicked. It would take me hours to go back to sleep."

"I remember."

"I wanted my mom so bad, but she was barely managing and I didn't want to bother her with it."

"So you told me about it instead."

"And you were such a good listener." Her thumb swept along his cheek. "We'll figure this out, Ty. I'm not going to let you drown."

He drank her in. Her reassuring words, her resolute tone, her tender expression. And the weight he'd carried only moments before seemed to take flight.

Now he was only thinking about Jenna and how she'd always been there for him. Their senior year when Danielle had dumped him and spread rumors about him—Jenna dressed her down in front of the whole cafeteria. Last year when he'd found out Britt was cheating—Jenna drove back to the island and was on his doorstep that very night. And now here she was, reminding him his failure wasn't final.

He pressed his own palm to her cheek. He didn't have the words. And even if he did, his throat was too clogged with emotion. Instead he said it all with his eyes. *You're always there for me. I don't know what I'd do without you.*

Her expression offered compassion, grace, and affection. Her thumb swept over his cheek again, making each cell quiver with life. Then she leaned forward, her breath whispering over his skin.

His lungs stuttered and his lips tingled in anticipation.

The kiss landed on his cheek near the corner of his mouth.

His heart thunked heavily to the bottom of his chest cavity. He could've wept with disappointment.

She drew away and made herself very busy with the seam of the throw pillow. "I—I should go. I have to be up early for a tour, and the game—" She gestured toward the screen. "Well, it's not exactly in jeopardy, is it?" Her chuckle choked off as she rose to her feet and gathered her purse. "Plus it's getting late and you obviously need some sleep."

He stood, his legs a little unsteady.

She was at the door already and exiting by the time he got there. "Thanks for having me over. We'll chat soon."

He barely had time to say good-bye before she was down the porch steps.

Chapter 17

Jenna had tossed and turned all night, reliving the moments leading up to the kiss she'd given Tyson on the cheek. The way he gazed at her. The awareness crackling between them. Then the roughness of his jaw on her lips.

It was official: She wasn't imagining these renewed feelings for Ty. And it seemed she wasn't the only one experiencing them. The question was, what should she do about them?

That was what she'd pondered all day as she led her tours. And now, as she stacked the wet kayaks, the thoughts were still heavy on her mind.

The late-May heat made sweat bead on the back of her neck. The temperature was in the eighties and there was no breeze to cool her skin or clouds to offer a temporary reprieve.

Why had she gone and kissed Ty's cheek? Sure, she'd been trying to comfort him. But come on. She'd never done anything like that before. The kiss had landed only centimeters from his mouth—no accident.

She shook her head at her own foolishness. She'd done it because in the moment she'd wanted to. Because her stomach fluttered and her pulse thrummed, and she wanted what she wanted, doggone it. But now, with a little time and space, well . . . it had been a reckless move.

The reasons were aplenty. Her friendship with Tyson was too special to ruin with a romantic fling. It was bound to go awry eventually after all. They'd end up bitter and resentful toward each other, spoiling her oldest and dearest friendship.

Furthermore, she was in no position to start another relationship. She still had to figure out why she'd settled for a relationship with Jason for so long. Until she got to the bottom of that, she was likely to hurt someone else—and God forbid that person be Tyson.

Besides that, she'd always maintained a hard-and-fast rule against dating firefighters. That dangerous occupation had already stolen her father. Her heart couldn't stand another loss like that. Best just to avoid that treacherous situation altogether.

Three strikes and you're out.

So that settled it. Entertaining a romantic relationship with Ty was a terrible idea. She just had to stifle these new feelings. Smother the sparks until they lay like cold ashes at her feet. She'd done it once before. She could do it again.

"How'd your tours go today?" Miss Molly exited the building and began helping Jenna stack the kayaks.

"Those middle schoolers were a fun bunch. Well behaved and curious."

"That youth group does a tour this time every year. Always have a good turnout." Miss Molly pushed her glasses in place. "I wanted you to know I *am* trying to find a replacement for you. I thought I had one—he gave a great interview and had a solid work history—but when I called yesterday to offer him the job, he'd already taken another position."

Jenna wiped her forehead with the back of her hand. "I'm sorry to hear that. But I don't want you to worry on my account. I enjoy the tours, and I don't mind sticking around the island for a while." What did she have in Alexandria other than an empty apartment?

Miss Molly squeezed her arm. "I'm so glad to hear that. I've really been sweating it."

"Well, you can ease up on yourself. I'm fine with the status quo for now. If and when I decide to return to Alexandria, I'll give you some advance notice. How does that sound?"

"Like a dream! Thanks, honey. Any chance you might want some extra hours next week? Paul and I are supposed to go to Asheville to watch the grandkids during my daughter's surgery."

"I'm happy to help out in the office when I'm not giving tours."

"You sure? I know I'm asking a lot."

Jenna gave the woman a side hug. "You kidding me? I love it here. It feels like my second home."

"I'll pay you for the office hours, of course."

"Go to Asheville and take care of those kiddos. Tina and I will hold down the fort."

Chapter 18

A funny feeling gnawed at Tyson's stomach as he headed home from work. He was meeting Jenna there to research Gordon. He was running late because he'd had trouble starting the Weed Eater, so he'd sent Jenna a text. But that wasn't why his stomach quivered.

It was because he was seeing Jenna again.

Since when did seeing his best friend rattle him? And why had he relived that kiss on his cheek a hundred times in the past twenty-four hours?

He already knew the answer to that question.

But these feelings had to be nipped in the bud. Jenna and him as a couple? Bad idea. What if they got together and things didn't work out? He didn't want to ruin their friendship. Not to mention he wasn't ready for a romantic relationship with anyone. His marital heartbreak was still in his rearview mirror, reminding him of the gut-wrenching loss and rejection he'd suffered. When someone who was supposed to love you discarded you so easily, it left a mark.

It had taken him months to see that Britt's leaving had picked at the emotional scars from his father's abandonment. Had left him feeling unworthy. He'd dealt by distracting himself. But that wasn't a fix. He had to work on himself. And he needed to be single for that.

Also, he wasn't in a hurry to go through that kind of pain again.

He just needed to ignore these weird feelings for Jenna and keep things as normal as possible. Just because they were both single and available for the first time in years didn't mean he should be thinking of her this way. Maybe his season of dating around was responsible for this sudden attraction. He'd gotten into a routine of noticing and appreciating women, and now he'd turned that attention on Jenna.

If that was true, it was a bad habit he needed to break. So no more gazing into her eyes. No more vulnerable revelations that stirred her empathy and resulted in comforting touches.

No more touches period.

He pulled into his driveway and exited his Silverado. He was glad he'd arrived before Jenna at least. As he rounded his vehicle he spotted an irregularity on his passenger-side door and stepped closer. Probably just a bit of dirt. But he was soon corrected of that assumption. He frowned as he ran his finger over the half-inch divot in the door.

Jenna pulled in beside him. Her smile fell as she exited her car. "What's wrong?"

"Looks like someone opened their door into mine and dinged it pretty good."

"Where'd that happen?"

He shrugged. "Not sure. Could've been at the B and B. Or maybe it didn't even happen today. Might've been a day or two ago and I'm just now seeing it."

"I'm sorry." She followed him up the walkway to his house.

"It's probably not even worth getting insurance involved."

"Probably not. Hopefully it won't be too expensive to fix."

"I have a buddy at a repair shop. He'll give me a good deal. It's just the fact that someone had to know they did it and didn't say anything." Islanders were generally respectful and considerate.

"It would be nice if people always did the right thing."

"Right there." Jenna's finger shook as she pointed to the laptop screen where Whitepages.com was open. "'Gordon Smith, sixty-one years.' Has to be him, right?"

"We're about to find out." Ty clicked on the link and a page opened, full of basic information. "There's his address, and a few relatives are listed."

"None of them live in DC, which is where he said his daughter lives."

"But this Joe Smith lives in Detroit."

Jenna perked up. "Has to be his son. This is definitely the right Gordon then."

"We're making progress." Ty clicked a button that read *View Two Background Records*, which opened another screen: *Unlock Gordon's Full Report*. When he clicked he got a list of plans and their prices. "It's only twelve dollars—a literal bargain."

"I'll pay you back." Jenna's leg jittered against the sofa seat as Ty went through the payment process using Apple Pay. How would her mom react if Gordon had a criminal record? What if even that didn't dissuade her? What if Mom confronted him and he just fed her some flimsy explanation and she believed him? Anxiety snaked through Jenna's system at the thought.

She shook her head as the program downloaded the results of the search. She was getting way ahead of herself.

Tyson set his hand on her knee. "Settle down. It'll be okay."

She hardly heard what he said because the heat of his palm burned into her bare skin. Her heart gave a few hard knocks against her ribs before he cut her an awkward glance and withdrew his hand. There was that awareness again. The one she'd committed to squashing.

But the memory of that kiss on the cheek resurfaced even as the scent of his cologne wafted over her. In her attempts to see the screen she'd moved in close. Her upper arm was flush with his, and their legs . . .

The warm press of his thigh was suddenly the only thing she could think about. That point of contact usurped every brain cell. She glanced down at his muscular legs, nicely tanned, just a sprinkling of dark hair.

"Here it is."

Jenna blinked away the thoughts and focused on the results of Gordon's background check. Ty slowly scrolled through Work History, Education, Credit History, and finally reached Criminal History.

A big fat zero sat beside the last listing.

Jenna's heart sank. That was not what she'd expected. "There's nothing here."

He scrolled back up for a closer look at the other sections. But there was nothing of substance. "Doesn't seem to be."

"Are these things even accurate? How do we know they're complete?"

"I guess we can't be 100 percent sure. But just because someone doesn't have a record doesn't mean they're not a criminal. It just means they haven't been caught."

"I thought for sure we'd find something." Jenna fell back into the sofa, feeling heavier than ever. She'd been depending on this to give her proof. Proof that the new man in Mom's life was a bad guy. She flung her hand over her face. "I was actually hoping he was a criminal. I'm a terrible person. What is wrong with me?"

"Hey. Nothing's wrong with you. You weren't hoping he's a criminal. It just feels like something's off, and you're worried about your mom and trying to protect her."

Jenna gestured to the screen. "But I seem to be protecting her from a perfectly nice person."

"Your suspicions didn't appear out of nowhere, Jenna. There are plenty of red flags here. He came to live with your mom after meeting her on a one-week cruise. Your mom is footing the bill for everything they do. He supposedly doesn't have a credit card. And he told someone on the phone he's in Maine."

Okay, maybe she wasn't a terrible person. Maybe she *should* trust her gut. "Thank you. I needed to hear that. But where do we go from here? In my mind this was my big plan, and it turned out to be a nothing burger."

He gave her a sympathetic look. "It's not nothing. We have a lot of information here. Let's think about how we can leverage it."

Chapter 19

Tyson went in for an easy layup and winced as the basketball hit the rim and bounced to the ground. He and Luke were at Veterans Memorial Park, a seaside playground that was uncrowded on this Wednesday evening. Gleeful sounds carried from the children frolicking on the nearby monkey bars, and a soaring seagull's cry pierced the air.

"You're off your game today." Luke took the ball out. "That's the second layup you've missed."

Tyson guarded him as he dribbled toward the basket. Layups had always been his thing in high school. Either he was getting old and out of shape or . . . he was just distracted by thoughts of Jenna. Disliking the thought, Tyson swiped the ball from his friend mid-dribble.

"Guess you're *not* asleep at the switch."

"Don't underestimate me." Ty tried to dart toward the basket, but Luke blocked his move.

"I was going to let you win anyway."

"As if I'll give you a choice in the matter." Ty regularly schooled Luke on the court. But Luke almost always beat him at pool.

"I want you feeling good by the time we're done anyway—I have a favor to ask."

"I always feel good after I beat you fair and square." Ty darted around Luke and put up a jump shot. It hit the backboard and whooshed through the net. "And just like that I'm up by four."

"Lucky shot." Luke's face and neck were pink from exertion as he worked his way toward the post. The evening was warm, though a nice breeze came off the water.

Ty gave him some coverage, his foot- and arm-work automatic. So automatic, his thoughts went straight back to Jenna. Turned out nipping these feelings in the bud was easier said than done. Only two days ago he'd committed to *no touching*, and he'd held his ground so far. But the other night she'd been the one to close the space between them. Albeit just to view the laptop screen. He could still feel the warm press of her leg against his.

In an uncharacteristic move, Luke bolted around him and put in an easy layup. He caught the ball as it fell from the net. "Man, you are distracted today. What gives?"

"Just a little tired, that's all." That was no lie. He'd hoped telling Jenna about the accident might magically make the nightmares disappear. No such luck. "How'd your date with Trinity go?"

A smile bloomed on Luke's face as he dribbled the ball in place. "It was good. Real good. I enjoyed talking to her, but . . ."

"What?" Ty asked when Luke didn't continue. "Trouble in paradise?"

"We're both introverts so there were some awkward silences. I'm just not smooth like you."

Ty smirked. "I'm not smooth."

"Better conversationalist. Whatever."

"So you don't think it'll work?"

"Oh no, I want it to work. She's great. Really sweet and smart and interesting. We had some really nice moments. We just need a little help getting things going, I guess." He shot Ty a sheepish look.

"Why do I get the feeling that favor's about to come into play?"

"If we just had some other people along, it would kind of smooth things over. I was thinking we should plan a double date."

Ty wiped the sweat from his forehead with the tail of his tee. "Sorry, pal. I'm on a dating moratorium, remember?"

Luke's eyes pleaded. "Come on. It's just a onetime thing."

"That's what my date with Marissa was supposed to be, and look how that turned out. Why don't you ask one of the other guys? Wheeler's got a girlfriend."

"I barely know him, much less his girlfriend."

"Drury then. He's dating that insurance adjuster from the mainland."

"Or you could just make an exception. Trinity already knows you, and you're good at keeping the ball rolling, conversationally speaking. It's the perfect solution."

Tyson frowned. He really didn't want to start something with another woman. He was still paying for the last time. Although it could also serve as a distraction from his unsettling feelings for Jenna.

The basketball thumped rhythmically on the pavement while they caught their breath. "Come on. You could even bring Jenna if you wanted."

Ty's gaze shot to Luke, searching. Had he read Ty's mind? Did he know Ty was having weird thoughts about Jenna?

As Luke searched his eyes a speculative look appeared. "What's going on?"

"What?"

"You have a funny expression on your—" Luke narrowed his eyes. "Is there something going on here I don't know about?"

Tyson swatted the ball away from Luke and dribbled it out, then turned back toward the basket.

Luke hadn't moved from his spot near the post, but his face had broken out in a wide smile. "There *is*. There's something going on between you and Jenna."

Ty's face heated. "Nothing's going on. Now are you gonna get down here and guard me, or should I just make the basket and put you out of your misery?"

"You always change topics when you're uncomfortable with the subject. When did this happen? And why didn't you tell me? I think it's great."

Ty dribbled toward the basket. "It's not great. It's not even happening."

"Well, why not?"

Ty barely spared Luke a glance as he put up a shot—and missed.

Luke gave a smug grin as he rebounded the ball. "You're flustered. Jenna Greene's got you flustered."

"I'm not flustered."

"And protesting an awful lot. Look, you and Jenna would be great together. She's perfect for you. Why are you fighting it?"

"She's a good friend. I'm not giving that up."

"You wouldn't have to give it up, dork. You'd just have to embellish it a little. And from that hot-and-bothered look you're wearing, I don't think that's going to be a problem."

Ty scowled. "I'm not hot and bothered. And I'm not ruining a great friendship for some temporary romance."

"Who says it has to be temporary?"

"It's not worth the risk."

"Does she feel the same way?"

"I don't feel any way!"

Luke chuckled. "All right, buddy. Have it your way." He smirked as he drove in for a layup. The ball swished through the net. "Then since she's just your friend, you won't mind helping out your old pal with a double date, will you?"

Chapter 20

A niggle of envy wormed through Jenna as she watched Luke and Trinity swaying on the dance floor. When the couple wasn't engaged in conversation, they were simply gazing into each other's eyes.

Chatties was crowded on this Saturday night of Memorial Day weekend, and a popular local band played country music. The lead singer stood in a puddle of light, belting out the ballad's chorus.

The smell of seafood pervaded the space, offending Jenna's full stomach. She pushed her empty platter away, then turned to watch Luke and Trinity again. "Why are we here again?"

Tyson followed her gaze. "To pave the way for romance."

As the band segued to the second verse, Luke gathered Trinity closer, and she set her head on his shoulder.

"Mission accomplished." Jenna saluted him with her Diet Coke, then took a sip. "I have to admit they're pretty cute together."

"Luke's a big weenie."

"I think it's sweet the way he's so nervous around her. And did you see the way she looks at him? Luke deserves someone like that."

"He's had a crush on her for months."

"Well, seems like our work here is done." She'd been reluctant at first when Ty suggested the gathering. But hey, this was a good cause and Chatties made for a fun friend night. Also, she couldn't help but notice how handsome Ty looked in an oatmeal button-down that flattered his skin tone and contrasted with his dark hair.

"Hey, guys!" Seth said in greeting, then sat in one of the empty seats at their table. "How you doing? Didn't know you'd be here tonight."

Ty nodded toward the couple on the dance floor. "We're with Luke and Trinity. What are you doing here?"

"This band's my favorite and I was craving some crab cakes, but all the tables are full."

"You can join us," Jenna said. "We've already eaten, but that's okay."

"Thanks, guys. I'll take you up on that." Their server showed up and Seth ordered. After she left, he turned to Ty. "Any developments on the pony bet?"

"Nothing significant. But I made sure Mom knew I'd be happy to feed and care for another one."

The brothers high-fived while Jenna shook her head disapprovingly.

"What?" Ty's grin was mischievous.

"You're incorrigible."

Seth shrugged. "All's fair."

The ballad trailed off, morphing into a rollicking version of "Country Girl."

Jenna bolted upright. "My favorite song."

"All right then." Seth extended his hand. "Let's go, gorgeous!"

Ty scowled as Jenna followed Seth to the dance floor. Jenna's red top hugged her small waist and her jeans showed off her trim figure. Ty's brother looked every inch the city boy in a white button-down, navy khakis, and tan oxfords. He grabbed Jenna's hand and spun her around. He was a slick dancer and moved Jenna around the floor with grace and confidence.

Ty's frown deepened. What if Seth asked Jenna out? What if she fell for him and they ended up together? A pit opened in his stomach. Maybe Ty and Jenna were a bad idea, but Seth and Jenna were a terrible idea. The thought made him sick.

And what does that tell you, huh?

More than he wanted to know, that was for sure. When Jenna threw her head back in laughter, Ty glanced away. If he didn't see it, it couldn't bother him.

But a minute later that plan didn't seem to be working. Ty's palms sweated just sitting here thinking about Seth holding her hand, touching the small of her back.

You're an idiot, Parker.

Of its own volition his gaze skated back to the couple just as Jenna glanced his way. Beaming at him, she waved him toward the dance floor. That sounded like a miserable idea if he'd ever heard one. But no more miserable than watching his brother show her a good time.

If you can't beat 'em, join 'em.

Seth wasn't the only one who could be fun. Ty got up and joined them as the final chorus kicked up. He wasn't a bad dancer himself and couldn't help showing off a little. He grabbed Jenna's hand and spun her out. Her hair whipped around her shoulders as he spun her back in, and he relished her wide smile and sparkling eyes.

For a minute he let himself forget Seth, forget the tension that had been bubbling up since Jenna's return to the island, and just enjoyed her company. And it was working great.

Until the music segued to a slow song.

"Hey, I gotta go talk to Nick Voigt," Seth called over the music. And then he was gone.

The couples around them were pairing up as the opening strains of "Die a Happy Man" swelled. Like a glutton for punishment, Ty held out his arms.

Jenna stepped into them, her eyes still sparkly and alive. Her hands landed on his shoulders while his settled at her waist. His body responded to her nearness, her touch. His heart pinged around his chest like a pinball.

Great idea, genius.

But here was the thing: It *did* feel like a great idea. It felt like the best dang idea he'd ever had. She felt perfect in his arms. He tucked his knee between hers, and they moved together like two halves of the same whole.

As the verse led into the chorus, she shifted closer until her temple brushed his jaw. He moved his hands to the small of her back. He caught a whiff of something sweet and pleasant. Something all Jenna. A wisp of hair tickled the side of his face. It felt so good to have her in his arms. He couldn't remember ever feeling this good.

And yet, this was *Jenna.*

Jenna, who at thirteen had insisted on playing tackle football even though he and his brothers outsized her. Jenna, who'd been so brave in the face of her father's heroic death. Jenna, who'd comforted him when he confided in her about his biological father's abandonment one night on her front porch.

The dichotomy between his feelings then versus now nearly gave him whiplash. But there was no denying the enormous shift that had somehow taken place in his heart. How had this happened? And how was she in his arms again after he'd committed to keeping a physical space between them? He couldn't seem to help himself.

Her fingers skated inadvertently over his nape, and a wave of gooseflesh swept down his arms. He was uber aware of each place where their bodies connected. The rhythmic brush of their thighs. The soft press of her temple to his cheek. The slight weight of her forearms on his shoulders. His arms practically vibrated with the urge to pull her against him. He squeezed his eyes shut.

This is Jenna.

This is Jenna.

This is Jenna.

He had to think about something else or he would end up doing something he'd regret. He spotted Luke and Trinity a short distance away, swaying to the music in their own little bubble. The romantic sight did nothing to distract him from his thoughts of Jenna.

A muted Braves game played on the big-screen TV in the corner. It was five-four in the third inning. The Braves were up to bat with empty bases and two outs. The game broke for a commercial.

His gaze drifted to their table, where Seth was digging into his appetizer. Remembering the way he'd flirted with Jenna, Ty pressed his lips together, and his arms tightened protectively around her.

She set her cheek against his shoulder and wrapped her arms around his shoulders.

His legs went weak. His pulse thrummed at his neck where her breath feathered his skin. Sweet heaven.

This was not good.

And yet . . . this was *so* good.

He was losing his ever-loving mind. But the song was winding down now, heading into the final instrumental. He was only a dozen seconds or so away from the end of this sweet torture. Might as well enjoy it while he could.

The emergency siren blared over the sound of the music.

The rest of the room carried on as usual, used to the air-raid siren. But Ty's thoughts shifted quickly to work mode. He reached for his phone, putting space between them. "Two-car accident on Circle Drive."

"You have to go," Jenna said.

"How will you get home?"

"Seth can take me."

He didn't have time to argue. He just squeezed her hand. "Thanks for coming tonight."

Worry creased her brow. "Be safe, Ty."

Chapter 21

At the ring of the phone Jenna darted from the brochure rack toward the office. But Miss Tina beat her to the call. Jenna sighed as she continued restocking pamphlets, casting a longing glance out the window. She'd been filling in for Miss Molly in the mornings and doing tours in the afternoon. But today Miss Tina had a dentist appointment, so Jenna was stuck in the office till three.

It wasn't as if it was torture. She was good at administrative tasks and the air-conditioning felt nice. But she missed the ocean breeze and the in-depth conversations with customers.

Plus it gave her too much head time. She kept remembering the way she'd felt in Tyson's arms at Chatties four days ago, and that wasn't helpful. Hadn't she promised herself she'd think of him only as a friend? Why did that suddenly seem impossible?

Because being in his arms had felt even better than she could've dreamed. She'd wanted to stay there in the safety of his embrace all night.

But his embrace wasn't safe. He was a firefighter and therefore in regular peril. Losing a friend would be hard enough. If she let herself fall in love with him and she lost him the same way she'd lost her dad, she'd be left in ruins.

It was unthinkable.

Jenna was just entering the house when she noticed a voicemail on her phone. She frowned at the foreign number as the screen door fell shut behind her. Probably just a credit card company with a onetime offer.

"Hi, honey!" Mom called.

"Hi, Mom." Jenna joined her mother in the kitchen where she and Gordon were unloading groceries. "Hi, Gordon."

He smiled as he withdrew from the fridge. "Hi, Jenna. How was your day? Your mom told me you've been working in the office this week."

"It was good. Miss Molly had to make a quick trip, but she'll be back tonight."

Jenna helped empty the last bag as Gordon grabbed an onion and knife and began chopping it up on the cutting board. He sure did know his way around their kitchen.

"Would you look at this guy?" Mom rubbed Gordon's back, gazing at him affectionately. "So sweet of him to take on the onions. He knows they just wreck my eyes. We're making meatloaf tonight—Gordon's special recipe. I hope you can stay."

Sadly she had no other plans. "I think I'm free. Can I help with supper?"

"Thanks, but we've got it under control," Mom said.

"You've been working all day," Gordon said. "Why don't you go put your feet up?"

Five minutes later Jenna had freshened up and settled in the living room before remembering she had a voicemail. She opened it and listened.

"Hi, Jenna. This is Nancy Orcutt with Alexandria Parks and Rec-

reation. I'm calling regarding an application you submitted recently. We're interested in doing an interview if you're still available and interested in the management position. Please give me a call at your convenience. I look forward to chatting with you."

Pleasure bloomed inside as Jenna lowered her phone. *Yes!* Finally, an opportunity for a position that felt like a great fit. She was beginning to wonder if she'd ever get another interview, much less for the position she'd been most excited about. And honestly, it was nice just to be wanted.

Mom passed by, drying her hands on a towel.

"Hey, Mom, I got an interview."

"That's wonderful, honey!" Mom darted toward her and Jenna popped to her feet to intercept the hug. "Which position?"

"The one with Parks and Rec to manage the athletics department."

"That sounds perfect for you. They'll be lucky to have you."

"I have to *get* the job first."

"They'd be crazy to turn my girl down." Mom's smile slipped a bit.

She was no doubt thinking about Jenna leaving the island. If Jenna was honest, the thought of leaving also weighed on her. She hadn't realized how much she'd missed her island, her people, until she returned home. "You know, Mom, I plan on coming around a lot more often in the future. And when I'm not here I'll be calling and texting you. You'll hear from me so often you'll get sick of me."

"Not possible, my sweet girl. But you know I only want what's best for you." A twinkle entered her pale blue eyes. "Sooner or later you'll figure out that's the island."

Jenna chuckled. "Not that you've got an opinion or anything."

"Oh, I'm chock-full of opinions." She snapped the towel at Jenna before she ducked from the room.

Jenna redialed Nancy's number and got her on the phone right away. The woman sounded warm and friendly. The person currently holding the management position was seven months pregnant and not planning to return to work. P and R wouldn't need a replacement until the beginning of July. That was a whole month away, but Jenna couldn't just ignore this opportunity.

They scheduled the interview in a week and a half, which was the soonest opening Nancy had.

Jenna was still wearing a smile as she opened her text app and typed out a message.

I got an interview!

Ten seconds after she sent it, her phone buzzed with an incoming call. She rolled her eyes even as her heart kicked into gear. "Don't you ever just text?"

"News like that deserves a phone call," Ty said. "Congratulations, that's great news. Which position?"

She caught him up to speed on the job. "I'm so excited just to get my foot in the door someplace."

"I'm excited for you." There was a smile behind his words. "Seems like the job would be perfect for you. Though I've gotten so used to having you around, I can't imagine you leaving again."

She was having a little trouble with that one herself. But a little distance between them might be a good thing—since she couldn't seem to control her thoughts. "I have an empty apartment just sitting there and a lease through the end of summer. I need a paycheck and soon."

"What if you get the job before we figure out what's going on with Gordon?"

"Hang on a second." Jenna slipped upstairs to her bedroom, closed the door, and lowered her voice. "I don't know. Guess I'll cross that bridge when I come to it. But even if I get the job, we still have a month. Although he's already been here almost that long, and I haven't heard a peep about him leaving anytime soon. You'd think the man would have some obligations back home."

"Have you done any more research on him?"

"Not really. I've been pretty busy the past few days. You?"

"I looked up his home on Zillow. It's a Federal-style row house in what seems to be a nice neighborhood."

"Just like he said. That can't be cheap in DC."

"Oh, it's not." He named the value listed by the site. "It's a three-bedroom, three-bath home. The interior looks to be well kept if a little dated. I'll send you the link."

A moment later the text arrived and Jenna clicked on the link. It was an attractive brick row house sitting several feet higher than the sidewalk. A cobblestone retaining wall fronted the home, and steps led from the sidewalk to a small porch. The home was two stories tall. "Seems like a big house for just one person. And it's just sitting empty? He can afford to keep up with the bills?"

"Maybe it's paid off. And it's not like it's costing him anything to be here."

True enough. Jenna scowled. They had to get to the bottom of this. "Maybe we should make a trip out there. It's only a few hours away."

"What would you hope to uncover once we're there? Where would we even start?"

Good question. "I don't know. Let's give it some thought."

"Maybe Gordon will say something that sparks an idea or gives us some kind of direction."

That would be helpful. But summer was busy for Ty. Plus he was dealing with a lot of fallout from that accident. "You know, you'll be really busy this month. If it seems like a trip would be helpful, I can just go alone."

"I don't like the idea of you poking around DC alone, especially when we don't know what you'd be getting into. Besides, we're in this together."

"You've got a lot on your plate, Ty."

"Believe me, I'd rather stay busy. And I care about your mom too. I want to make sure she's not getting scammed."

Jenna could hardly argue with that. "Okay, let's give it some thought and see what happens."

Chapter 22

The briny scent of the ocean hung in the air, and the roar of the crashing waves carried up the beach where the Parkers and Greenes had situated themselves. A pair of giggling preteen girls passed on their way to frolic in the water.

Rick stood from his lawn chair. "I'm going for a walk. Anyone want to come?"

"I'll go," Alex said.

Seth joined them. "Me too."

"I'm feeling lazy." Jenna closed her eyes, basking in the sun's warmth and the gentle breeze cooling her skin.

"I'll keep Jenna company," Ronda said.

"We'll be right back."

The two women watched the men disappear down the shore.

"There's no way they'll be right back," Ronda said. "Once Rick heads down the beach, he has to keep going until he reaches the end."

"Good thing it's not that far away." Jenna shaded her eyes as she scanned the shoreline for Mom, who'd decided to wade into the water. She was up to her waist in the surf. Gordon had gone to the restroom a while ago.

Ronda tilted her sunglasses onto her head, exposing her deep-set brown eyes. She checked her phone, then glanced up, nailing Jenna with a look. "Okay, what is going on with my boys?"

"What do you mean?"

"Seth just texted me projections about how the ponies will pay for themselves if we market them for the business correctly."

Jenna shifted in her chair. "Uh, well . . . that seems like good business sense, I guess."

"And yesterday Alex sent his dad a link to an article on how much horses cost annually."

Jenna bit her lip. "Oh, really?"

"And Tyson's been dropping hints about Patches seeming lonely when Penny's in a mood."

"Well . . ." Jenna had nothing.

"Those boys have a bet going, don't they? Don't you lie to me, missy. I know all your tells."

Jenna held up her hands, palms out. "You didn't hear it from me."

"Those boys. I thought they'd outgrown this nonsense." Ronda narrowed her eyes on Jenna. "Or are you in on it too?"

"Oh no. I had nothing to do with this."

"Good girl. Remember when Ty had to do Seth's dishes for a year?"

"Or when Alex had to clean Ty's room for six months?"

"What do they have riding on this little bet of theirs?" Ronda said.

"A hundred bucks."

"Those scoundrels." Ronda shook her head disapprovingly as she stared off into the crowd. A moment later her gaze shot back to Jenna, an impish light in her eyes. "Get 'em to raise the bet."

"*What?* Why?"

"By the time their dad and I are done with them, they'll be so sure of themselves they'll at least triple that amount."

Jenna's lips twitched. "What do you have up your sleeve?"

"You don't raise three boys without having a few tricks of your own." Ronda offered her a smug grin that reminded Jenna of Ty's.

Jenna smiled. "This is going to be entertaining."

"Just leave it all to me."

Speaking of Tyson, Jenna spotted him down the beach in conversation with a couple of friends. His tan did nice things for those wide shoulders and tapered waist.

"So, your mom and Gordon seem to be hitting it off. I haven't seen her so happy in years."

"Yeah, she seems really cheerful lately." Mostly because she had her head in the sand.

"And Gordon's certainly solicitous of her. He seems like a good guy."

He was good all right. "He's very attentive and helpful around the house." As he should be since he was basically freeloading off her mom.

Ronda's focus burned into the side of Jenna's face, but she was determined not to confess her suspicions. At least, not until she had concrete evidence. Ronda and Jenna's mom were close, and Jenna didn't want to put her in an uncomfortable position.

Gordon returned, but instead of joining Ronda and Jenna, he headed straight for the water.

A text came in and Jenna checked her screen. Tyson.

Meet me at the restrooms.

She glanced at where she'd last seen Ty, but he was gone.

Okay.

She turned to Ronda. "I'm going to the restroom real quick."

"All right."

Concern knotted her brow as Jenna traipsed down the beach to the walkway that led to the restrooms. It had to be important if he wanted to talk right now.

She found him in the shade of the building. "Everything okay?"

"I was just getting ready to enter the restroom, and you'll never guess who was inside talking on the phone."

"Gordon?"

"I slipped around the side and listened. It seemed like he was talking to a woman. His voice was all soft."

"I know what you mean. Did you hear anything important? What did he say?"

"Mostly he just listened. But at the end of the conversation it seemed like they were talking about when he was coming *home*. And he said 'I love you' before he got off the phone."

"Sounds like it's the same person he was talking to before." She tempered her response. "It could still be his daughter, though. Or any female relative really."

"Not unless she's living in his house. At one point he gave her instructions on some glitch with his microwave."

Jenna frowned. "His *microwave*?"

"No reason she'd need help with that unless she was living there, right?"

"I guess it's possible his daughter lives with him."

"Or it could be someone else."

Jenna's heart clenched. My gosh, what if he already had a girlfriend? What if he was already *married*? Could he be one of those men who created two separate lives, leaving both women in the dark about the other?

"It's not looking good. I hated to worry you like this, but I knew you'd want to know."

"I'm glad you told me." She *was* glad, even though she really hoped she'd be proven wrong.

Chapter 23

It didn't matter that it was a weeknight—Island Creamery was always a hive of activity in June. Jenna and her mom were lucky to snag a picnic table on the deck after waiting in the long line for homemade ice cream. The shop, with its appealing lighthouse exterior, was now run by the third-generation owners and was a favorite with Teaguers and tourists alike.

The sun was just setting and a warm breeze ruffled the colorful table umbrellas as Jenna took another lick from her Marsh Mud cone. She moaned as she savored the rich chocolate. "It's been too long. How have I been on the island over a month and not stopped in for my favorite flavor?"

"Now that you've had a taste, you'll find it hard to stay away. We should make it a regular event, just us girls." After a beat Mom rolled her eyes. "Listen to me, talking like you're staying forever when you're about to get that fabulous job in Alexandria."

"Let's not get ahead of ourselves. I haven't even interviewed yet, and let's not forget my previous employer is unlikely to recommend me."

"Oh, you can explain all that. You're a shoo-in for that job, and I'm happy for you, truly. But I sure will miss you around here."

"I'll miss you too, Mom." This was a good opportunity to swing the conversation to Gordon. "But you have Gordon to keep you company."

Mom lowered a spoonful of Orange Juice Sorbet. "He's great company. I've had so much fun since he got here. I didn't even mind when the cruise ended once I knew he'd be coming back to the island with me."

The richness of the chocolate suddenly became too much. Thankfully Jenna was almost finished. "What are your plans? Have the two of you talked about the future?"

"We're just playing it by ear for now. But . . ." Her eyes went all soft and warm. "I'm falling for him, Jenna. He's such a wonderful man, and he's so good to me."

"Wow, Mom." Jenna forced a smile. "I can see he makes you very happy."

"Oh, he does. In so many ways." Mom sobered as she grabbed Jenna's hand. "I know you're skeptical, but he really is a good person."

"I understand. It's just fast, that's all. It's been less than six weeks since you met. I don't want to see you get hurt."

Mom gave Jenna's hand a squeeze and scooped the last of her sorbet. "You're sweet to be worried about your old mom. But I have a lot of life experience and I have a good feeling about this." She popped the bite into her mouth, her blue eyes lighting and crinkling at the corners. "When you know, you know."

Jenna's stomach twisted as she took the last bite of her cone. "You'd mentioned taking a trip with Gordon to DC. Is that in the works?"

"There's nothing on the calendar yet, but we'll definitely get around to that. I used all my PTO for the cruise. Besides, I don't want to take a trip while you're here and miss out on time with you."

That was a blessing in disguise. Jenna didn't like the thought of Gordon taking her mom away on their own. Speaking of which, this would be a good time to gather more information. "Maybe when you go you can meet his kids."

"Well, certainly his daughter, Katie, since she lives in the city. But I doubt his son will be able to make the trip from Detroit. He has a job and a family."

"Gordon has grandkids?"

"He does. Joe has three kids: two girls and a boy. Gordon goes out there at least once a year to visit."

"How nice."

"They're one, three, and five and they're so adorable! I can't wait to meet them all." Mom grabbed her empty bowl and their napkins and stood. "I'll be right back. I have to use the restroom."

Jenna watched her go, her heart sinking like an anchor. She suspected her mom was very close to being in love with Gordon. Jenna and Ty had to figure this out before Mom got in any deeper. They might have to make that trip to DC. Gordon had left a piece of mail on the table last week, which confirmed that his name and the address they had for him were correct. So that took those concerns off her list.

"Hey there." A smiling Sofia stopped by Jenna's table, looking carefree in a breezy white top that complemented her deep skin tone.

"Well, hello." Jenna jumped up and hugged her friend. "Where's Jack?"

Sofia gestured at the end of the long line. "Over there, holding our place."

Jenna and Jack exchanged waves and smiles, then Sofia joined Jenna at the table.

"Did you come alone?" Sofia asked.

"No, Mom just headed inside for the restroom."

"Good." Sofia waggled her brows. "It'll give us a few minutes to chat."

Jenna cut her a sideways look. "Did we have something to chat about?"

"Well, yes. I've been dying to know if you've kissed him yet."

Jenna jolted backward. "Kissed *who*?"

"Don't be coy with me. It's been two weeks since you and Ty were flirting right out in the open, and yesterday Linsey Burkett told me you two were looking pretty cozy on the dance floor Saturday night at Chatties."

Jenna gave a mock scowl. "This island is way too small."

"You're dodging the question . . ."

"I have not kissed Ty." But then Jenna remembered the kiss she'd given him on the cheek. She could still feel the roughness of his jaw, and the mere thought of it made her lips tingle.

"Are you lying to me right now? Because you're biting your lip again."

Drat. Jenna let loose of her lip. She had to get that stupid tell under control. "It was just a kiss on the cheek. Happy now?"

Sofia's face fell. "Not really. I was hoping for something a little more scandalous."

Jenna chuckled. "Stop it. We're just friends."

"So you keep saying." Sofia's gaze traveled over Jenna's shoulder. Her mom must be returning.

Sofia stood, giving Jenna a knowing look. "Keep me in the loop."

"There is no loop."

"Oh, there's a loop." Sofia beamed at Jenna's mom as she neared. "Hi, Mama Dee."

"Sofia, honey, so good to see you. How's your mother? I haven't seen her since the Christmas tree lighting."

They caught up for a few minutes, then Sofia returned to the line while Jenna and her mom headed back to the car. On the way home Jenna shook Sofia's ribbing about Ty from her mind and forced herself to think about Mom and Gordon instead. At the rate their relationship was progressing, they would have to level up their research and quick.

We need to put a rush on our research.

Ty pulled his hand back from stroking Penny, and she pawed the ground in protest. Mama Dee must've said something when they went for ice cream tonight. Ty tapped on Jenna's contact and put the phone to his ear.

She answered on the first ring. "Seriously, what have you got against texting?"

"What did your mom say?"

Jenna sighed. "She's falling hard for the guy. Like, she's on love's doorstep here. We have to be more proactive. Gordon has no plans to leave anytime soon. I wish I could just tell her my suspicions, but she's so far gone, I don't think it would do any good."

"Have you given any more thought to that DC trip?"

"I want to do it. Worst-case scenario, I don't learn anything helpful. I have to at least try."

"Let's figure out a time that works for us both. Better if it's before the end of June when the carnival kicks up." The fire company was in charge of that monthlong event leading up to Pony Penning Days.

"Sooner is better for me too. I'm sure Miss Molly will give me time off. My interview is next Monday. We could do both at the same time since DC's so close. That would probably make it a two-day trip though. Would your parents give you time off?"

"Yeah, those are slower days at the B and B, and I haven't taken any vacation time this year."

"What about the fire company?"

He'd been a little overzealous lately about going on every call. And things were still uncomfortable with Marissa. Some of the guys had become pretty standoffish with him, making those interactions awkward. "Honestly, I could use a break from the firehouse."

"Are you sure?"

"Positive. Let's do it."

It wasn't until he was off the phone that he realized he'd just committed to two days alone with Jenna. And the thought of it made his heart gallop.

Chapter 24

Jenna ran her damp palms down the length of her jeans and tried to focus on the country tune playing in Tyson's truck. They'd kept up a steady conversation for the past four and half hours, which had helped keep her mind off the upcoming interview. But now that they were getting closer to Alexandria, the nerves were settling in.

"I can't believe I've never been to your apartment," Ty said.

They were stopping there first so she could change into something nice. "I haven't even lived there a year."

"This'll give you a chance to check on things anyway."

"I'm sure everything's fine. I've forwarded my mail to Mom's, and I only have one plant—which I brought to the island."

"You're keeping a plant alive?"

She wrinkled her nose in a mock scowl. Then a beat later confessed, "Okay, it's a succulent, but still."

He chuckled.

She swatted his arm. "Hey, at least I can keep a goldfish alive."

"I was thirteen. I thought I was doing him a favor with all those extra feedings."

Ten minutes later they entered her first-floor apartment. The familiar smell of new flooring and citrus cleaner welcomed her home. As she set down her things on the kitchen island, she tried viewing the space through Tyson's eyes: the ivory leather sectional with soft blue pillows, a cozy area rug, and wooden accent pieces. Its overall effect was slightly feminine, subdued, and inviting.

"This is really nice, Jen."

"Thanks. Definitely a step up from my last place. However, I'm not sure I'll be able to afford it on this new salary—if I even get the job."

"Well, money isn't everything. This position sounds more *you*, and you can't put a price tag on that."

"True enough."

His gaze homed in on her. "I'm proud of you, Jen. These past few months you've kind of had to pivot from the life you thought you'd have. That takes a lot of courage."

She hadn't thought of it that way, but it was true. Getting the rug pulled out from under her had been scary. "You'd know all about that since you've had to do the same thing. You expected your marriage would last forever and suddenly it was gone. I know moving on was hard, and I'm just as proud of you for having the strength to do it."

"I guess we've both faced a lot of loss and disappointment. Reinventing yourself is not easy."

"No, it's not. But having good friends to help you through is everything."

"You've got that right." Ty nodded.

She glanced at her Fitbit. "Well, I'd better go change. Don't want to be late. Help yourself to the Keurig, but fair warning—the cream's probably expired."

Almost two hours later Tyson waited in a coffee shop just down the street from the building where Jenna was interviewing. While he waited he answered some texts. One from Luke, who was excited about his relationship with Trinity. A couple of messages from his mom regarding a reservation for the upcoming weekend.

When he wasn't on his phone, he flipped through a copy of *The Alexandria Times* someone had left on the table. But he was only skimming the newspaper. He couldn't focus well enough to actually read the articles.

He was too nervous for Jenna. Or maybe it was just jitters from the caffeine. Yeah, that was it. Couldn't be worry that the new job would take Jenna away from the island again.

The image of her emerging from her apartment hallway flashed in his brain. Her brow furrowed, she'd stopped and smoothed the skirt of a dress that somehow managed to appear both businesslike *and* sporty. It offered a conservative view of her slim arms and tanned, toned legs.

"Is this okay?" she asked. "Is it too much? Not enough?"

He jerked his gaze from her legs. "It's perfect. You look great." He handed her a mug of hazelnut coffee. "Energy in a cup."

Since creamer was his thing he'd skipped the coffee, but he was making up for it now with the large cold brew. He checked the time. Must be going well if the interview was lasting this long. She would get the job, and he'd be back to irregular visits and sporadic texts.

His phone vibrated and a notification appeared on the screen. Jenna.

I'm done.

He replied,

Be there soon. Want a coffee?

No thanks. Too jacked up on adrenaline!

He left the shop, and unable to wait any longer, he sent a text on his way out to the truck.

It went well then?

She responded as he got in his truck.

Very well! I'll tell you all about it on the way to DC.

Chapter 25

Jenna couldn't believe how well the interview had gone. She and Nancy hit it off from the start. They connected over the Braves, and the woman's aunt vacationed on Chincoteague every summer. Nancy had even visited a few times herself.

Furthermore, the position seemed perfect for Jenna. She'd be responsible for overseeing the coaches of all the adult sports. She'd be accountable for the venues and equipment. The only negative was the reduction in salary, which would likely mean giving up her new apartment. But the pay was comparable to what she'd been making before the last pay raise Jason had given her.

When they'd gotten around to talking about Jenna's dismissal from Fleming Orthodontics, Nancy seemed to accept Jenna's explanation—and even sympathize—about the workplace romance gone awry. She'd apparently had a similar thing happen years ago. And even though she'd connected the last name with Mayor Fleming, she seemed unconcerned about the association. The interview only got better from there.

Jenna spilled every detail to Ty on the drive to DC, and retelling it only amped her up more. "She didn't commit to anything because she still has a few more people to interview—including one person on staff. I'm most worried about that. But I'm still hopeful."

"That's great, Jenna. Sounds like it couldn't have gone better."

Jenna beamed. "It felt like a really good fit."

"She'd be crazy to hire anyone else."

"Thanks, Ty." She glanced his way. It had somehow helped knowing he was just a few miles away rooting for her. "I'm glad you came with me today."

"I'm glad too."

But as they headed into DC proper, the pep in Jenna's step began to fade. A job was important, but it was just a job. Their mission now was to figure out who this Gordon guy was so she could protect her mother. It was going on six o'clock and DC's rush-hour traffic was living up to its bad reputation.

They'd put Gordon's home address into the GPS, and now it was only twelve miles away, but it would apparently take almost an hour to get there at this rate.

"What would you think about stopping for supper?" Ty asked.

She was eager to stake out Gordon's home, but she was also hungry—they hadn't eaten since before the interview. "That makes sense. Maybe some of this traffic will clear up by the time we're finished."

The two-story row house looked much as it had online, but viewing the neighborhood granted Jenna additional perspective. The homes were well maintained, and the neighbors coming and going seemed like regular, upstanding people.

When Ty and Jenna first arrived, they simply drove past the home as there were no parking spots available. Then they parked a block away and strolled past the house. The curtains were drawn except for one upstairs window, and there were no signs of life.

A while later a parking spot opened a few houses down. They snagged it and had been surveying the house ever since. But there was no movement in or around the home that they could see. They'd talked about ringing the doorbell, but Jenna hoped to avoid that.

The notion triggered a thought. Jenna reached into her purse, removed the binoculars, and pressed them to her eyes.

"You brought *binoculars*?"

"What's a stakeout without binoculars?"

"Where did you even get those?" he asked.

"Dad and I used to go bird-watching sometimes. We saw a flamingo once near Wallops Island."

"That's cool. Are you hoping to spot the rare speckle-throated nightflutter?"

"That's not a thing." She adjusted the focus. "I'm trying to see if . . . Oh good. They don't have one."

"Don't have what?"

"One of those doorbell cameras that record everyone approaching the house. As far as I can tell, he doesn't have any kind of camera." If they approached the door, Gordon would recognize both of them.

At the sound of pedestrians approaching on the sidewalk, she lowered the binoculars. "Last thing we need is to get hauled in for stalking."

"We could call your mom to bail us out."

"Funny."

His phone vibrated as a text came in. "It's Mom. Look, she sent a picture of the foal she's eyeing. Look at her."

Jenna lowered the binoculars and leaned in to see the filly. She was a beautiful bay with a white blaze and spindly legs. "Aw, she's so cute."

"It'd be nice having another foal on the property." He shot Jenna an impish grin. "Dad's sunk. I'm going to send this picture to Alex. A little gloating never hurt anyone."

She remembered her conversation with Ronda. "Or . . . you could not tell Alex and just get him to raise the bet."

The look in his eyes shifted to one of admiration. "You're a genius." He started texting.

Jenna turned her attention to the neighborhood. A streetlight kicked on nearby. The sun was setting and a cloak of darkness would soon fall over the neighborhood.

A few minutes later Ty pocketed his phone. "Done. Got him to three hundred."

"*Three* hundred? I thought it was one hundred."

"It was, but Alex got us up to two hundred last week."

That tricky, tricky woman. Jenna stifled a grin.

Ty nodded to the binoculars. "Give me those things."

She handed them over, then let her gaze drift back to the house. "Is that a light in that upstairs window? A faint one?"

He aimed the binoculars that way. "Maybe. I can't really tell yet. But it's getting darker by the minute."

"Even if a light is on, that doesn't mean anyone's home. He could've just left it on for security."

"True. Are you thinking we should ring the bell tonight?"

Mostly she just wanted to make sure he lived alone. "I think so. If someone does come to the door, should we just ask for Gordon?"

"Maybe not. They might tell him someone was looking for him, and they'll want to know who we are."

"We could ask for his daughter, Katie."

"That might work."

Jenna swung her gaze back to the second-story window, which now appeared brighter as darkness fell. "There is a light on."

He lowered the binoculars. "Should we knock on the door before it gets darker?"

"Good idea." She'd already changed into comfortable clothing at the restaurant. Now, just in case, she withdrew a ball cap from her purse, threaded her hair through the back, and donned the hat. After flipping down the car's visor, she tucked the stray hairs away and pulled the cap low on her forehead.

"Got a fake mustache in there?" Tyson wore an amused look.

"I'm afraid you're on your own. If anyone answers, I'll do the talking. People are more apt to trust a woman."

"It's all yours, Sherlock."

The streets were quiet as they approached the house. The evening air was thick with the scent of roses. Ivy roped the stone retaining wall leading up the lawn. They crossed the sidewalk and went up the five steps, then followed the short walkway to the porch steps.

Jenna's heart knocked against her rib cage. She wasn't sure what she was more afraid of: that someone would be home or that this whole trip would turn out to be a dead end.

At the door she shot Ty a nervous glance before she rang the bell. She listened for activity that might indicate someone was beyond the door but couldn't hear anything for the cars passing by and the distant wail of a siren.

After waiting a minute she knocked on the door. Ty was trying to see through the slit in the curtains, but it seemed dark inside. Jenna glanced around the porch for clues about the occupants. Two sturdy chairs sandwiched a small round table. A well-used broom leaned against the brick exterior, and two dead ferns sat on the thick porch ledge like sentinels who'd long ago given up the guard.

Jenna knocked again, harder this time, then waited impatiently. "It doesn't seem like anyone's home."

"No, it doesn't." Tyson pushed the lid of the wall-mounted mailbox upward and it squawked in protest.

"You can't do that! Tampering with mail is a federal offense."

"I'm not tampering. I'm taking a peek."

Jenna glanced around. There was no one that she could see. Plus it was getting pretty dark and the porchlight was off.

Tyson held up the mail so the nearest light shone on the letters. "A piece of junk mail addressed to Gordon Smith or current resident. Royal Caribbean, addressed to Gordon Smith. Draft Kings, Gordon Smith." He stopped on a postcard from some retailer, staring at it like it might hold the answers to life's greatest questions.

"What? What is it?" Jenna leaned closer, squinting, but couldn't make out the name.

After a beat he turned a worried look on her. "This one's addressed to a Rosalind Smith."

Chapter 26

"I don't understand." Jenna leaned into Tyson for a better view of his laptop screen. "There doesn't seem to be a Rosalind Smith anywhere in DC, much less at Gordon's address."

After finding the suspicious piece of mail, they'd staked out the house until after eleven before giving up for the night. Then they checked into a nearby hotel.

"It is odd. But Rosalind wasn't on the house's deed, and Gordon wasn't listed as married on that background check. Plus we never found a current certificate of marriage for him, all of which indicates he's likely unmarried."

"We only got a conclusive result on the marriage certificate from the county website, though. He could've been married anywhere else."

"That's true," he said.

"And there does seem to be a woman with his last name living in his house."

"That seems pretty damning. But there are other explanations. It could be his ex-wife. Or maybe his son and daughter-in-law used to live here. Smith is such a common name, it could even be a previous owner."

"I guess those things are possible. But I don't think they're the most logical explanations. Too bad he's not on social media—Rosalind would be listed among his friends."

They'd found plenty of Rosalind Smiths on Facebook but none living in the DC area. Then there were the Roses, Rosas, and Rosies. Tracking down the right person with so little information seemed daunting.

Jenna leaned back into the cozy outdoor love seat. The calming scent of lavender drifted from the flowering patio border, soothing her nerves, and a warm breeze ruffled her hair. "I thought for sure we'd find something."

"Don't lose hope. Even if we strike out online, we're not done. We still have tomorrow and we can head back over to the house." They both had to return to the island tomorrow night in time for work Wednesday.

"Presuming she works outside the home, we should get there early, maybe catch her as she's leaving."

"Would you want to approach her?" he asked.

"I think we should. If she's off to work, we won't get another chance before we have to leave. If she doesn't leave for work, we can wait until a respectable hour and knock on the door."

"Sounds like a plan."

The low timbre of his voice was pleasant and inviting. The breeze carried the scent of his familiar cologne, and Jenna drew a deep breath. It was even better than the lavender, beckoning memories of quiet talks, good-natured teasing, and boisterous laughter. He'd always been such a fun, easy person to be around. A good companion.

She cut him a sideways glance. The golden patio light sparkled like copper in his hair while the glow of the laptop lit his facial features. His brows drew together as he searched yet another social media platform for the elusive woman.

He shifted his arm, bringing it in contact with hers as his fingers hunted and pecked across the keyboard. Such nice hands. Big and masculine, with fingers that tapered to squared-off tips. His palms sported calluses from tasks both on the job and with the fire company. He'd never been afraid of hard work.

And here she was, gazing longingly at his hands. She shook her head. So much for conquering her thoughts. She was losing her mind—and this battle.

"Maybe this one?" Ty clicked on a profile of a woman who seemed about Gordon's age. "She's from DC and studied at the University of Maryland, DC."

Jenna skimmed the profile and pointed at the screen. "But she currently lives in Pittsburgh."

Tyson sighed. "You're right." He toggled back and continued scrolling through the Rosalind Smiths. "She has to be here somewhere."

Jenna's fingers itched to smooth his brow. He was going above and beyond to help her, taking two days off work. Driving all the way here. He was such a loyal friend.

Friend.

Because that's the kind of thoughts you're having about him.

She rolled her eyes. Friends didn't notice hands or long to smooth brows. They didn't savor the feeling of their arms pressed together or relish the tones of each other's voices.

Somehow this summer, her feelings of friendship had been on a slow, steady slide into something more. Something romantic. Something alluring and yet scary.

Something completely irresistible.

As if sensing her appraisal he turned her way. His gaze swept over her features, concern flickering in his eyes. "Don't be discouraged."

"I'm not. I'm really thankful, Ty. I can't tell you how much your help means to me." She leaned forward and planted a kiss on his cheek and savored the instant reward—the warmth of his body, the scent of his skin, the roughness of his jaw.

But as she withdrew, worry washed over her. She'd kissed him on the cheek *twice* in a matter of weeks. What was wrong with her? She was about to ruin the best thing she had going.

The heat of Jenna's lips was like a brand on his cheek. Tyson's heart stuttered at her nearness. This lingering kiss, like the last one, landed so close to his mouth it pained him. Why hadn't he turned just a fraction of an inch and captured that kiss with his lips? But it was too late now. She was already retreating.

Her breath whispered across his skin as she withdrew, eyes still closed. His gaze dropped to those lips. Before darting back to her eyes, which now opened slowly.

Their gazes locked. Was that desire shimmering on the surface? The thought of it buoyed him. But the glimmer was gone in an instant. Replaced by something less welcome.

"I'm sorry. I don't know why I keep—"

He stole the words with his mouth. He brushed his lips over hers slowly. Carefully. And then she responded. A fire kindled inside him as their lips mated in a sensuous dance. He held on to his restraint. Even when her palm pressed against the skittering pulse at his neck.

His hands found the curve of her waist as everything around them evaporated. It was just the two of them and this mesmerizing moment.

It was enthralling.

It was perfection.

He never wanted it to end.

How could this be Jenna? He'd never even thought of her this way until recently. Not even back in high school when they'd shared that prom kiss. His brain had been too full of Danielle Collins to consider anyone else. But now he felt as if he'd die the second this amazing kiss ended. "Wild," he whispered against her lips.

"Hmm?" Her murmur vibrated against his mouth, the sensation electric.

"This is wild."

She hmmed again and he continued his soft exploration. His brain shut off as all his other senses took over. Her lips were so warm and inviting. She tasted of mint and honey. Her touch on his skin sent ripples of pleasure down his spine. She emitted a little mewling sound that just about drove him over the edge.

It was then that, most inconveniently, his brain engaged.

This is Jenna.

Jenna, his best friend.

And they were kissing each other without regard for the future. They'd crossed a line that couldn't be uncrossed. He couldn't bring himself to regret that right now. But it was a huge shift in their relationship. A relationship that was very important to him.

They needed to talk.

It was the last thing he wanted to do.

Even so, he mustered every ounce of restraint and put a centimeter of space between them. He kept his eyes closed, for fear he'd see regret or something worse in her eyes. Their breaths clashed in the space between them. "We're—we should talk about this." Gathering courage, he opened his eyes—and met her sleepy-eyed gaze. Not a shred of regret there. Not even close.

Have mercy.

His will tottered. "Shouldn't we?"

Her eyes dropped to his lips. "I'd rather just keep kissing."

"You're killing me, Greene." And yet, how could he refuse such a sweet request? He resumed the kiss, pouring himself into it, and she returned the favor. Her hand drifted to his nape, her fingers sliding into his hair, shocking every hair follicle to life. He moved his hands around, pulling her closer as he deepened the kiss. Their breathing accelerated. "I can't seem to stop."

"Who asked you to?"

Laughter bubbled out.

Then she initiated a long, searching kiss that flung all humor to the other side of the universe. She'd never been timid. Not the girl who'd fielded line drives and swung for the fences. Certainly not the woman now in his arms. And he'd never been more thankful.

She withdrew long enough to tilt her head the other way. "How'd you get so good at this? Never mind. Don't want to know."

Their lips came together like magnets. He couldn't get close enough to her.

But her last words hovered in his mind like an annoying fly. They'd both had recent relationships—and both had ended badly. He was still healing and she'd said the same of herself. This kiss had ushered them into foreign territory, and what if it was too soon for both of them? What if he ended up hurting her? He couldn't bear the thought.

He palmed her cheek and put a sliver of space between them. "Is this . . . a bad idea?"

"Doesn't feel like it." She brushed his nose with hers. "Does it?"

Her warm breath against his lips tantalized. "I'd tell you, but I can't seem to think straight."

"We're just kissing . . ."

"I think we're making out at this point."

"Fair. But I'm good with it if you are. Just for now?" She brushed his lips with hers.

The caress eradicated all common sense. All sense period. "What—what do you mean? Like just this once?"

"Just tonight. Kissing only. Get it out of our systems."

He wasn't sure it worked like that, but . . .

Then her eyes opened lazily, filled with hope and desire. And when she smiled at him like that, he could refuse her nothing.

He dove his fingers into her hair. "Deal."

Chapter 27

Jenna's alarm dragged her from the oblivion of sleep. She grappled for her phone and turned off the alarm. Memories of the night before washed over her like warm waves. Tyson and his languid, breathtaking kisses. Tyson holding her and touching her as if she was precious and important. As if he couldn't get enough of her.

She stretched languorously in the king-size bed as a smile spread across her face. The sentiment went both ways. She'd never been kissed like that before. Who'd have thought the two of them would ignite like a lit match on gasoline?

Parting had been sweet torture, especially since they'd agreed the extracurricular activity would be confined to last night. They'd shared at least a dozen one-last-kisses before they'd finally parted ways. Then she'd fallen asleep in a cocoon of warmth and wonder.

The cold light of day didn't leave her with regret so much as a profound sense of unfulfilled longing. Her smile wilted at the thought.

Who wanted to leave behind something so wonderful? But she was a sensible woman. There were reasons she'd suggested that time limit on their very nice canoodling. Reasons that still applied, unfortunately.

Heaving a sigh, she slipped her legs over the edge of the bed. She could be a grown-up about this and keep to their agreement because it was in their best long-term interests.

She didn't have to like it though.

Nerves didn't take hold of Jenna until she began getting dressed. They'd agreed to meet in the lobby at six thirty, and now her heart ricocheted through her chest like a rubber ball in a racquetball court.

How was Tyson feeling this morning? Did he regret the make-out session? Would he ever be able to see her as his old buddy again? Did she even want him to?

She stuffed the questions down even as she stuffed her belongings in her duffel bag. They *had* to go back to friendship. She wouldn't risk hurting Ty with her fickle heart. Last time it was Jason. But before that there was Spencer during her freshman and sophomore years of college and Ian during her yearlong internship. All long-term relationships that never fully engaged her heart.

And there was no way she was getting involved with a firefighter and ending up heartbroken and alone like her mom. She couldn't imagine building her whole life around a man and losing him so suddenly and tragically. Not to mention the many anxious nights spent waiting and watching for his return.

So it was back to the friendship track. The good news was, they seemed to be on the same page.

She was zipping her duffel when a knock sounded. She couldn't imagine anyone but Ty coming to her door this early. So she grabbed the bag and shouldered her purse on the way to the door.

She steadied her breath—if not her heart rate—and opened the door. "Good morning."

"Morning."

She caught just a glimpse of sleepy eyes and tousled dark hair before she slipped into the hall and pulled the door shut.

They headed silently down the hallway, which seemed to stretch ahead of them like a runway. The flap of her flip-flops was loud in the interminable quiet. She could practically hear her heart beating.

Jenna searched for something to say, but her mind was blank. Should they address last night, or would that only make things more awkward? Could things even *be* more awkward?

What was Tyson thinking over there? She hadn't been able to tell much from that glimpse. Only that he seemed to have had a rough night. Was that because of their kissing? Had she messed things up for good? Her thoughts spun out of control from there as the distance between her room and the lobby seemed to lengthen despite their progress.

"So . . ." Ty said into the void. "I guess that happened."

Their gazes met.

His eyes crinkled at the corners in that familiar way. He was okay. And somehow that made her okay too.

"And hey . . . it was pretty awesome, Greene."

"Well, now that you mentioned it." The smile they shared made her heart bloom with color.

Chapter 28

Jenna licked the deliciously sweet chocolate from her fingers. To save time Ty had gone out early and hit a neighborhood donut shop before they met up. He'd bought her favorite: Boston cream. She wiped her fingers on a napkin and stowed it in the empty bag.

The morning had dawned sunny and beautiful. This bustling area of DC was a far cry from their quaint little island. Traffic was challenging, but they were less than ten minutes from Gordon's house. It had been just enough time to polish off the donut while making small talk with the man she'd made out with last night.

She shook away the thought—and the remnants of those amazing kisses. Time to focus on their mission.

It was six forty-five when they stopped at the red light just before Gordon's row house. She zeroed in on the porch, three houses from the end of the block. All seemed quiet.

Movement pulled Jenna's attention to the porch, where a woman emerged from the shadows.

"There she is!" Ty said.

"She's leaving." The fortysomething woman had short auburn hair and wore business-casual clothing. She was already down the porch steps and striding across the strip of lawn. Then she was heading down the steps toward the sidewalk. "She's getting away."

The cross traffic at the intersection still flowed. A car waited in front of them for the light to turn. Jenna glanced at the traffic signal. They were stuck. *Hurry, hurry!*

Rosalind approached a car parked at the curb across from the house. If they didn't stop her, they wouldn't have another chance to confront her.

Jenna flung off her seat belt. "I'm going after her."

"Be careful!" he called before the door shut.

She dashed toward the corner. There was no time to wait for the Walk signal. At the first pause in traffic she darted across the street. She lost sight of Rosalind behind a group of tall shrubs. But when Jenna reached the other side of the street, she glimpsed Rosalind getting into a car.

No, no, no!

Jenna booked it down the sidewalk. But as she neared, the woman took off in her white Toyota, heading toward the light where Ty waited.

Jenna started to run back toward Ty's truck, but she only got a few yards. The light had turned and his truck advanced quickly. He pulled to the curb near Jenna and she jumped in. "Let's go after her."

Jenna buckled up while Ty waited for a break in traffic. When it came he whipped the vehicle in an illegal U-turn. Jenna couldn't even complain. Rosalind had already gotten a head start. They'd have to hurry if they had any chance of catching her. "If we follow her to work, we can approach her there."

He accelerated until he came to a slow-moving SUV and navigated around it. "What will we say?"

"I don't know. We'll have all day to figure that out if we can just find out where she works."

"There!" Ty pointed out the windshield.

She glimpsed a white car about ten cars ahead. "Has to be her. Maybe she'll get stopped at the next light." *Please, God.* A face-to-face meeting was their best chance of figuring out who she was.

A break in the right lane allowed Ty to shoot ahead a few cars before he jogged back into the left lane. The white car was only half a block ahead now. But they were momentarily stuck behind two slow vehicles, and Jenna feared *they* would be the ones caught at the next light.

She held her breath as they approached the signal, but they made it through just as the light turned yellow. Jenna craned for a view of the white car. "The next light just turned red. She has to stop."

They slowed for two cars turning into a plaza and Ty switched lanes. They would be coming up alongside the vehicle at the stoplight. But as they approached, Jenna got a better view of the car. It wasn't even a Toyota. Her heart sank. There were no white cars ahead at all. Rosalind must've turned off somewhere.

Jenna's sigh seemed to come from the soles of her feet.

When Ty's gaze met hers, his expression echoed her feelings. "We lost her."

Ty made another turn, glancing this way and that for the Toyota. They'd been driving around the area for ten minutes. The futility of the situation had already settled in for him, but he didn't want to give up the hunt until Jenna was ready. He hated disappointing her. He should've whipped the car around at the intersection near the row house once the light turned green. But he hadn't wanted to leave Jenna standing on the sidewalk by herself.

At this point, though, that's probably what she wished he'd done.

A minute later she sagged into her seat. "She's long gone. Probably at work by now."

He hated the surrender in her voice and body language. "Maybe we can figure out where she works some other way."

"How? We couldn't even find her online."

"We could look some more. We could even do a background check on her. Or we could delay our return tonight." He had to be at the B and B by 5:00 a.m., but he was willing to do about anything to erase the disappointment from Jenna's eyes.

She stared out the passenger window for a while. "We already know a woman's living in his house. And it's not his daughter—Mom showed me a picture of her. Maybe this is God's way of telling us to go home. I can have a talk with Mom, tell her what we found out. Surely that'll be enough for her to confront Gordon about it."

"And if he lies?"

"Why else would someone named Rosalind Smith be getting mail at his house? We *saw* her. There's no getting out of this."

He noodled on that for a minute. "I know we only saw her from a distance, but didn't she seem a little young for him?"

Jenna rolled her eyes. "Pretty typical, though. Seems like men often marry women half their age."

He nudged her playfully. "Hey."

"Present company excluded, of course."

'Cause, yeah, the woman he'd married was actually a couple years older. Although that hadn't worked out so well.

He drove in silence for a minute, leaving Jenna to sort out her thoughts. He knew just how to cheer her up. The neighborhood sported a lot of restaurants and retail shops, so he wouldn't have to look too far. A few blocks ahead he pulled into a coffee-shop parking lot.

She tossed him a grateful smile. "You read my mind."

They exited the shop with steaming cups of their favorite beverages. Jenna already seemed a little less disappointed. The coffee had lifted her spirits, but he knew exactly what would refresh her mind and body. "Do you still want to head back to the island?"

She nodded. "I'll just have a talk with Mom when she gets home from work, and hopefully I'll be able to get through to her."

"She'll have to take you seriously now." He glanced at his watch. "We have plenty of time before we have to head back, though." After they returned to the truck he glanced her way. "What would you think about taking a little hike?"

"Um . . ." Jenna made a show of glancing around them. "You know we're in DC, right? One of the most densely populated cities in the US?"

He offered a furtive smile. "It so happens I know just the place."

Chapter 29

Jenna inhaled the calming scents of pine and earth. The forest canopy cocooned them from the city's sights and sounds. Out here there was only the rush of Rock Creek, the sunlight dappling through the trees, and a million shades of green.

It was a full ten degrees cooler in the depths of the park. The roar of the rapids absorbed the sounds of their footfalls. The weight of her upcoming conversation with her mother seemed to have fallen off a couple miles back. This outing was exactly what she'd needed. Time in nature to soothe her mind and ease the tightness from her shoulders.

As they followed the trail, Tyson gave her the time and space to work out her thoughts. He knew her so well. Knew just what she needed—sometimes before she did, apparently. That was the benefit of knowing someone for so long. The blessing of having someone care enough to pay attention to your needs. What a gift that was, to be known and understood in such a way.

A rush of affection swelled inside, compelling her to reach out. She took his hand and threaded her fingers through his. She caught his startled look from the corner of her eye and held her breath. Then his hand tightened around hers and her lungs began functioning again.

They continued along the dirt path, linked in a way that felt so natural, even though this was a first for them. He must be wondering why she'd reached for him. It was the gesture of a girlfriend, and they'd agreed to leave the more-than-friends activities behind last night. But in this moment she simply felt so grateful for him. She wanted his touch, this connection.

Was that so wrong?

Maybe not *wrong* but probably confusing. Which was apropos since she *was* confused. Confused as to why making out with Tyson Parker had affected her on a level she'd never experienced before. She thought back to last night. To his passion, tempered with gentleness. His touch, restrained by will. His words, imbued with caution. He cared about their relationship enough to stop what they were doing—as wonderful as it was—and consider the risks. Even though it also made her wonder—what would it be like to see him lose control and know she was the one who inspired that?

One touch of those lips and she'd lost all reason. She cast him a glance from beneath her lashes. Was he remembering those kisses too? Why had they made that stupid arbitrary agreement, limiting their kissing to such a stingy fragment of time? It just hadn't been enough.

She wanted another kiss more than her next breath. She pulled him to a stop.

He turned, a question in his eyes.

She answered by rising on tiptoes. Brushing his lips with hers. When had she gotten so bold? It must be Tyson. She was so comfortable, so at ease in her own skin with him. She could hardly regret her fearlessness when he responded so fervently. The kiss lingered a heartbeat before she drew back.

His expression held surprise along with warmth and affection. Then another question flickered in the depths of his gaze. "I thought . . . ?"

She'd thought too. Yesterday's kisses had opened a Pandora's box, but she didn't want to think about the ramifications right now. She only wanted to feel close to him again. "I just figured since we're still in DC . . ."

He searched her eyes for a long, hopeful moment. "So when we go home, things go back to normal. But until then . . ."

"Until then . . . we do as we like?"

The corners of his lips lifted ever so slightly, and he leaned close enough that his breath whispered across her lips. "Is this what you'd like?"

In lieu of an answer, she welcomed his kiss.

They spent the morning walking, taking selfies on Boulder Bridge, and of course kissing. They held hands as they strolled and chatted about their families, work, and old times, falling into a familiar rhythm derived from years of friendship.

When morning melded into afternoon, they found a snack bar at the tennis center and settled at a secluded table for an impromptu picnic. Afterward they rented a canoe, and Tyson gave her palpitations when he stepped in wrong and nearly tipped them into the river.

By the time they exited the park, Jenna felt so refreshed and joyful that she hated to leave. Hated the thought of that conversation she had to have with her mom. Hated the thought of returning to the island because that would burst this bubble of intimacy she'd enjoyed with Tyson.

As he turned onto the highway, she glanced his way. In roughly three and a half hours they'd be home, and they'd go back to the way things were before. Back to being only friends.

The thought left her hollow. But as much as she'd enjoyed these hours together, not to mention the monumental kisses, she couldn't escape the fact that she couldn't be with Ty.

As they headed back to the island, heaviness swelled inside the cab. There was little conversation. Obviously she wasn't the only one with conflicted feelings. She could read the tension in Ty's body language. See that the sparkle in his green eyes had dimmed.

They hit a drive-thru for supper, and when they were an hour from home, he gave her a sidelong glance. "Want to talk about what's going on?"

She held his gaze for a long beat. "I'm not sure it would do any good."

He turned his attention to the road. "Probably not."

"We can just, you know, carry on as usual. We've been friends for a long time. It's familiar ground."

"I'm not sure it'll be that easy for me," he said quietly.

Or for her. A frisson of fear passed through her. The closeness they'd shared might've changed everything between them. And the thought of losing what they'd had before the past twenty-four hours knocked the wind out of her.

Chapter 30

It was dark by the time Jenna approached her mom's house. Her mind was still on the awkward good-bye hug she'd shared with Ty. He still sat at the curb, waiting for her to enter the house. Ever the gentleman.

As she stepped onto the porch she gave him a wave.

With the weight of everything that had happened, she'd decided to put off her talk with Mom until tomorrow. Maybe arrange another girls' night at Island Creamery. A little something sweet to help the bad news go down. Sure, that would help.

Her mother's car wasn't in the drive anyway. But when Jenna entered the house, she found Mom curled up on the sofa, watching a reality TV show. She looked younger than her years with her stubby ponytail and pale blue loungewear. The familiar smell of molasses and vanilla reached Jenna's nose.

"Hi, honey." Mom jumped up and embraced her. "I'm so happy the interview went well. I can't wait to hear all about it."

"I can't wait to tell you." Jenna had only texted broad details about the interview.

"Ty's not coming in? I have a fresh batch of oatmeal-raisin cookies cooling on the stove."

"His favorite. He said to tell you hello but he had to get going."

"I'll just take some over tomorrow. Ronda likes them too. I made some without raisins for you and Gordon." The man had a huge sweet tooth, which might account for the uptick in Mom's baking this summer.

"Thanks. I'll have one later."

They settled on the sofa as the program broke for a commercial. Jenna answered all Mom's questions about her conversation with Nancy and the job particulars. So much had happened in the past twenty-four hours that the interview seemed like it had taken place a week ago.

"The job sounds perfect. So you think you'll get it?"

"It seems promising, but she's not finished interviewing so I don't want to be too optimistic. Where's Gordon?"

"You just missed him. He went to Island Foods for basil. He's planning to make his homemade spaghetti sauce tomorrow, which apparently has to simmer all day."

Island Foods was a twenty-minute errand at most. Maybe that was Jenna's cue to have that talk with Mom. But Jenna had already been here ten minutes, and this wasn't a conversation to rush.

Mom's phone vibrated and she checked the screen. "They didn't have fresh basil, and the man refuses to use dried herbs. He's heading to Food Lion."

The store was off island, a twenty-minute drive. Plenty of time for that talk now. But Jenna's heart thumped with dread. The thought of hurting her mother pained her. She'd clearly grown very fond of Gordon. Was probably in the early stages of love. But that gave Jenna even more reason to divulge the truth. Even though it would be hard, it was the loving thing to do.

The program was back on now, but her mother had muted the show long ago. Mom was apparently texting Gordon back. When she set down her phone, Jenna took the opportunity. "Mom, can we talk a minute? I—I have something I need to tell you."

Her mother's pale blue eyes sobered. "What's wrong, honey? Are you okay?"

Of course Jenna would be her first concern. It only made her feel worse about what she had to say. "First, I have a confession to make. Ty and I did go to Alexandria for my interview, but after that . . . we swung up to DC."

A glimmer of joy entered Mom's eyes as a smile bloomed on her face. "I knew it! I could just tell something was brewing between you guys. It's about time!"

Jenna parted her lips but couldn't seem to formulate any words. Her mom had been expecting a romance to develop between them? Jenna thought she'd put that dream to bed long ago.

"So you went on a little romantic getaway?" Mom turned fully toward Jenna, pulling her knees to her chest. "Tell me everything. I'm so excited it's finally happening."

"Oh, Mom, no. That's not what—" Well, it kind of *was* what happened. But that particular situation was complicated—and beside the point! She had to get this conversation back on topic. "That's not why we went to DC."

Mom's face fell. "Oh. Then you're not together?"

"No, we're not."

"Then why did you—?" In a matter of seconds her mother's eyes went frosty and her expression closed. "Please tell me your little excursion had nothing to do with Gordon."

"Before you get upset—"

"Too late."

"—hear me out. Please. You know we only have your best interests at heart."

Mom faced forward, lowering her feet to the floor. "So Tyson's in on this too. The both of you are conspiring against Gordon. What in the world could you possibly have against him? He's been nothing but kind to me—and to you."

"Perhaps, but there've been a few red flags, Mom. Don't you see how fast this is moving? Plus I heard a suspicious phone call between him and someone—he said 'I love you,' and I got the feeling something wasn't right."

Mom scowled. "Oh, he said 'I love you' to someone on the phone. How heinous! He does have family, Jenna—did you think of that?"

"Of course I did, but—" Jenna gave her head a hard shake. "Just listen. We discovered something in DC. Something that's going to be difficult to hear. The last thing I want to do is hurt you, but you need to know the truth."

Mom crossed her arms and leveled an impatient look at Jenna. "Well, go ahead then. Tell me whatever it is you think you know."

Jenna winced. This was harder than she'd expected. She was about to break her mother's kind, soft heart. But it had to be done. "Ty and I went by Gordon's house. There's a woman living there, Mom. Her name is Rosalind Smith. We didn't speak with her, but we saw her exiting the house early in the morning. And the mailbox had mail addressed to her." There. It was done. She set her hand on Mom's. "I'm really sorry to have to tell you this."

Mom stared at her for ten full seconds, her expression blank. Jenna couldn't even guess what she was thinking. She was probably in shock, registering what Jenna had said. Processing what it meant.

"And the two kids?"

Two kids? Jenna blinked. "What two kids?"

"The two teenagers who also live there. Didn't you find any mail for them while you were rooting through his mailbox?"

Wait. Her mom knew about Rosalind? And they had kids together? None of this was making sense. Had Jenna misunderstood?

Mom huffed. "Rosalind is Gordon's *sister*, Jenna. She's divorcing her two-timing husband and living at Gordon's house with her kids until things settle down."

His *sister*?

Rosalind was Gordon's *sister*? Could Jenna really have gotten this so wrong? It all lined up: the piece of mail, the "I love you," the woman living in his house. But what if he'd only told Mom that to cover the truth? It was possible, wasn't it? But Jenna had to tread carefully here. "Okay . . . but if she's married, why's her last name still Smith?"

Mom narrowed her eyes. "Because she never took her husband's name. Are you seriously doubting him even still? Even though I'm sitting here giving you a perfectly reasonable explanation?"

"Well, I— It's just . . . he never mentioned her, that's all."

"Well, he mentioned her to *me*. He's opened his home to them even though her teenage boys drive him up the wall. It so happens he's a humble man, so no, he doesn't go around telling everyone he's helping her out. It's also why he's in no rush to get home. We didn't realize you needed a notarized letter explaining his situation."

Warmth flooded Jenna's face. Still . . . it was possible he wasn't telling her mom the truth. The sister thing could just be a cover story for the wife and kids he had back home. There was still that comment Jenna had overheard about him being in Maine. What was that all about?

"Oh, for heaven's sake! I've seen pictures, Jenna. Pictures of his sister and nephews before the divorce. I saw her wedding photo. Do you need visible proof? I'm a grown woman and I'm perfectly capable of handling my own love life. You have got to drop this right now."

Ouch. That kind, soft heart Jenna knew and loved was nowhere to be seen now. Not that she deserved to benefit from it at the moment. Apparently she *had* been wrong about Gordon. Somehow she jumped to the wrong conclusion and started seeing danger around every corner. Maybe Gordon really was just a nice man who didn't own a credit card and opened his home for his brokenhearted sister and her kids.

Oh boy, had she messed up. She gave her mom an apologetic look. "I'm so sorry. I really thought—"

"You have been suspicious of him from the start, Jenna Mae Greene."

The full name. Jenna winced. "You're right. It just happened so fast . . ."

"I'm getting awful weary of that tired old line."

"You're right, you're right." Jenna rubbed the back of her neck. "I don't know what's gotten into me." She'd done a background search on the man! Maybe her breakup with Jason had messed her up somehow. Or maybe no one would ever measure up to her father. But that wasn't Gordon's fault. "I really am sorry, Mom. I'll try to do better."

A bit of the starch left her mother's posture, and the smallest of smiles lifted her lips. "Do more than 'try.'"

Chapter 31

Tyson lifted the eight-year-old girl from Patches' back while her dad spotted her ten-year-old brother on the dismount.

"That was so fun!" Addy said. "Can we do it again tomorrow, Dad?"

"If Mr. Tyson says it's okay."

"There's plenty of room in the schedule. Just pick a time on the sign-up sheet."

Elijah gave Penny one last stroke. "She likes me."

"She definitely likes you. I can tell by the way she nickers."

"Thanks again for taking the time," their dad said. "This is the main reason we booked here. The girls are wild about these ponies."

Tyson heard that a lot. It wasn't every day you got to ride a genuine Chincoteague pony. "My pleasure."

The group scuttled off while Tyson began unsaddling and grooming the mares. They complained each time he gave the other attention. Finally he shook his head at them. "You're like a couple of jealous wives."

Penny snorted as he led her back out to pasture. Patches followed along, as he'd known she would. He gave them both a little affection before he headed toward the house. The scent of grass still permeated the afternoon from yesterday's mowing.

As he rounded the house he caught a glimpse of Mama Dee's

place across the street. He hadn't seen Jenna since they'd returned to the island three days ago. She'd texted to brief him on the conversation with her mom. He'd wanted to call her and have a real talk. Especially since it had gone so poorly.

But common sense reined him in. He was having trouble navigating his thoughts about Jenna. Trying to sort out his feelings for her. The memory of her kisses, her affection, the way she gazed up at him kept him up at night.

As if the nightmares didn't do enough of that.

When he entered the house Mom was descending the stairs with a load of dirty sheets, her gray hair piled on her head. But she beamed when she spotted him. "Those Carter kids couldn't stop talking about their pony rides. They're begging their parents to come back for the Pony Swim."

"They'd be hard-pressed to find a place at this late date."

"I told 'em as much and suggested they make plans for next year. We still have two rooms left that week."

"Good idea." Ty nodded.

"Hey, there's a light bulb out in Driftwood—tableside lamp—and a dripping faucet in Pasture View. Both rooms are currently empty."

"I'm on it."

"Thanks, honey."

He headed upstairs and grabbed a bulb from the supply closet. He was exchanging the bulbs when a text came in from Luke.

> I was at Teaguer's with the guys last night and there was some stuff going around about you and Marissa—someone insinuated you slept with her. Thought you'd want to know.

Ty frowned.

Who said that?

I was away from the table at the start of the conversation. It didn't go on long once I got back, and I did defend you. Just wanted you to know what was being said.

Those guys act like a bunch of old biddies sometimes.

Kind of made me wonder if it's coming from Marissa.

Why would she lie about that? He shot back a text.

Think so?

It just seems like this whole thing should've passed over by now. Gotta run. Boss sending me on an errand.

See ya.

Tyson was getting a little tired of the drama. He'd done everything he could think of to fix things, but it didn't seem to make a difference. Maybe he should try apologizing to Marissa again.

He mulled over the idea as he went for his tools and headed to Pasture View to check on the dripping faucet. As he loosened the set screw, his thoughts turned to Jenna and those two days they'd had together. Being with her like that, especially that last day when he'd felt free to take her hand or touch her cheek, had given him a small taste of what a relationship with her might be like.

And a taste hadn't been nearly enough.

He'd missed her these past few days. Like an actual physical ache in his gut. He wanted to call her up and ask how her day was going. Wanted to run across the street the minute she got home.

And what would you say, idiot?

She'd always claimed she'd never date a firefighter—and that's who he was down to his core. He planned on being an active member of the fire company as long as he was able, just like Dad had been.

Plus he was a little wary about putting his heart out there again. Britt's desertion had left him feeling unworthy and rejected. He'd responded by going a little crazy. But maybe he'd just been proving to himself that he could leave people before he got left. Maybe it gave him a sense of control for a while. It certainly gave him the time and space to get over Britt. But look where his shallow lifestyle had led him.

Jenna wasn't his feckless biological father, however. And she certainly wasn't Britt. He knew her inside and out. She would never treat him so callously. Which brought him to the whole friendship thing. How could he take the chance of souring their relationship?

But that excuse was starting to wear thin. Especially in light of their time together this week. What if it was worth the risk? What if a romantic relationship with Jenna turned out to be the best thing that ever happened to him? To them? And how would they ever know if they weren't willing to put it all on the line?

He removed the handle and found the adjusting ring loose. A simple fix. He tightened the ring and put the handle back on. When he turned on the water, the drip was history.

He cleaned up his tools and stowed them in the closet, then stopped in the kitchen to see if Dad needed help—though heaven knew food prep wasn't Tyson's forte.

Dad turned down the offer but was happy to catch up while he punched down the dough for tomorrow's cinnamon rolls. Mom joined them after a bit, and they talked until they were interrupted by a call from someone wanting to book a weekend in August.

Tyson was just about to head out front to pull weeds when he got a call from Fish & Wildlife. He stepped out onto the porch and took the call. "Hey, Greg, how's it going?"

"All right, all right. Busy day out here on the refuge. Seems we had a little skirmish between two stallions. They're fine, but one of the mares got in the way. Got a little scraped up. Nothing too serious by the looks of it, but we probably need to get the vet out here to take a peek at her."

"Sure thing. Where's she at now?"

"We've got her in the south corral with her foal. She's a little shaken up. It's Dream."

Jenna's buyback. He sure hoped Greg was right and it was nothing serious. "Her foal all right?"

"Yeah, she's unharmed."

"Okay. I'll make a call and we'll get out there ASAP."

"Thanks, Ty."

Tyson ended the call and reached out to the vet, who agreed to meet him at the pen in an hour.

Once he got off the phone he glanced across the street. Today was Jenna's day off, but her car wasn't in the drive. Still, if she wasn't in the middle of something important, she wouldn't pass up the opportunity to see Dream and her foal up close and personal. Make sure they were all right.

Before he could stop himself, he placed the call. It had nothing to do with missing her. At least that was what he told himself as the phone rang. Once. Twice.

"Hey, Ty, what's up?" Jenna answered in her normal tone.

"Not much. Where are you?"

"Running a few errands. I'm currently finishing up at the post office. Why do you ask?"

"Just got off the phone with Fish & Wildlife. There was a little run-in with a couple stallions, and Dream got in the way. Sounds like she's fine, just a little scraped up."

"Oh no. Are you sure she's okay? And her foal?"

"The foal wasn't involved and Jerry doesn't think Dream's injuries are serious. But just as a precaution I'm meeting the vet at the refuge. Thought you might like to ride along."

Chapter 32

Jenna pushed back her nerves as she shifted in Ty's truck. She was worried about Dream, that was all. If anything happened to the pony, it would be like losing her father all over again.

But it didn't sound as if that would happen. "*Only a little scraped up*," Fish & Wildlife had said, and Ty had spent most of the drive reassuring her.

But part of her nerves had nothing to do with Dream and everything to do with the fact that the last time she and Ty had been together, they were all over each other. A rush of heat swamped Jenna's cheeks at the thought. The past few days the memories had never been far from her mind. Not while she was guiding kayak tours and certainly not when she was lying in bed late at night.

"How are things between you and your mom?"

"You know Mom. She can flare up pretty good, but she forgives quickly." Jenna thought back over the summer. "I just can't believe I had it so wrong. I'm usually better at reading people." Why had she been so quick to doubt Gordon? Sure, she was protective of her mother, and the romance had progressed quickly. But sometimes they did.

"There were some red flags."

"Sounds like they weren't so red after all." She'd been extra nice to Gordon this week—her way of atoning. It wouldn't do her mom's relationship much good to admit how far she'd gone to prove he was up to no good.

She stared out the window as they crossed the bridge to Assateague. At the end of the bridge a line of cars stretched from the entrance gate. But Ty went through the unmanned lane, offering a wave to the rangers. He followed Beach Road to the south pen, where cars lined up along the road's shoulder to snatch pictures of Dream and her foal.

Some had approached the wooden rails, putting them within a few yards of the wild ponies even though park rules required a forty-foot distance from them. "You'll need to move back to the road, folks," Ty said as they approached the pen.

They followed his direction even though he lacked a uniform or even a badge. Ty had a certain presence that conveyed authority. It was an admirable and attractive feature.

With the crowd dispersing, Jenna visually examined Dream's form. A jagged wound near her left flank was easily visible against her white coat. "She's bleeding."

Ty opened the gate, letting Jenna go first. "I'll go check it out."

Engagement with humans was kept to a minimum to preserve the ponies' wild nature. And even though Jenna would've liked to interact with the ponies, she stopped just inside the gate.

Ty approached the pair for a closer look, talking in a low, soothing tone. Dream's ears perked up as she nickered. Her foal came closer. The filly was adorable with those spindly legs and bore the markings of a pinto. She had her mama's white tail and mane, though.

"She seems all right," Ty called over his shoulder as he watched the pony move. "Cut doesn't look too deep."

The sound of an engine alerted them to the vet's arrival. Lloyd

Phillips was a crusty old-timer with stooped shoulders, white hair, and a sharp tongue. But the second one of these ponies needed him, he was there.

Jenna's heart gave a sigh as the man stepped up to the pen. Dream was in the best of hands.

The sun was ready to set by the time Dream was resting comfortably at the Chincoteague carnival grounds, where injured or sick ponies were rehabilitated. The mare had been deemed clear of internal injuries. Doc sutured her up, and now Dream and her foal roamed the fenced-in pasture on the northeast side of the property. Although it was easily accessible by road, most tourists didn't know to look here for the Chincoteague ponies.

Jenna leaned against the railing, watching as the mama nursed her foal. The mare nickered softly, and the sound carried across the pasture. Jenna breathed in the scent of fresh hay and horseflesh, then exhaled, relief flowing through her.

Dream's going to be okay, Dad. And do you see her baby? She's just beautiful, isn't she?

It seemed like just last week Dream had been a foal herself. Jenna laid down her savings to buy back the pony. She wished Dad could be here to see how Dream had bloomed into such a beauty. Such a good mama. Even though she'd been through an ordeal today, she watched over her foal, groomed her, fed her with care.

Footsteps approached and Jenna turned to see Ty heading her direction. He'd stepped away to return the horse trailer. A certain weariness infused his slow strides and lingered in his eyes. Was he getting any sleep? Or were those nightmares still plaguing him?

Her chest tightened and she squeezed the fence post to keep herself from reaching for his hand. As he leaned on the gate beside her, she noted the downward tug of his eyes and the remnants of dark circles beneath them. He couldn't go on like this. He was always there for everyone else, even the ponies. Especially the ponies. He needed to take better care of himself.

"She doing okay?" he asked.

Jenna dragged her gaze back to Dream. "She's doing great. Both of them are. I'm so relieved it was just a minor injury."

"She's a tough girl. With a soft heart." Ty's searching gaze was like a laser on Jenna.

Her cheeks heated in response. Her heart felt very soft and squishy at the moment. Tyson did something to her. He made her feel things she'd never felt before. Want things she'd never wanted before. Her heart thundered in her chest like a stampede of wild ponies. When she couldn't take his scrutiny anymore, she turned to face him.

And promptly fell into his heated gaze. Those green eyes held all the moments they'd shared in DC. Moments that couldn't be undone, ignored, or forgotten. Couldn't be shoved into some box never to be reexamined again. What happened between them had changed things.

No, those things had begun shifting weeks ago. What happened in DC had just been a manifestation of those changes within her. Within *them*.

The past few days she'd grappled with all of it, with longing and regret. Not regret that it had happened. But regret that it wasn't happening still. She'd been the one to propose a deadline on their romance. An idea that seemed more idiotic by the minute. This thing between them was as unstoppable as a riptide. Fighting it seemed futile.

And now, looking him in the eyes, seeing all her thoughts mirrored back, she couldn't deny herself—or him—any longer. "I miss you," she said softly.

Something like relief fell over his expression. "I miss you too. You know, Dream's only half the reason I called you today."

His words curled around her heart like a soft hug.

"I know what we said in DC, about leaving it there. But I can't stop thinking about you."

The smile started inside and worked its way to her lips. "Who asked you to?"

Humor flared in his eyes. "I don't want anything to come between us ever."

"We won't let it. Our relationship is too important. No matter what, we preserve our friendship." Perhaps an oversimplification. But it was also a decision they could make. No matter what happened.

"Agreed." He leaned closer, palmed her face. Swept his thumb over her cheek, bringing every cell to life. "Are you sure about this?"

She answered the question with a brush of her lips against his. And then all the questions disappeared in a haze of want and pleasure, the likes of which she'd never known.

Chapter 33

It had been Jenna's idea. She thought it would be enjoyable to surprise their families with the new development in their relationship, and Ty agreed. The family gathering had already been scheduled, and their families would be thrilled with the match.

The garlicky aroma of Cosa's pizza hung in the room. Ty's parents had kept it simple since the B and B was full tonight. One of their part-time team members was holding down the fort so the families could gather in peace. Mama Dee brought her delicious brownies, and they'd just taken down the whole pan.

By the time they headed to the patio, the sun was setting, the evening cooling off. There was no need for a fire on this mid-June night. The white lights shone over the patio and the scent of salt lingered in the air.

"I was hoping you'd bring your new girlfriend, Alex," Mom said. "We've barely even met her."

"She had plans with her family."

Mom smiled. "Well, I do like that she's a family girl."

"I'll bring her next time."

Tyson was the last in the circle to be seated, and as planned, Jenna dropped into his lap, draped her arms around him, and gave him a big smooch.

The kiss effectively absorbed his attention for a moment. But the resounding quiet around the firepit soon claimed his attention. The startled pause was followed by loud whoops and hollers.

The kiss ended when Jenna laughed, a sound so filled with joy and pleasure, he couldn't help his own grin.

And then everyone seemed to speak at once.

"When did this happen?"

"Finally!"

"What took you guys so long?"

Seth was beaming like all the rest. "About time, you two!"

Ty sent him a mock scowl. "Maybe now you can stop flirting with her."

"Who, me?"

Ty scooped up a wood chip and flung it, hitting Seth in the chest.

"Hey! I was just trying to wake you up."

"Boys!" Mom called. "Behave."

At the prodding of their families Jenna and Tyson told the story of their trip—leaving out the part about DC. The family pummeled them with questions. It was enlightening to hear Jenna's thoughts on the getaway and their separation once they'd returned home.

"And then last night," Ty added, "when we were at the carnival grounds with Dream . . ." His gaze fell on Jenna.

"We just couldn't be apart anymore."

"Aw . . ." Mama Dee said. "I couldn't be happier."

Gordon chuckled. "I was oblivious to the whole thing."

Mom preened. "Well, *I* knew it! The way you two have been looking at each other this summer—"

"It was inevitable." Mama Dee gave Ty's mother a nod. "Whenever Ty would come around, Jenna's face would get all flushed."

"Mom!" Jenna said. "It did not!"

Ty let his gaze rove over her face, noting her heightened color. "Don't look now," he teased quietly.

"Hey. You're supposed to be on my side."

"Oh, I'm on your side."

"Well," Dad said, "can't say I saw it coming either, but I couldn't be more thrilled. This happy development deserves a toast." He held up his glass. "To new adventures with old friends."

Everyone joined in. "Hear, hear!"

Much later, after everyone had left, Ty walked Jenna across the street. The house's windows were darkened, but Mama Dee had left the porch light on. A warm breeze skated by, carrying the fresh fragrance of Jenna's shampoo.

He took her hand, twining his fingers through hers. When she cast him a sweet smile, he felt it in his gut. Would he ever tire of being with her this way? Of having the right to reach out and take her hand? To lean in and claim her lips in a kiss?

He hoped not. It was such a great feeling. He wanted to shout from the rooftops that she was his and he was hers.

"Tonight was fun," she said as they stepped into the glow of the porch light. "I only wish I could've witnessed the looks on their faces when they saw us kissing."

He grinned. "You could've heard a pin drop."

"And then we couldn't get a word in edgewise. They seemed pretty delighted."

He squeezed her hand. "They're not the only ones."

"Aw . . ." She turned to him with affection in her eyes. "I never knew you could be so sweet."

He slipped his arms around her waist. "That's because you weren't my girlfriend." He realized his mistake as the word left his mouth. They'd barely begun dating and certainly hadn't discussed exclusivity. Hadn't had time to, and now he'd just blurted it out like it was a foregone conclusion.

"Girlfriend, huh?"

"Did I speak out of turn?"

She gave him a coy look as she snaked her hands up his chest and over his shoulders. "Nope."

"Whew. I was hoping you'd say that. I shouldn't have made assumptions about you, but *I'm* not interested in anyone else."

"That goes double for me."

"Glad to hear it." He laced his hands behind her back. "And while we're on the subject . . . We haven't really talked about what the future might entail—what with your life in Alexandria and a potential job on the horizon."

"That might be an obstacle, but it's not an insurmountable one. I have to make a living, and if I get the job, I wouldn't be that far away."

"We'll figure it out." Three hours seemed like a lifetime away. And their work schedules wouldn't help. She'd have weekends off, but those were his busiest days. But he didn't want to worry her about the obstacles right now. He was already too deep into this to back out, and he hoped she was too.

"I know I've always said I'd never date a firefighter. But I guess I'll just have to come to grips with it—because I can't seem to stay away from you."

Touched by her words, he pressed a kiss to her forehead. It wouldn't be as easy as she'd made it sound. Her father's death had left its mark. "I know that'll be a tough one for you. I want you to know I'm always careful. I don't take anything for granted."

"I appreciate that. And it's not like we live in New York or Chicago. My father was the only Chincoteague firefighter to ever lose his life."

"It was an extraordinary circumstance." A warehouse fire had escalated due to the chemicals stored inside. Her father was killed following an explosion, and several other firefighters were injured. "As you know, most calls on the island are car accidents, small kitchen fires, pretty routine stuff. My life really isn't on the line every day." They only had a couple fires a year on the island, though they were sometimes called to the mainland to assist with bigger emergencies.

"I'll try to keep that in mind. I know firefighting's in your DNA. I'd never want to take that away from you."

"You know me well."

She flashed a flirty smile. "I do know you well. I know all your weak spots, Parker, and don't you forget it."

"And I know all your ticklish spots, Greene." Just to prove it he poked at the one in her side.

"Hey!" She tried to squirm away.

But he tightened his arms around her, holding her fast, and she quickly gave up the fight. "This feels so natural. So easy."

She pressed closer. "It feels right."

"And you're sure this isn't too fast for you? I don't want to rush you."

"We've known each other since we were twelve, Tyson. I don't think anyone would call this fast."

He chuckled. "True, but we did share our first real kiss only five days ago."

"Hmm . . . why *did* we wait so long?"

"Why, indeed?"

They didn't wait even another second for their next one.

Chapter 34

Tyson felt great as he exited the meeting room at the firehouse. He couldn't wait for Pony Penning Days next month. The volunteers were finalizing plans for the Pony Swim and carnival. The saltwater cowboys had the schedule for the festivities. It took a lot of dedicated people to pull this off, and he was proud to be part of it. This year's event promised to be well attended, and the funds raised would go a long way toward keeping his beloved community safe.

Luke caught up with him in the hallway. "Headed back to work?"

"Yeah, in a minute. Thought I might track Marissa down and try to make peace with her again."

"You're a bigger man than me. I'll wait for you. I haven't gotten the scoop on you and Jenna yet. Although I'll definitely take partial credit since I did set up that double date a few weeks back."

"Take all the credit you want. I'm too happy about it to care."

Luke chuckled. "I haven't seen this side of you in a while."

Yeah, the past year had been a rough one with Britt's infidelity and their divorce. And if Ty was honest, the year before that hadn't exactly been a walk in the park. It felt good to be happy again. To feel optimistic about the future. To know Jenna wanted to be with him as much as he wanted to be with her.

Every day was like a gift. And even though they'd jumped head-first into an exclusive relationship, they'd decided to take things slow in other ways. He didn't want anything ruining what they shared.

Luke followed Ty onto the apparatus floor but hung back as he headed toward the 3–1 ambulance where Marissa mopped down the vehicle.

As he approached she turned a sour look on him before returning to her task.

Ty managed to maintain a congenial smile. "How's it going, Marissa?"

"Fine." Her flat tone left little doubt about her current feelings toward him.

"I understand you guys have been busy this week. Heard you had a great save with a heart attack victim yesterday."

"That was 3–2."

"Oh. Well, a save is good for everyone, right?"

His question was met with silence.

Okay . . . He shifted. Rubbed the back of his neck. "Listen, we never really got a chance to finish the conversation we started before, and I just wanted to clear the air. Make sure things are okay between us. I heard there were some rumors flying around the firehouse, and that's not good for the company."

She nailed him with a look. "Are you accusing me of starting rumors?" Her raised voice echoed through the bay.

He kept his tone low and moderated. "No . . . I didn't say that."

"That's how it sounded to me."

"That's not what I meant, Marissa. You're twisting my words."

"And *you're* harassing me. You've approached me four times about this, and I've been as nice as I can be. But you never seem to get the message, so I guess I just have to be direct—I need you to leave me alone." Her eyes glazed with actual tears.

He blinked. "Whoa. I was just trying to make peace with you. I don't want hard feelings between us, that's all."

"There aren't any feelings at all between us. And if you don't leave me alone, I'll have to report you."

He gave his head a shake. What was happening? Where was this coming from? Clearly he wasn't helping the situation. He put his hands up, palms out, and turned away—only to find a dozen or so volunteers at the back, hanging on to every word. Great. Just what he needed.

Luke followed him into the hallway. "What the heck was that?"

"That's what I'd like to know."

"What did you say to her?"

It had been a mistake to speak quietly. He'd been trying to de-escalate the situation, but the whole group had heard only her accusations. Never mind that they were entirely unfounded. He explained the whole conversation to Luke, who seemed just as bewildered by her reaction as Tyson.

"Man, that woman's got some issues."

"I'm the last person to call a woman crazy, but that was not normal."

"What are you going to do?"

"Stop trying to make things right for starters. Obviously that's not helping. And the last thing I want is to get reported."

"Chief Jones wouldn't pay much mind to a new paramedic, not when you've built up so much trust around here. You've got a great reputation."

Ty glanced back toward the bay. "Yeah, but Geena doesn't know me very well." The new EMS director had been here less than a year. "And a bunch of the guys just heard Marissa pretty much accuse me of harassment."

"Just because she said it doesn't make it true." Luke shook his head. "If I were you, I'd stay away from her. I know *I* will."

Chapter 35

When Jenna returned from work on Monday she was on cloud nine. Who was she kidding? She'd been on cloud nine all weekend. Even Miss Molly had known something was up when Jenna walked into work this morning with a giddy smile.

On Sunday Jenna had had coffee with Sofia and relayed the good news. Her friend was thrilled for the couple and didn't hold back on the teasing or I-told-you-sos. Jenna was too blissful to mind either.

Even though Ty had been busy with the B and B over the weekend, he'd made time to talk on the phone. They texted each other throughout the day. This slide from friendship to more might have happened quickly, but it felt so right.

With Jason—and the others before him—she'd had anxiety about growing closer. A feeling that as the relationship progressed, she was getting backed into a corner. A stifling, suffocating feeling that had her putting up walls.

She hadn't been able to put words to the feeling until now. Until she felt only excitement about a future with Tyson. Being with him was worlds different from being with anyone else. No one understood her the way he did. No one made her feel the way he did.

Sure, it wouldn't be easy if she moved back to Alexandria. But she might not even get that job. And maybe she could find something here on the island. She hadn't really poured herself into that yet.

And Ty had been right about his position as an active firefighter. He'd never even been injured beyond a minor burn. If her anxiety over his volunteer spot became a problem, she could always seek counseling. Their relationship was worth fighting for.

A welcome waft of cool air brushed her skin as she entered the house. She needed a shower after being in the sun all day. She and Ty had plans to meet up later for supper at Captain Zack's. The casual restaurant had been a favorite for years.

The house was quiet—but then again, Mom's car hadn't been in the drive. She and Gordon were probably out enjoying the summer evening.

But as Jenna started to head upstairs, she heard the floor squeak in Mom's room and turned that direction. She found her mom standing in her bedroom, staring at her phone. "Mom?"

Her mother startled. "Jenna. I didn't hear you come in."

That wasn't like her at all. Jenna paused in the doorway, noting Mom's blanched face. "You okay? You seem a little upset."

"Oh, I don't know. I'm fine, I guess."

Jenna entered the tidy bedroom, the familiar scent of Chanel No. 5 washing over her. "You don't seem fine. Did something happen?"

Mom stood frozen for a few seconds, then dropped onto the edge of the bed, pressing her hand to her chest. "My heart's beating a million miles an hour."

Alarm shot through Jenna. "Are you having chest pains?"

"No, no, it's not that. Not a medical event. Something else entirely."

Jenna lowered herself beside her mom. "What is it then?"

Mom's brows squished together, and a bewildered look shadowed her eyes. "I just—I was taking some clean towels up to Gordon's room, and it was just sitting right there on the bathroom vanity. It didn't even register at first—I just started to hang the towels . . ."

"What didn't register?"

She turned and met Jenna's gaze. "It was a credit card statement. It didn't dawn on me until I was putting the stack of towels in the closet: He had a credit card bill, and he told me he didn't have a credit card."

A pit opened in the bottom of Jenna's stomach. "Oh, Mom. Maybe there's some other explanation."

"I looked at the statement. The card's in his name. And Jenna . . . the balance is almost *thirty thousand dollars*."

Thirty thousand dollars? She couldn't imagine being so deeply in debt. No wonder Gordon had wanted Mom to pay for everything.

"See for yourself." She shoved her phone at Jenna.

Mom had taken a picture of each page. The bill was addressed to him, and the total amount owed . . . *Yikes.*

Mom put a hand to her forehead. "I'm losing my mind. I can't even imagine that he would lie to me like that. I *know* him. Or maybe I just thought I did. Maybe my judgment was clouded and you were right about him all along." Tears seeped from Mom's eyes.

Jenna's heart gave a hard crack. "I'm sorry, Mom. I admit it doesn't look good. But if he's so deep in debt, it's no wonder he wouldn't want to charge anything else."

"But he didn't have to lie about it. If he lied about this, what else did he lie about? Maybe I don't know him at all." Mom gave her tears an angry swipe. "And why would he go on an expensive cruise when he had this kind of debt? That's just irresponsible."

Jenna's mind spun for a reasonable explanation. But obviously Gordon had been dishonest. "You should confront him about it. Hopefully there's some kind of explanation." But a memory flashed in Jenna's mind—his phone conversation where he'd claimed he was in Maine. She didn't want to lay anything else on her mom, but it was relevant to the conversation. He'd lied to someone on the phone about where he was.

"What?" Mom asked. "What are you thinking?"

Jenna grimaced. "I just remembered something. Something I overheard when he was on the phone. It didn't make sense at the time. It still doesn't, but it might be nothing."

Mom's shoulders straightened and her chin went up. "Tell me. I need to know everything. If I've been a fool, I'll just have to face it."

Jenna took Mom's hand. "It was shortly after I arrived on the island. He told whoever he was talking to that he was in Maine. Does that mean anything to you?"

"*Maine?* Why would he say he was in Maine?"

"I don't know. It raised a red flag for me. He also told the person that he loved them. When I discovered he was living with a woman, I assumed he'd lied to her about where he was for some reason. Then when I found out he was living with his sister, I just put the Maine thing aside. But now . . . I was hoping you might have some insight."

Mom gave a self-deprecating laugh. "I'm starting to think I don't know anything at all. I should've listened to you and instead I let my emotions run away with me. And now I'm in love with a man I can't even trust." More tears leaked from her eyes.

The hurt in her eyes was like a sucker punch. "Oh, Mom. I'm so sorry this is happening."

The rumble of an engine sounded outside the window, growing nearer.

"He's home." Mom straightened her slumped shoulders and wiped her eyes.

Jenna gave her hand a squeeze. "What are you going to do?"

"I'm going to ask him why he lied to me. Do I look okay?"

Her eyes were slightly red and turned down at the corners. "You look fine. You've got this." Jenna gave her a hug, wishing she could imbue Mom with strength. Her mother lingered in her arms for a moment.

At the slam of the car door, they eased apart.

"My heart's pounding. I feel sick."

"You'll be fine, Mom. You're a strong woman. Tell him what happened and give him a chance to explain." Though Jenna wasn't too hopeful he'd have a reasonable excuse. "I'll run across the street and give you two some privacy."

"No." Mom grabbed her hand. "Can you just . . . hide somewhere? Maybe listen in? If he comes up with some cockamamie tale, I don't know if I'll be able to tell if it's the truth. I don't know which end is up anymore."

"Whatever you want. You've got this, Mom. I'm here for you no matter what." Jenna squeezed Mom's hand one last time before she slipped from the room and down the hall. She slipped into the bathroom and whispered a prayer for her mother. Jenna's own heart ached in sympathy.

She left the door cracked so she could hear. The front door opened and Gordon greeted her mom. There was a slight pause before he asked, "What's wrong? Are you okay?"

"I have something I need to ask you about." Mom's voice sounded stilted.

"Okay . . ."

"I was taking towels up to your room and I saw the credit card statement you left in the bathroom." Her voice trembled at the end of the sentence.

The long pause didn't exactly alleviate Jenna's fears. She clutched the collar of her shirt.

"And you think I lied to you."

"You *did* lie to me."

Another pause followed. "The credit card might be in my name, honey, but it isn't mine." He sighed. "Can we sit down and talk about this?"

The muffled sound of footsteps reached Jenna's ears, followed by the slight squeak of Mom's recliner.

"I've told you a little about Katie—how she's had some problems."

Katie—his daughter who lived in DC. His voice was hushed and Jenna had to lean into the door's crack to hear.

"I told you about her alcoholism and that she'd had a little trouble with the law over the years."

"Minor stuff, you said."

"Yes, minor stuff. But what I didn't tell you was that while she was staying with me last year, trying to get back on her feet, she took out a credit card in my name. She transferred debt from her own credit cards to the one in my name and then paid the minimum payment for a while. Since she intercepted the mail, I never knew about it.

"I didn't lie to you, Dee. I don't have a credit card anymore. Obviously I froze this one, once I found out about it. But unfortunately Katie stopped payments on it months ago. She tanked my credit. I'll be paying off the debt—I've got money set back for retirement obviously—but it's currently tied up in investments."

Jenna weighed his words, and Mom must've been doing the same because quiet echoed throughout the house.

"Why didn't you just tell me about this?" A hint of distrust lingered in her mom's voice.

"I was embarrassed. My own daughter exploited me. *Me,* a retired accountant. The whole thing is humiliating. But . . . I would've told you eventually. Time just got away from me, I guess."

He sounded so sincere, even Jenna was inclined to believe him.

"Why did you go on that cruise if you had a pile of debt back home?" Mom still sounded guarded.

"Rosalind transferred that cruise to me. She and her husband planned to go for their anniversary, but then things fell apart. And it was too late for a refund. She insisted I go to thank me for taking them in."

"You never mentioned that to me."

"Why would I? It seemed irrelevant at the time."

A long silence ensued. Jenna leaned closer, feeling like an eavesdropper. But Mom had asked her to listen in.

"Why did you tell someone on the phone that you were in Maine?"

Another pause indicated he'd been caught off guard. "That was Melanie. I told you about her. She vacationed in Maine as a child, so now she refers to every destination as Maine. When I went out of state for work, I was in Maine. When I was on the cruise, I was in Maine. It's what she understands."

It sounded as if Melanie might be a special needs adult. Likely a relative since he'd told her he loved her.

"Oh." A load of regret packed her mom's one word.

Jenna winced. Mom wasn't the only one dealing with that particular emotion. Everything Gordon said made sense. He couldn't have made all that up on the fly, could he?

"Listen, Dee," he said gently. "I can see you have some reservations about me. About us. Maybe it's time I went back home."

"That's not what I want." Mom's voice wobbled pitifully. "I'm sorry I jumped to conclusions. I just saw that statement and I—"

"We haven't known each other very long, and maybe we rushed things. Got a little excited to have found someone we connected with.

But I admit I'm feeling pretty hurt right now. I probably should've told you about Katie and the credit card debt, but I would've hoped you'd at least give me the benefit of the doubt."

"I should've . . . I'm sorry."

"I appreciate that. But I think maybe we should take a little break here. I've probably overstayed my welcome."

"That's not true. I've loved having you here."

"I've loved every minute, Dee. I really have."

"Please don't leave like this."

A moment of silence passed before Gordon responded. "Honestly, Dee, I'm feeling a little . . . uneasy. It's probably me. Maybe I've got some issues of my own to deal with. But right now I need some space. I never intended to stay this long anyway, and I should probably get back home to my sister and nephews."

The sound of footfalls suggested Gordon was heading toward the door and Mom was following. "I'll go on up and schedule a flight home."

"Oh, Gordy, I don't want you to go."

"It's for the best. I'm feeling . . . I think I need to leave, that's all. We'll talk later, okay?"

The door snapped quietly shut.

Jenna listened for her mother but heard nothing. Had she gone with him? Jenna opened the bathroom door and watched Mom disappear into her bedroom. The door closed and the muted sound of weeping soon followed.

Jenna palmed her forehead. She couldn't believe he'd responded this way. It seemed like such an overreaction.

But also, this was her fault. Her suspicions had brought this on. Mom never would've responded to that credit card statement suspiciously if Jenna hadn't planted seeds of doubt in her heart. Why had Jenna been so quick to jump to the wrong conclusion?

She wallowed in remorse as she gave her mom a few minutes. When Jenna couldn't take it another minute, she approached the door and tapped quietly. "Mom? Can I come in?"

Everything went quiet for a moment. Then a heartbeat later her mom answered the door, eyes red, lips quivering, and fell into Jenna's arms.

Chapter 36

A few days later the mood around Mom's house was still somber. Gordon had flown home the morning after their falling out and hadn't yet called, leaving Mom to wonder if the relationship was over. Jenna had apologized profusely about her part in the debacle. But Mom insisted it wasn't her fault.

Still, Jenna ached to see her mother so hurt. So lost.

Jenna drew comfort from Tyson, who also felt guilty about his part in the whole fiasco. He encouraged Jenna to give herself some grace and distracted her with ice cream runs and delicious kisses.

On Thursday she was starting her car after work when a call came in. It was Nancy from Parks and Recreation. Jenna's stomach fluttered. She took a few seconds to settle her nerves before answering.

"Hi, Jenna, this is Nancy Gillespie from Parks and Rec. How are you?"

"I'm doing well, thank you. How are you, Nancy?"

"Doing well. The office has been quite busy this week, but I actually prefer it that way. Keeps things more interesting."

"I like staying busy myself."

"I had that feeling when we spoke last week. I enjoyed our conversation and I'm pleased to offer you the position. I feel you'd be a great

fit around here, but I also realize you might have other opportunities you're considering."

A smile spread across Jenna's face. She made an effort to temper her enthusiasm. "I appreciate the offer. I do feel the position at Parks and Rec is ideal for me, but I would like a few days to consider all the factors."

"Of course. I can send you the paperwork detailing the benefits and salary. I'm hoping that'll be all the incentive you need. While I realize this would be a pay cut for you, we do offer terrific benefits for our team."

"That would be helpful. Thank you. I really enjoyed talking with you last week, and I'm sure I'd enjoy working for you as well."

"We did hit it off, didn't we?" Her tone was conspiratorial.

"We sure did."

They chatted a few minutes about the Braves' recent series, the conversation flowing as easily as it had during the interview.

When Jenna hung up, she was grinning from ear to ear as she pulled the car from the lot. She couldn't wait to tell Tyson.

"We have you right here in the Seashell Room." Tyson unlocked the door and held it open for the middle-aged couple from Pennsylvania. They were celebrating their thirty-fifth anniversary.

"Aptly named," Mrs. Turner said, referring to the wall decor. "These paintings are gorgeous."

"They were done by a popular local artist. You can see more of her work at the Osprey Nest Art Gallery in the village."

Mr. Turner set down his duffel. "I know where we're going in the morning."

"You know me well."

"The village has some quaint shops with great local finds, a nice bookstore, and a coffee shop. If you're looking for lunch or dinner and enjoy seafood, you can't go wrong with Don's."

"I guess I know where we'll be *all day* tomorrow."

Mrs. Turner offered her husband a coy smile. "Don't be silly, we have to make time for the ponies."

"You definitely don't want to miss that. Let me know if you need any help with a boat or kayak tour."

"Given the heat, I think we'll just drive over to the refuge and scout out the ponies from the comfort of our car."

"That works too. If you need a wildlife refuge map, we have them downstairs, and anyone at the desk can tell you all the best pony-viewing spots."

"I can't wait." Mrs. Turner removed her baseball cap, letting her brown hair fall into place around her shoulders.

Time to wrap it up. "We serve a continental breakfast in the dining room from seven till eight, and the Wi-Fi password is on your key card. If you need anything else, feel free to call down to the front desk or shoot us a text—that number is also on the key card."

"Thank you, Tyson," Mr. Turner said.

"Enjoy your stay." With a parting smile Ty closed the door and headed downstairs. The steps creaked here and there, something his dad was always after him to fix. But Ty loved those familiar creaks. Reminded him of all the times he'd run up and down these stairs as a boy. All the times he and his brothers played hide-and-seek in this big old house.

And the handful of times he'd dodged those squeaks as he sneaked out at night to meet friends. They went fishing at Tom's Cove or just hung out at Veterans Park. One time when he was fourteen he'd sneaked out, crossed the street, and tossed pebbles at Jenna's window. She came to the opening a minute later, frowning down in the moonlight, her hair in a messy cloud around her face. "What are you doing here?" she hissed.

"Come outside."

She crossed her arms against the cool night air. "Are you crazy? It's after midnight and I'd fall to my death trying. And if that didn't kill me, my mom would."

"Aw, come on, Greene. She won't find out."

"Famous last words. Anyway, it's fifty degrees outside and I have an English test tomorrow."

"So?"

"So I need my sleep."

He rolled his eyes. Such a rule follower. "Or we could go hang out at the park for an hour, and you'll still get an A-plus tomorrow."

She hesitated. Glanced back into the room. He'd thought he had her talked into it. But then she turned back. "No way. Not worth getting grounded for two weeks. I have volleyball matches coming up, and if Mom tells my coach, she'll bench me for sure."

"Aw, you're no fun."

She reached for the window sash. "Go coerce one of your brothers into your silly shenanigans."

"Look at that vocabulary. You'll ace that test no problem."

"Good night!" The sash snapped into place.

Now Tyson smiled as he headed toward the front desk. He loved all those sweet memories with Jenna. Loved that they'd built and maintained a solid friendship for years before progressing to something more.

When they'd first met she had braces and a constant sprinkle of acne. He could only silently commiserate as he shared the same misfortune. She was built like a filly: tall, lean, and all legs. But she could run like the wind and throw a football like a boy. He was impressed, though he wasn't about to let her know it.

Eventually she had the braces removed, passed the acne stage, and grew into her legs. He could hardly miss that she'd turned out to be rather pretty. And if he hadn't noticed on his own, he had plenty of friends willing to point it out.

But Jenna had been the neighbor girl who ran round in jeans, a T-shirt, and a sloppy ponytail. She was the girl with whom he tossed the football and argued sports.

Not the girl he asked out on a date.

As their friendship morphed easily into adulthood, they'd shifted into more mature roles. Once he'd started dating Britt, he'd stepped back a little. Britt was jealous of his relationship with Jenna. But Jenna seemed to understand. Once Britt left him, he'd turned to his old friend, and she'd become his buddy and confidant once again. Nothing more, nothing less.

He shook his head. He wasn't sure how his feelings had changed. It was as if someone flipped a switch, allowing him to see Jenna in a whole new light.

And what a vision she was.

The past week had been one of the happiest of his life, despite the drama at the firehouse. When he wasn't with Jenna, he was looking forward to seeing her again. The sight of her name on his phone screen sent his heart pinging around his chest. Being with her made him absurdly happy. It was pretty ridiculous.

But he didn't care as long as she was his.

Tonight they were heading to the carnival grounds to visit Dream and her foal. The vet wanted her to heal there for a week or so, then she'd go back to the refuge. Her sutures would be fully healed in time for the Pony Swim, which was less than five weeks away.

The front door burst open—and there was Jenna, beaming from ear to ear.

Just like that his day went from good to great. "Well, hello there."

She launched herself into his arms.

He caught her, chuckling as warmth spread through him. Everything was right in the world when Jenna was in his arms. "What's all this?"

"I got the job!"

Apprehension slipped through a crack in his heart before he self-corrected. "Jenna, that's amazing. Congratulations." He placed a quick kiss on her mouth.

Her brown eyes sparkled, and her pearly white smile was on full display. "I can't believe it."

"I knew you'd get it. They'd be crazy to hire anyone else."

She slipped her hand down to his chest. "I'm pretty stoked. She's sending the package to look over, but I already know the basic offer, of course."

"It's official then." The apprehension oozed into all the spaces around his heart. They'd only briefly discussed how this long-distance thing might play out. What if it didn't work at all?

"I didn't commit yet. Told her I'd let her know in a few days."

"You'd consider turning it down?" He hated himself for the bubble of hope that swelled inside. She deserved to have fulfilling work. He wanted that for her.

Her smile dimmed. "Well, if I'm honest, I don't relish the thought of being so far away from you."

At least she was having the same concerns. That helped. But he didn't want to dissuade her from a job she might truly enjoy. "I feel the same way. But you have to earn a living, and this job does seem perfect for you."

"I just wish it were *here*."

"Me too, honey."

Her expression softened. "Aw . . . you called me honey."

His face heated. Which was stupid, considering the hours they'd spent in each other's arms.

She palmed his cheek. "I liked friend Tyson a lot, but I like boyfriend Tyson even more."

"Yeah?"

"Oh yeah. I might even start calling him honey. Or sweetie. Or babycakes."

He winced at the last suggestion.

"You're right. No babycakes." She brushed his lips with hers. "Besides, I like calling you Parker."

He'd been calling her Greene so long, he wasn't sure he could break the habit. Or if he even wanted to.

Jenna eased away and patted his chest. "I think I'll spend the next couple days seeing what's available on the island. Or even on the mainland."

"I can ask my family to put their feelers out." They knew everyone in the business community.

"That'd be great. Thanks."

He hated that her unmitigated joy was gone. He cupped her cheeks. "I'm proud of you. I know you'll make the right decision. And no matter what, we'll make it work."

She smiled into his eyes. "Yeah?"

"Absolutely. Now that I've had a taste of you, there's no turning back."

A grin split her face as she radiated joy once again. "Tyson Parker, you always know just what to say." And then she rewarded him with a lengthy kiss.

Chapter 37

Jenna's thoughts grew heavy as Tyson drove her home. They'd grabbed supper at Steamers and spent the rest of the evening sitting at a picnic table that overlooked the pasture where Dream foraged near her foal.

Ty was still experiencing nightmares. He'd fallen asleep again during the Braves game last week. It warmed her to know he felt at peace enough to sleep in her presence. But she wanted to kiss away the dark circles under his eyes. If only it were that easy. That stupid Marissa at the firehouse wasn't helping matters. The thought of leaving him this way made Jenna's heart shrivel up in her chest.

She'd talked big about finding work on the island, but deep down she knew what a long shot that was. Still, she'd start searching online tonight.

But housing was so expensive. Of course, her mom's attic apartment was now available. But she'd refurbished the space for extra income—not to let her daughter freeload off her. With island wages, no way would Jenna make enough to pay what that space was worth.

Her trust fund could go a long way toward opening a business of some kind, but it wasn't nearly enough. On average, start-ups took two to five years to become profitable. She couldn't sponge off her mother that long.

But the thought of being away from Tyson made her heart hurt. Being with him this way was everything she'd been missing with her previous boyfriends. She was happy and at ease. She wanted to be with him all the time. When they weren't together she wanted to tell him everything that happened while they were apart. She was excited about the present and had a hopeful outlook on the future.

In short, she was beginning to understand that she'd never had a commitment problem at all. She just hadn't had the right man. But he'd been right under her nose the whole time. She couldn't help but smile at the thoughts swirling through her head.

Shells popped under the tires as Tyson pulled into Mom's drive.

"Want to come inside? Looks like Mom's still up. She made blueberry scones yesterday and they're delish."

He put the truck in Park. "Thanks, but it's getting late and five o'clock comes early. I'll walk you to the door."

They exited the truck and met up around the front, automatically joining hands. "You just know Mom'll bring them over to you guys tomorrow anyway."

"She sure does spoil us."

At the door he turned toward her, a serious expression falling over his features. "I've been thinking . . . Maybe in time I could move to Alexandria. Mom and Dad can afford to replace me, and . . ."

Jenna shook her head. "I don't want to take you away from your family, Ty. Not to mention the fire company."

His eyes twinkled. "Hey, I've got an idea. Maybe Alexandria has a fire company."

"You know it wouldn't be the same. You're part of something special here. You love overseeing the ponies, being a saltwater cowboy. You love this *island*. Maybe something will turn up for me here." Though likely nothing as perfect for her as that Parks and Rec position. "I'll start looking tonight."

He placed his hands on her hips. "Listen. I think you want this job. I want you to promise that if nothing exciting turns up, you'll take it. You deserve to have rewarding work you love."

"Don't I also deserve to have the man I love?" Her heart leapt from her chest. *Oh, crap.* Yes, it was true. But also so, so fast. And she hadn't wanted to be the first to say it. "Did—did I just say that out loud?"

A smile was already stretching across his lips. He framed her face with his palms. "You did. Say it again. This time on purpose."

She wasn't sure exactly when it had happened. But it had. And from the look on his face, he was in the same boat. Nevertheless, her heart beat up into her throat as she peered up at him. "I love you, Tyson Parker."

"And I love you, Jenna Greene." He kissed her then. A slow, luxurious kiss that made her knees go weak.

It was a long while before Jenna watched Tyson's truck disappear down the street.

She pressed her palm to her chest, unable to calm the silly organ. She felt almost dizzy with all the feelings coursing through her.

She was in love with Tyson Parker. And even more miraculously—he was in love with her. Life would be perfect except for the minor little detail of her vocational future.

Ugh. Why did this island have to be so expensive?

Her thoughts came to a halt when she spotted Mom on the sofa.

Mom winked. "That was an awful long good-bye."

Though her mother tried for a bright smile, Jenna couldn't miss her bloodshot eyes.

"What's wrong? Did Gordon call?" Jenna took a seat beside her.

"No, he didn't. But he did send me this handwritten missive." She handed Jenna a white envelope.

Jenna pulled out the contents: the itemized list of what he owed her mom—753 dollars, a check in that same amount, and a thank-you card bearing a watercolor painting of the Assateague Lighthouse.

"He bought those cards the day we visited Assateague." Her mom's tone was flat. "Go ahead, read it."

The small, tidy printing matched that of the itemized list. It didn't take long to read the four lines of standard thank-you etiquette. The words were kind and gracious. But after the closeness he and Mom had shared, Jenna could see why this note—and the accompanying check—might feel like a slap in the face.

"Emily Post would certainly be proud," Mom said.

"Who?"

"He said he'd call! And instead he sends me this generic thank-you card and the money he owes me. I don't even want the money. He's such a kind, gentle man. How could I have ever thought he was trying to deceive me? No wonder he hates me." The tears were back.

"Oh, Mom, I'm sure he doesn't hate you." Jenna had been so stupid and stubborn. All that time she'd been trying to prevent her mother's heartbreak, and instead she'd actually effectuated it.

Ouch.

She squelched the urge to apologize again. This wasn't about her. "You did have a viable reason to confront him. His reaction seems over the top. Maybe you should just call him. Tell him how you feel."

"I'm afraid of what he'll say. I don't want to hear him tell me it's over. I don't want it to *be* over."

"Maybe he just needs a little more time. It's only been three days. And he would've had to mail this a couple days ago. He might feel differently by now. Surely he can see now why you had some reservations."

Mom wiped her tears away. "I'll think about it. I can't call him tonight, though. I'm a mess." Her tears evolved into weeping. "I can't seem to stop crying. This heartbreak stuff is for the birds."

Jenna's gut clenched. "Oh, Mom." She put her arm around her mother and pulled her close. All she could do was offer comfort—and it just didn't seem like enough.

Chapter 38

"It's just as dismal as you said." Tyson's hopes dwindled as he scrolled through the available jobs posted online. He and Jenna were cozied up on his sofa while the Braves game played on the TV.

"I don't seem like front desk material?" Jenna said.

"You're overqualified for everything."

"There is a general manager position open."

"I doubt Dollar General pays a living wage." Perhaps the salary would be enough to make ends meet elsewhere, but not on the island. He stifled a yawn. The sleepless nights were taking a toll.

"It's getting late and you're tired. I should go." She started to ease away.

He held her fast. "Game's almost over."

"You need your rest." Her gaze sharpened on him. "Are you still having nightmares?"

"Some." Nearly every night, but who was counting?

"You can't go on like this forever, Ty."

"I know. I'll look into some counseling if it doesn't get better soon." These days he felt like a zombie when the morning alarm went off, and he was dragging a bit through the day.

"I'll hold you to that."

At the crack of a bat they glanced at the screen where the Braves runner on third brought in the tying score. It was the bottom of the ninth.

They high-fived each other as the station broke for a commercial.

"Did you check out the management position at the visitors' center?" His mom had mentioned the opening.

"It's been filled. Same for the office manager position at that occupational therapy place Alex suggested. Speaking of Alex, he seemed pretty confident about that silly bet you guys have going when I spoke to him yesterday."

Ty snorted. "*Over*confident, you mean. I won't mind taking five big ones from him on auction day."

"*Five?* What happened to *three*?"

"Like I said, *over*confident—and I found the big-screen TV I want. It'll take up half that wall. Be like watching the game in person."

"You guys are ridiculous."

"Alex is ridiculous. I'm clever."

She chuckled.

"Something funny?" He poked the ticklish spot on her side.

"*Hey.* Watch it, buddy."

He would've pushed his luck but decided she felt too nice curled against his side. He pulled her closer instead and ran his fingers through her silky chestnut hair as the Braves brought in another run, ending the game eight to seven.

"Good game," she said.

"Good series. I like their chances for the playoffs this year."

"I do too, but it's early yet."

It was so much easier to talk baseball than the subject at hand. But Jenna had to give an answer on the Parks and Rec position tomorrow, and the job started a week from tomorrow. How had time passed so quickly? As much as Ty hated it, the right answer seemed crystal clear. He set the laptop aside and turned to her. "Jenna, you should take the job."

Her brown eyes dimmed as she held his gaze. "I don't want to leave you."

The admission made his dopey heart buck. "We'll figure it out. We're both committed to making this work."

She was quiet for a long moment, seemingly considering what a long-distance relationship might look like. "It wouldn't have to be forever."

"Absolutely. Maybe something will open up here that would be perfect for you. Or maybe I'll move to Alexandria after all. These aren't decisions we have to make right now."

With a quiet sigh she let her head fall to his shoulder.

"I really do think you'll love that job. And Nancy seems like she'd be a great boss."

"I know. I should be more grateful instead of focusing on the drawbacks. It's just that . . ." Jenna raised her head and met his gaze. "We just found each other."

The way she looked at him made his skin go warm. "I don't know how it can feel that way when we've known each other for years, but it does. How did these romantic feelings just hit us out of nowhere?"

She bit her lip as her eyes shifted away. "I don't know."

He knew her well enough to know when she was holding something back. "What?"

"What *what*?" A pretty pink flushed her cheeks.

"There's something you're not telling me. What is it?"

When her gaze found his again, she looked a little sheepish. "Those feelings didn't really hit me out of nowhere. Remember back in high school? That prom kiss?"

"Yeah . . ."

"I might've caught some feelings for you after that."

A startled chuckle escaped. *"What?"*

"Just for like two minutes!"

"You were into me and you didn't even tell me?" The whole idea delighted him. He couldn't erase the grin from his face.

"Because you got back with Danielle Collins three seconds after that kiss!"

"You were *jealous*."

"No, I wasn't. Well, maybe a little. But I got over it quick enough."

He couldn't stop staring at her. Couldn't stop marveling over this new information. "I can't believe you never told me."

"I can't believe I'm telling you now."

Laughing, he pulled her into his side, gazing down at her with eyes that surely told her he now returned every ounce of affection. "I'm going to hold that over your head every chance I get."

"Don't I know it."

He gave those pouty lips a little kiss, the whole thing still sinking in. When he drew away they were both smiling. "I love that I'm still learning new things about you. I want to learn everything there is to know."

Her expression softened. "Me too. But being apart will make that harder."

"Don't worry. We'll figure it out. I'll talk to Mom and Dad and see if my schedule can be shifted to free up some weekends."

"That would be nice. Then you could come see me, or I could come here."

"See? This is totally doable. In between we'll FaceTime and text. I'll call so much you'll be sick of me."

She turned her lower lip down. "But I won't be able to kiss you over FaceTime."

"You'll just have to save them up for the weekends." Brave talk, but he'd gotten used to having her here. To being together every day. He only had to walk across the street to see her.

She regarded him for a long moment, sadness lingering in her eyes. "All right," she said finally, her tone resolute. "I'll take the job."

Chapter 39

Jenna's mood grew heavy as she watched Tyson head toward the bar with Jack. She was leaving tomorrow. Where in the world had this week gone?

Chatties was packed and the noise level seemed to increase by the minute. The band was taking a break between sets, giving the patrons the opportunity to catch up with their friends and neighbors.

She and Ty had decided to go out with friends tonight, keep things light. But it was hard to keep her spirits up when she would soon be living three hours from Tyson.

This was their first double date with Sofia and Jack, although they'd all known each other since high school. They'd already eaten their fill of seafood, and the aroma of fried fish made Jenna's stomach churn.

"What's that look about?" Sofia called over the cacophony.

"This past week went so fast. I can't believe I have to leave tomorrow."

"Do you regret taking the job?"

"It's not that. It was the right thing to do. I'm just dreading leaving, that's all. I believe I'll like my new job, but I'll sure miss you and my mom and Ty and being out on the water every day."

"I'll miss you too. It's been fun catching up. How'd Miss Molly take the news?"

"She was sad about it, but she knew it was coming. She already has someone lined up for my spot." Jenna glanced around at her friends and neighbors. This island had laid such a great foundation for her. She admired its hardy people, its unique history, its beautiful scenery, and its wild ponies. "I really do love this place."

Sofia tilted her a look. "And *Ty*?"

A dreamy smile curled Jenna's lips. "Especially Ty." Ever since their declaration a week ago, the two had been trading "I love yous" on the daily. It was nice. More than nice. The relationship felt so different from what she'd had with Jason and those before him. Her feelings for Tyson were on an entirely different scale. It was exhilarating and awe-inspiring.

And, if she was honest, a little scary.

Maybe a lot scary. Doubt edged in at the thought of their separation. Fear of losing him the way she'd lost her father wrapped around her like a tentacle, squeezing until she could barely breathe.

But she couldn't see Tyson and *not* want him. *Not* need to be with him. It wasn't even a choice.

"You guys are really good together," Sofia said.

"It's so easy with him."

"I love the way he looks at you when you're not looking."

"How's that?"

"Oh, you know . . . like he can't believe you're his."

Jenna went soft inside. "I'm the lucky one. I've always known he was a great guy, but he's an even better boyfriend. He sent me flowers this week. They're so beautiful. I put them in my room so my mom wouldn't have to see them."

Sofia gave her an empathetic look. "How's she doing? Did Gordon ever call back?"

Mom had called the day after she'd received his check in the mail but had gotten voicemail. "He did, but he's still uncertain about their future and dealing with some pretty heavy issues from his past." Apparently his ex-wife had had major trust issues. He caught the fallout from that, and he was wary about navigating those waters again. Of course, Mom didn't actually have trust issues. "I never should've made her doubt Gordon."

Sofia took her hand. "Don't be so hard on yourself. You were just trying to protect her."

"And look how that worked out. She's utterly heartbroken."

"Is it over for good then?"

Jenna gave her head a shake. "He said he'd like to keep in touch. I'm still praying he comes around."

Tyson and Jack appeared, drinks in hand. They took their seats, still engaged in a conversation about the upcoming football season. Jenna took a sip of Diet Coke as the band headed back to the stage.

The air-raid siren blared and the noise level in the room decreased.

Tyson whipped out his phone and checked the screen. "There's a fire over on Willow. Sorry, guys, have to go." He reached for his wallet.

"I've got it," Jenna said. "Go ahead."

"Thanks. Call you later." He gave her a peck on the lips, then took off toward the stairway, already in firefighter mode.

Willow Street was just down the road, but he'd have to go to the firehouse for his turnout gear. The whole thing shredded Jenna's nerves.

Sofia patted her hand. "He'll be fine."

"Of course." But that didn't stop the niggle of worry that wormed through Jenna's veins.

The engine's siren wailed as it cut through traffic on the way to the scene. Adrenaline pumped through Tyson's veins as he watched the houses speed by.

EMS had reported that the scene was a working fire with smoke coming from the eaves. The unit slowed as it came to Willow and made the turn. Smoke billowed skyward and flames shot from the windows.

The situation hadn't gotten better. Hopefully everyone was out of the house and they could knock the fire down quickly.

As soon as the engine rolled to a stop, the crew jumped from the rig. Across the street one of their medics restrained a frantic woman from entering the blazing structure.

"3–1 and 3–6, set up water supply!" Chief Jones called. "Parker, O'Neil, mask up. Victim inside—fourteen-year-old girl, possibly in the bedroom upstairs on the south side. Window inaccessible. Let's go! Let's go!"

The crews went to work.

Tyson's heart jackhammered as he and Luke geared up with oxygen tanks and masks and headed in. The smoke was already thick, the air hot, the house fully involved.

"Fire department, call out!" Tyson said as they headed through the living room. They searched through the smoke for movement. Where was she? Seeing no one, they moved toward the steps and started up.

At the top landing he called out again. The only response was the roar of fire and the sound of his breathing. The smoke was thicker up here. The landing led to a long hall. Flames shot out of the doorways.

Ty used his com. "Chief, we need a knockdown."

"Copy. They're coming. What's the situation?"

"Upstairs hallway is partially collapsed. We can get through if we can get this fire knocked down." He was tempted to make a dash. But the hallway was long and narrow, and the collapsed beam would slow them down. Egress with a victim would be hazardous.

He glanced down the stairs for the firefighters. *Come on, come on.*

A lifetime later Riggs and Novak showed up on the nozzle. They aimed the spray at the first door, knocking the flames down quickly, and the crew progressed down the hall.

"Don't like the looks of this." Riggs glanced at the ceiling where smoke rolled. "It's not stable."

"We have time," Ty said. They had to. He wasn't about to let a fourteen-year-old kid die in this blaze. Not when they were right here. An image of that dead seventeen-year-old boy flashed in his head. Anxiety threaded through Ty.

That was not happening today.

"Two minutes!" Chief called over the com.

Riggs and Novak advanced down the hall, knocking the fire down as they went.

"Fire department, call out!" Ty and Luke swept the two rooms on the way to the southernmost room. But they were empty.

Just before they reached the last room, a loud crack split the air. Novak and Riggs dove out of the way just in time. Another beam dropped, raining down smoke and fire.

"Riggs!" Ty checked the downed firefighter.

"I'm fine. Novak?"

"I'm good," he called.

They cleared the debris and helped the men to their feet.

"Parker, report!" Chief Jones called.

"We're all good, Chief." The ceiling had come down, but there was still space to get to the bedroom.

"Get out of there now!"

"Copy that," Riggs said, and the other three turned back toward the stairs.

Ty couldn't just leave the kid! He glanced toward the bedroom, panic bombarding his every thought. "Fire department, call out!" He listened intently.

There. Had that been a voice?

"Call out!"

"Help!"

He sprang into action. Squeezed through the debris from the collapsed ceiling. The heat was suffocating, the smoke blinding. He slipped through the doorway. Flames engulfed the room. "Call out!"

"Over here."

He headed toward the voice. The coughing. There was the bed. He squatted next to it and the teenage girl grappled for his boots.

"Found the victim," Ty reported.

"Get her out the front. Move, move!"

Ty pulled her out and lifted her to her feet. But she was too weak to stand. Wracked with coughing. He pulled off his mask and put it over her face. "Hold it."

She grasped the facepiece, and Ty swept her up in his arms. "Hang on!" Heat seared his lungs. Fire roared along the walls, nearly engulfing the exit. He had to get her out of here and fast.

"Parker, report!"

Ty ducked low, dashed through the doorway. A crack sounded. He hunched over, pushing forward. But a force from above shoved him down. The ground closed in.

Then there was only darkness.

Chapter 40

Jenna must've finally dozed off because the buzzing of her phone startled her awake.

Tyson. The fire must be out. He was calling to set her mind at ease. She grabbed for her phone and blinked at the screen.

Ronda?

She could think of only one reason Ty's mom would be calling her at this hour. Jenna sprang upright, her heart thrashing as she stabbed at the Accept button. "What's wrong?"

"Jenna, it's Ty. He's on his way to Riverview Shore."

"What happened?"

"I'm not sure exactly. I was so flustered. Chief said something about smoke inhalation and a head injury. Rick and I are getting ready to leave now."

"I'll be right over." Jenna disconnected the call, flung off the covers, and jumped from the bed. She was halfway down the steps when she realized she was still in her pajamas.

Think, Jenna!

She quickly changed into the clothes she'd worn that night, grabbed her purse, and made it all the way to the front door before remembering her mom.

She rushed into her mother's room and tapped her shoulder. "Mom. Mom, wake up."

"Huh? Jenna? What's wrong?"

"Ty's headed to the hospital. He got injured on a call. I'm riding with the Parkers."

"Wait." Mom sat up. "I'll go with you."

Mom would hold them up by at least ten minutes. And Jenna didn't want to put her through another stressful wait at the hospital. "No, stay here. I just wanted you to know where I was." Jenna backed to the door. "Pray for him, Mom."

"Of course, honey. Let me know when you get there."

Jenna dashed from the house and tore across the street, panic rising with each step. The Parkers were exiting their house, rushing toward their crossover as frantically as she was.

As they converged on the vehicle, Rick fumbled with his key fob.

"I can't believe this is happening," Ronda said.

"He'll be okay," Jenna said by rote. He had to be. She couldn't lose him. Her heart couldn't take it.

The doors finally gave a click and they all piled in, Jenna in the back.

Rick started the car and backed out onto the street. Then they lurched forward.

Jenna pressed a hand to her chest. Tried to slow her breathing. *Please, God. Let him be okay.*

It would be a long forty-minute ride to the mainland hospital.

The clock read one o'clock and still they'd had no word. Luke and a handful of firefighters kept Jenna and the Parkers company in the emergency waiting room. They'd gotten the gist of the story from Luke. Tyson had been rescuing a teenage girl from the fire when the ceiling collapsed. He was briefly unconscious, and Riggs and Novak pulled him from the flames.

By the time they loaded him in the ambulance, he'd taken in a lot of smoke, but he was coherent.

But smoke inhalation was tricky. The high temperatures could burn the airways. Low levels of oxygen could lead to seizures or even a coma. Plus he'd been knocked out by falling debris, which meant he also had a traumatic brain injury. A TBI could present all kinds of problems, up to and including death.

Panic squeezed her chest, making it hard to breathe. She flashed back to fifteen years ago when she'd sat in the ER with her mom, waiting for word on her father. Flashed back to the nurse who came to speak with them, the bad news written all over her face.

No. No, that wouldn't happen to Tyson. He was young and healthy. He hadn't been involved in a chemical explosion.

Jenna wanted to run from the building and keep going till her legs gave out. But that was stupid. Instead she closed her eyes, shutting out all the movement around her, and said a prayer for him.

She had to stop thinking the worst. Be positive. Any minute now a nurse would come and tell them he was fine and would be discharged soon.

But the memory of that long-ago night played in her mind, terrorizing her. Making her short on breath. Long on panic. She jumped to her feet, startling Rick and Ronda.

"I'm going to— I have to move around." Or she was going to jump right out of her skin.

She paced the short hallway near the front desk where a patient filled out forms. Her stomach gave a rumble but she couldn't even think of eating.

What if Ty had taken in too much smoke? And what about carbon monoxide poisoning, one of the most immediate causes of death following smoke inhalation?

Tyson could die.

She moved her hand to her throat. As she turned to retrace her path, a nurse came through the double doors and headed toward the waiting room. She could be going to talk to anyone, but Jenna quickened her steps anyway and arrived as Rick and Ronda stood in front of the nurse.

"Mr. and Mrs. Parker?"

"Yes," Ronda said. "How is he?"

"He's going to be okay. We're treating him for smoke inhalation, but his airways aren't compromised. The X-ray checked out and he's on supplemental oxygen, but he tested negative for carbon monoxide poisoning."

Ronda nearly wilted with relief. "Thank God."

Jenna's breath rushed from her lungs. She pressed a hand to her chest. *Thank You, Jesus.*

"What about his head injury?" Rick asked.

"He has a concussion and nausea, which we're treating him for, but he's coherent and his CT was clear. For a couple days he'll need physical and mental rest. That means steering clear of stimulation like the TV and his phone. No screens or reading. We'll be dismissing him soon, but he should make an appointment with his doctor in the next week. Lung injuries can take time to show up. But overall, very good news."

"Thank you so much," Rick said. "Can we see him?"

The nurse glanced around at the relieved firefighters, many of whom still had soot on their faces. "Keep it to just a few of you. Right through those doors, room 118."

The Parkers and Jenna were already moving that way. Ronda gave her hand a squeeze. "He's going to be okay."

"Yes, he is." Jenna's legs wobbled so badly they nearly gave out as they headed down the hallway.

Moments later they entered the room and found Tyson sitting up in bed, looking safe and healthy. Except for the nasal cannula and sooty face, he could've been home on his sofa, watching a Braves game instead of receiving emergency medical care in the hospital.

"Honey, we were so worried." Ronda gathered her son awkwardly into her arms.

Rick patted his arm. "Your mom's been squeezing my hand so hard, it's lost circulation."

"Sorry about the scare. As you can see, I'm fine." Over his mom's shoulder Ty's gaze found Jenna.

She averted her eyes. She didn't want him seeing the fear that paralyzed her. What was wrong with her? She should be over by his bed, offering comfort like his parents. But instead she was stuck in her own head, her feet rooted to the floor. She had to actually think about drawing a breath.

I could've lost him. Oh God, I could've lost him.

Tyson caught them up on the medical side of things, coughing intermittently. He asked about the teenage girl, who they'd heard was doing well and also about to be discharged.

"Good, good. I'm so glad." Ty's voice was hoarse, but he did seem fine otherwise.

His gaze suddenly sharpened on Jenna and something flickered in his eyes. He held out his hand. "Come here."

She eased her way over to the bed.

"Your hand is freezing," he said after he'd taken it in his.

"The waiting room was cold." Or was it? She couldn't remember. All that panic sluicing through her had consumed her. And now that the good news had been delivered, she was in some kind of freefall.

The aftermath of the adrenaline rush? Whatever it was, it left her body heavy and sluggish, her brain foggy.

His parents were talking, his dad getting all the details of the fire, and Jenna tuned them out. She didn't want to hear about the blaze Tyson had been in or a play-by-play of his accident.

Because it turned out that even though the emergency had passed, the panic had not.

Chapter 41

Jenna awoke groggy and weighted by the sound of rain pattering the roof. She noticed the suitcases by the door and her stomach sank.

She hadn't gotten to bed until after three. Ty's parents had settled him in their house where they could keep close watch on him. When Jenna got home her mom was awake, and Jenna filled in the details missing from her texts.

She rolled over in bed, trying to wake up. It was now going on ten. She was supposed to have been on the road to Alexandria by now. Her new job started the next morning, and she'd wanted time to settle into her apartment and mentally prepare. She was keeping the apartment until the lease expired at the end of August—already had her eye on a more economical option.

But it was hard to focus on any of that right now. Across the street Tyson lay recovering from a head and lung injury. He'd been knocked unconscious during a fully involved blaze.

And now that she was removed from the emergency, the chatter from the firefighters the night before was slowly sinking in. Tyson had defied orders to exit the structure. The chief deemed the building unsafe, and while the other firefighters headed to safety, Tyson went back for the teenager, endangering his own life. On top of that, he'd given the girl his oxygen. If Riggs and Novak hadn't noticed him missing and turned back, this could've ended very differently.

The girl and her parents were no doubt grateful beyond measure for his actions. The *Eastern Shore Post* would certainly declare him heroic when the paper released Friday.

But all Jenna could think was, *I could've lost him.*

It had been so brave of him. Tyson would always do the courageous thing, even if that put him in jeopardy. The thought put that familiar pinch in her chest. The one she had when she remembered the painful loss of her dad. And this summer she'd let herself fall in love with a firefighter.

It had been a terrible mistake.

She'd allowed herself to go down a road that could lead to the same horrible heartache she'd spent her life avoiding. And now she couldn't bear to do anything but put space between them. Protect her heart from what could happen. No amount of therapy could help her if she just wasn't strong enough to suffer another loss like that.

But she also couldn't admit her feelings to Ty. Not now. She had to put them on the back burner until he healed.

Her phone alerted her to an incoming text, and her arm felt heavy as she retrieved it. Tyson.

You up?

Her mouth felt dry and that pinch grew stronger.

Yeah. Just woke up.

Thank God. Come rescue me from Mom.

Ronda was probably hovering with ice packs and Tylenol and snatching away all the reading materials.

Be there in twenty. And get off your phone!

Oh God, save me from my mother.

For the moment Tyson's prayer went unanswered. Mom fluffed the pillow beside him and tried placing it behind his back. If he stayed in this bed another minute he would lose his mind. "I think I'll just move to the sofa, Mom."

Her brows crinkled. "You should stay in bed and rest, honey."

He swung his legs over the edge of the bed. "I can rest just as easily on the sofa."

"Wait, I'll get your dad to help you."

"I can walk across the room on my own." He proved it by coming to his feet and heading toward the living area of the guest room.

Mom dashed to his side—just in case.

"I feel fine this morning. My headache's gone and I—" As luck would have it he broke out into a coughing fit.

Mom scowled at him. "You feel fine, huh? How did you boys get so stubborn?"

Oh, he could hazard a guess.

After he was settled on the sofa, Mom headed toward the door. "I'll be right up with some nice green tea to soothe that cough. It's good for the lungs. Mind you don't turn on that TV," she called over her shoulder, then closed the door behind her.

Ty dropped his head against the seatback and flung the throw pillow over his face. He needed Jenna. Once she got here, Mom would stop fussing around.

Jenna.

He'd been thinking of her since he'd awakened at seven o'clock this morning. He hadn't missed the sheer panic on her face last night. Even the good news about his lungs hadn't smoothed the creases on her forehead or chased the shadow of fear from her eyes.

Last night she'd faced her biggest nightmare. But he was fine. She'd surely see that even though he sometimes encountered dangerous situations, he and his crew could handle it. Just because her dad had died on the job didn't mean he would too. In fact, the odds were long against it.

Hopefully a good night's sleep had left her feeling more optimistic. He was strangely rested and refreshed even though he'd gotten little sleep. Perhaps because the sleep he did get was nightmare free. It was the most restful night he'd had in a while.

He thought of the girl he'd found huddled beneath her bed and allowed a sliver of a smile. Luke had texted this morning with an update. Her dad had appeared at the firehouse with donuts and a good report. He asked them to pass on his gratitude to Tyson.

He could be grateful for the save and still recognize that he'd defied orders and taken a risk because of his guilt over Andre Wallace. Maybe it had worked out this time, but it could've ended very differently. Very tragically.

He could never make up for the boy he'd lost, but he could go on helping people, saving lives. Just because he wasn't perfect didn't mean he couldn't be useful. But he needed help processing this guilt that had been weighing so heavily on him. He needed therapy. There was too much on the line to mess around with this any longer.

He would get help, get healthy, and then he would go on helping people as he was meant to do. Just having a plan in place made him feel better. Peace washed over him, healing a small tucked-away place inside him.

"Tyson?"

At the sound of Jenna's panic-laced voice, he ripped the pillow off his head. "Hey there."

Her brow was furrowed as she came through the doorway. "What's wrong? Why'd you have the pillow over your face?"

"Oh, you know . . . Mom."

Jenna's brow smoothed. "She's only trying to help. She sent this up for you with strict instructions that you drink it all."

Ty took the mug of steaming tea. "Yes, ma'am." He sipped, winced when it tasted like grass clippings, and set it on the coffee table.

"How's the headache? The cough?"

He spared her a look. "Don't pretend my mom didn't just give you a full report."

"Okay, fine, she did." Jenna sank beside him, careful not to jostle him, and too far away for his liking. "But I don't like hearing your voice so hoarse."

"It'll get better in a few days." He took her hand and found it cold, even though it must be ninety degrees out already. "You should be on the road by now."

She averted her eyes. "You couldn't think I'd leave you like this."

"You heard the doctor. I'm fine. Just need to lay low a couple days, and you know Mom will watch me like an eagle. God forbid she let me return to work if I have so much as a flicker of a headache."

"Nor should she." That panic still cowered in the depths of her eyes. Infused her tone.

"I'll be careful, Jen. I promise."

"You've already been on your phone."

"Just to text you. I turned it off." He squeezed her hand. "You can't miss the first day of your new job. There's no reason for that." It took a lot to say those words when he only wanted to pull her into his arms and keep her here forever. Especially because she hadn't willingly touched him since she'd walked in. Her hand lay lifelessly in his.

Ever since they'd grown closer she'd been so affectionate. So quick to grab his hand, touch his face, or press a kiss to his lips. She stared at him often, assessing him, studying him, admiring him. That she wasn't doing any of that now, when he'd just come through an emergency, was telling.

The realization sent a cold shiver of fear up his spine.

She handed him the mug, not sparing him more than a glance. "Maybe so, but if you want me to stay, I will. I'm sure Nancy would understand under the circumstances."

He sipped the tea, wishing he could swallow the terrible dread working its way up his throat. "I appreciate that, but I'll be fine. I don't want you to miss your first day."

"If you're sure. But I can still keep you company for a while." She settled back on the sofa with her phone. "I can read to you if you want. I have a ton of e-books on here. Or I can download a suspense novel. Do you have the new David Baldacci book?"

Her expression, her posture made it obvious what was going on inside her: The accident had terrified her, and she was already withdrawing from him. She was done.

But she wouldn't vocalize her feelings because he was healing. She'd wait until he had his strength back. The problem was, he couldn't live with this uncertainty for days on end. And he didn't want that for her either. They were only putting off the inevitable. He could see that quite clearly.

At the thought of her leaving him, a vise tightened around his heart, squeezing until his breath felt labored.

"It says right here it's riveting, engrossing, totally captivating. Sounds like just what the doctor ordered. What do you think?"

"Jenna."

"Have you already read it? There's always Ken Follett or Harlan Coben. Do they have anything new out? I know you liked the last Coben."

"Jenna."

He had her attention now. Her lips were parted, eyes questioning. Realization slowly settled in her features. Then a sadness crept into her eyes. And guilt. A heavy dose of guilt. His accident had scared her to death. She couldn't face a future where he risked his life—and her heart—on a regular basis.

He could try to talk her into it. He might even succeed. But he had multiple calls a week. It would be a perpetual conflict between them. Continual anxiety for her. Constant guilt for him.

For the first time he wished he could surrender the part of himself that felt called to the fire company. But he'd known since he was little that he was made for this assignment. It was part of who he was. Giving it up would be like giving up a piece of himself, and that wouldn't be right either.

Panic edged her eyes. She was petrified of the danger he faced. And after her father . . . how could he blame her? He loved her too much to put her through this day after day. He touched her cheek. "You don't have to say it, Jen. It's written all over your face."

"What do you mean? I'm fine. But *you* won't be if you don't finish your tea. Your mother was quite explicit in her instructions."

He set the tea back on the table without taking a drink. "Look at me, Jenna."

"What? I'm okay."

"You're not okay," he said gently. "Who do you think you're talking to? Your left eye is twitching like mad and your voice is all quivery . . ." He brushed a tear from her cheek. "And now you're crying. Talk to me."

Her mouth opened. But all that came out was a squeak. She closed her trembling lips as more tears followed.

Tyson gathered her into his arms. "Aw, honey. It's okay." It wasn't okay. Not even close. But he wouldn't guilt her for something she couldn't help. That childhood wound had left her scarred. She'd always been clear about that. He'd known all along he was taking a chance.

Even now he couldn't bring himself to regret it. Although losing her would be a kind of pain he'd never faced. He kissed the top of her head. And while she gave in to her tears, his own eyes burned. How would he go back to the way it had been before?

But it wouldn't even be that, would it? A friendship like they'd always shared wouldn't be possible when he loved her this way. Being with her would be too painful. He would always want more.

And someday she'd find someone else. He'd have to stand by and pretend to be happy for her while jealousy slammed into his heart. Because he couldn't even imagine these feelings for her fading away. Couldn't imagine feeling only friendship for her. He'd been naive to think things could ever return to the way they were before.

He wasn't only losing the woman he loved; he was losing the friend he'd always had. At the thought of letting go of her, his arms automatically tightened.

"I wish I could be as brave as you." Jenna's breath shuddered on the words.

He drew away, finding her eyes bloodshot and her lashes wet. "You had the courage to leave the island, go off and chase your dreams. A lot of people are too afraid to do that. I'm proud of you, Greene."

Her lower lip trembled. "I don't want to leave *now*. I'm afraid things will never be the same between us. I don't want to lose you."

"Hey, you haven't lost me. That'll never happen." He had no idea how he'd keep that promise, but he had to. He couldn't see a life without Jenna in it. He thumbed away her tears, trying to figure out how to fix this mess. "Okay, let's do this. Go back to Alexandria. Get settled in your new job. A little space, a little time might be just what we need."

Every cell in his body refuted the thought. Space and time away from Jenna was the very last thing he wanted. But he was glad he'd suggested it when a little hope surfaced amid the despair in her eyes. "It's going to be all right. It'll get better."

"You really think so?"

He tried for a smile. "I've loved you for years, Jenna. That'll never change." A fist tightened in his gut. Because now he was *in* love with her, and he was pretty sure he couldn't reverse that.

"I love you too."

He pressed a final kiss to her forehead. He wasn't sure how she'd meant those words. But he had a terrible feeling it would be the last time he ever heard her say them.

Chapter 42

The buzz of an incoming phone call sent a jolt of hope through Jenna. She closed the microwave door and checked the screen. Upon seeing the image of her mother, the adrenaline surge came to a crashing halt.

She accepted the call and injected enthusiasm into her tone. "Hi, Mom."

"How's my baby girl doing?"

"Just great. Had a great first week on the job, and I'm about to watch the Braves game."

"You're loving your job so far?"

"It's great!" Jenna rolled her eyes. Maybe she could say *great* one more time. "The people are nice and my boss is—terrific." Of course this week had mostly been spent learning what was what, which was never a true indicator of what a job would really entail. But she was trying to be positive.

"I'm so glad to hear that. I've been praying for you."

"I appreciate it." Jenna settled at the kitchen island where she could eat and keep tabs on the game. She let her warmed-up leftovers cool for a minute. "What are you up to?"

"Oh, I have the game on too. Just got back from the grocery, and I'm making a batch of oatmeal-raisin cookies." A lonely note lingered in Mom's voice. She'd gotten used to baking for Gordon's sweet tooth. But he was gone now. "I thought you might be going out somewhere fun to celebrate your first week on the job."

That was a great idea. Except she was basically starting over when it came to friendships. It was a bit overwhelming. And heartbreaking, since she'd left all those close relationships on the island for this. "I had some laundry to catch up on." Well, didn't that just sound pathetic? "I do have plans Sunday with a new coworker, though." She'd invited Jenna to church because yes, Jason had also gotten that in the split.

"That sounds wonderful. Just let me know when you're ready for weekend company. I'll come up and we can go on a shopping spree."

"I'd love that." Jenna paused as a Braves batter slugged a ball that went almost to the wall. Unfortunately it was caught by the center fielder.

"How are you doing otherwise, honey? You must be missing Tyson, hurting. I hate that for you."

Jenna didn't want to think about her heartache. She'd done everything she could to stay busy this week. And fortunately her new job made that easier. But the long weekend stretched ahead. "I'll be fine, Mom. I just need some time and space." She was clinging to Ty's words, though she doubted it would be that simple.

Leaving the island had been so much harder this time. Back then she'd had her whole future ahead of her. Now she could only think of the future she was leaving behind.

"Have you seen him? How's he doing?"

"He started back to work on Wednesday, though Chief Jones has him on light duty. I thought I'd take over some cookies tomorrow."

Jenna was glad Mom was looking out for him. "That's nice of you."

"You know how I love to bake."

And now she didn't have anyone to bake for. Thanks to Jenna.

She hated to ask because she was sure she already knew the answer. "Have you heard anything from Gordon?"

Mom sighed softly. "No, I haven't. I'm thinking he's probably moved on, sweetheart. I guess my doubt triggered all those issues from his marriage, and now he's just afraid to take a chance on me."

The sadness in her voice made Jenna's wobble. "I'm sorry, Mom."

"Well, aren't we a pair? But Jenna, *I* didn't have any choice in the matter. I made mistakes, but it wasn't my decision. You, though . . . that boy loves you."

Jenna shook her head. "That's not the problem, Mom."

"I know it must've been scary seeing him hurt in the line of duty. Trust me, honey, I know all about that. But love never comes without risk. As much as losing your father hurt, do you think I would've traded one minute with him? I treasure every day we had together."

Jenna wished she could view it that way. Maybe she wasn't as brave as her mom. Jenna shut down at just the thought of losing him. "I wish I could, but I just can't."

A beat of silence passed. "I won't press you. I hate seeing you so heartbroken, that's all."

Jenna could relate. Seeing her mom so despondent was hard to bear. Of course, some of that was brought on by the guilt.

They talked for a while about the goings-on around the island and the Pony Swim coming up in less than three weeks. But Jenna's mind was only half on the conversation.

The other half was problem-solving. She had a free day tomorrow and an idea that could possibly change her mom's situation. By the time she got off the phone, the plan was firmly cemented in her mind.

The row house appeared the same as it had a few weeks ago, except someone had removed the withering ferns from the porch. Jenna swallowed hard as she walked up the porch steps. Memories of her visit with Tyson intruded, but she shoved them firmly away. She had to focus on her objective.

Rosalind's car was out on the street, but Jenna had no idea what kind of car Gordon drove. She wanted to catch him at home, but also . . . *ugh*. This was not going to be fun. But the hope that she could repair the relationship between Mom and Gordon drove her on. And even if she couldn't, she at least owed the man a direct apology.

She knocked on the door, her heart hammering. A glimpse of the mailbox elicited an image of Tyson withdrawing the mail for his perusal.

Before she could follow the memory, the door opened and Rosalind appeared in a pair of denim shorts and a periwinkle tee. "Can I help you?"

"Uh, hi. I'm Jenna, a friend of Gordon's. Is he home by chance?"

"He is." Smiling kindly, Rosalind pushed open the screen door. "Come on in. He's out back trying to find some peace."

Music blared from upstairs. At least Jenna thought it was music. Hard to tell.

"I'm his sister, Rosalind," she said over the noise, then glanced at the ceiling. "And that's my son's loud, obnoxious music. Excuse me while I go handle that. Just go straight back and you'll find the door—and some blessed peace," she mumbled.

"Thank you."

A quick peek in the living room offered a glimpse of soothing neutral tones, brown leather furniture, and original mahogany woodwork. All in all a well-kept, inviting environment, if a little on the masculine side.

Jenna headed the way the woman had directed. Rosalind seemed nice. Just like Gordon. If only Jenna had taken him at face value all those weeks ago, she could've avoided all this pain and suffering.

When she reached the back door, she opened it and spotted Gordon sitting on a well-appointed patio. He was reading a newspaper, a mug of coffee resting at his fingertips.

The city noises infiltrated the shrub-lined yard, covering the sounds of her arrival. She stepped down onto the patio and closed the door behind her. "Gordon?"

He turned and his eyebrows hiked at the sight of her. "Jenna." He dropped the paper, and his chair scraped the cement as he stood. "What are you doing here? Is your mom okay?"

"She's fine." His obvious concern for her mother buoyed Jenna's spirits. The man must still have feelings for her. "I'm sorry to drop by unannounced. I needed to talk to you and I—I guess I was afraid you wouldn't see me."

"Of course I'd see you. Have a seat. Would you like a cup of coffee? It isn't as good as your mom's, but it's not terrible."

"Thank you, but I'm probably overcaffeinated as it is." Maybe that accounted for the way her heart jittered in her chest.

When he gestured her toward a chair, she took the one across the table from him and studied his face. Perhaps it was just the direct sunlight, but he seemed a little older. Perhaps a bit tired. But his eyes were kind and curiosity shimmered in the green depths.

This wouldn't be easy, but it had to be done. She took a deep breath and plunged ahead. "You must be wondering why I'm here. The gist of it is . . . I came to apologize."

His brows shot up again. "Whatever for?"

He seemed genuinely stymied. While she'd always been cordial toward him, she'd never exactly laid out the welcome mat. Shame pricked her skin. "I haven't been fair to you, Gordon. From the start I was . . . suspicious of you, I suppose is the best way of saying it. Your relationship with my mom happened so suddenly, and then you were moving in with her, and I started to wonder what you were up to."

His countenance fell, tugging on his skin as if earth's gravity had increased a hundredfold. "Oh. I didn't realize."

"I was worried about my mom. Afraid you were, perhaps, up to no good. I tried to share my concerns with Mom, but she wasn't very receptive." Jenna swallowed. "I was afraid you were rushing things along for some—some nefarious purpose. I didn't give you a chance, Gordon. I can see that now."

His brows furrowed. "Well. You didn't know me at all, and your mom and I did fall for each other rather quickly. Of course you'd want her to be careful with her heart."

Very gracious of him. Especially when she could see the hurt in his down-turned eyes. Jenna cleared her throat. "A while back I found out Mom was footing the bill for your outings, then I overheard you on the phone talking to someone, telling her you loved her."

"Probably my daughter."

"I realize that now. But at the time it just fed my distrust. I—I was so suspicious of your motives that I looked into your background."

He blinked. "Oh. I can't imagine there was much to find. I'm a pretty boring individual."

"That's not true. I mean, yes, there wasn't anything to find. But I've since come to believe you're a kind, decent man. I don't think there's anything boring about that."

"Well, thank you, Jenna." He scratched his head. "I guess."

"I'm afraid that's not all." She swallowed hard. This was where she'd gone way over the line. She dreaded telling him, but it had to be done. "Remember when I went to Alexandria for a couple days?"

"Yes, for your interview, with Tyson."

"Right. But Ty and I didn't just go to Alexandria." She forced herself to meet his gaze. "I also dragged him up here—to check out your story."

An excruciating beat of silence passed. "Well. My goodness. I don't know what to say."

She wished he'd get angry—she deserved it. But instead he just seemed befuddled. Saddened. She launched into the whole story. Arriving here, finding mail addressed to Rosalind. Seeing her leave the house the next morning. Jenna's suspicions about him having a wife. By the time she was finished, the temperature seemed to have shot up fifty degrees.

"I guess . . ." He gave his head a shake. "I guess I can see how that might've looked . . ."

"I'm sorry to say I went home and confronted Mom about my concerns. But she was quick to point out that Rosalind was your sister. She was very defensive of you and upset with me for interfering in her love life."

"She never mentioned any of this to me."

"I'm sure she didn't want to throw me under the bus—though I definitely deserved it. I'd learned my lesson by then. And that probably would've been the end of it, except—"

"The credit card statement." His tone was heavy.

"Right. She was upset when she found it. Confused. And I don't think I helped matters much. I remembered overhearing you tell someone on the phone that you were in Maine, and I told Mom about it."

"That was my niece."

"I realize that now. But it put doubt in her mind when she was already wavering. *I* put doubt in her mind. And when she confronted you, she was carrying the weight of *my* skepticism. Not her own."

Gordon sat back in his seat as his attention drifted over his small yard. "I see."

He didn't seem relieved. He seemed burdened and despondent, as if the memory of her mother's confrontation brought him great despair.

She had to make him see this was her fault. "Gordon, Mom told me a bit about your ex-wife. And I want you to know my mom is a very trusting person—almost to a fault. Without my interference she never would've jumped to that conclusion about the credit card bill. That was all my doing."

He seemed to be digesting her words. If only Jenna hadn't started down this road. If only she'd given the man half a chance. So what if they'd fallen for each other so quickly? Why had she been so determined to see fault in him at every turn? Sure, she'd wanted to protect her mother from heartbreak, but she'd gone way over the line.

That familiar pinch in her chest returned. Was she so afraid of grief and loss that she'd projected that fear onto her mother? Had Jenna been trying to protect her mom from her own paralyzing fears?

Oh, that was messed up.

Was she that troubled? That wounded? That she'd risk her mother's perfectly good relationship due to her own irrational fears?

Gordon leaned into the table. "I appreciate your honesty, Jenna. It took a lot of courage to admit what you did."

"Please don't hold my mom accountable for the way she reacted. She loves you so much. She misses you." Jenna's eyes burned with tears.

"I miss her too. I realize my sudden departure was a bit of an overreaction. I wish nothing but the best for your mother. But I have a lot to process. Some things of my own to work through." He gave a wry grin. "Believe it or not, I'm actually an analytical and pragmatic sort of guy. Falling for your mother so quickly was a complete aberration—although a very delightful one."

His gentle tone when he spoke of her mother gave her a smidgeon of hope. "I understand. I've dropped a lot on you. And in case I wasn't clear enough—I really am so very sorry for my actions. You didn't deserve my suspicion. I feel horrible to have come between you and my mom. She was so happy with you—happier than she's been in years, and I ruined it."

He reached across the table and patted her hand. "I appreciate your apology and I'll think about what you said."

But when they said good-bye a few minutes later, the lingering sadness in his eyes only left Jenna with a quiet sense of dread.

Chapter 43

If someone had told Tyson he'd be sitting across from his ex-wife in AmaRin a week after Jenna had left, he'd have told them they were crazy. When he'd spotted her in the coffee shop lobby, he came to a dead halt. His first inclination was to run—but then she saw him.

She convinced him to stay awhile, and he followed her to one of the back booths. It wasn't that he hadn't forgiven her. He just had no unfinished business with her. That season of his life was over. He'd learned from it and moved on.

Britt told him she'd arrived on the island yesterday with her parents and was staying through Pony Penning Days. She seemed to think he might be interested in all the goings-on in her life as she regaled him with them for the next thirty minutes. He'd forgotten how much she talked—and how little she actually said. His headaches had been gone for a few days, but he could feel another one coming on.

She was still very attractive with long blonde waves and sea-green eyes. But he viewed her differently now. She might be smart and talented, but she was also fickle and flighty, always fluttering after the next exciting thing. She would never be content with what she had.

The whole conversation made him homesick for steady, loyal Jenna, who'd shown him what true love really was. He ached at the thought of her. It seemed as if she'd been gone months instead of only a week.

He'd started to reach out a dozen times and stopped himself. How would he ever give her the time and space he'd promised her?

Britt cackled at something she'd said, and he tried to pay attention as she finished the story about her cat Isabella. Britt had always treated the feline like a princess, though she had only ever hissed at Tyson.

He drained the rest of his cold brew. He was searching for the words to make a polite escape when Britt finished her story and placed her hand on his. "I was planning to call you this week and set something up. But running into you has been so much fun. I've missed talking to you, Ty."

Oh boy. He tried to withdraw his hand.

But she held tight. "Don't you miss me? Miss our walks on the beach, the fun nights out"—she offered a coy smile—"the lazy Saturday mornings in bed?"

He leaned back in the booth, taking his hand with him. "We had it pretty good there for a while. But our marriage is over, Britt. We've both moved on."

Her gaze swept over his face, a decisive look coming over her features. "Do you want me to say it? Okay, I made a mistake. And I regret it. I never should've left you."

"But you did. And I've moved on."

She leaned into the table, her focus sharpening on him. "I'm asking for another chance, Tyson. We were good once before. We could be good again—you know it's true."

He blinked. He had not expected this. And he couldn't even entertain the idea. Not after what he'd had with Jenna. He had a fresh perspective on love, and it had changed everything. What he and Britt had before was a poor imitation of the real thing. He felt sorry for Britt that she hadn't yet realized that.

And even though Jenna wasn't able to go forward with their relationship, he still loved her. And that wasn't about to change anytime soon.

Britt gave a nervous chuckle. "You're awfully quiet over there."

He felt a nip of sympathy at the hope in her eyes. It was false hope. This was never happening. "Listen, Britt. I accept your apology. I made mistakes too, and I'm sorry I couldn't be the husband you wanted. I don't have any ill feelings toward you." It was true. The realization was freeing, like a breath of fresh air. "But I think we should leave well enough alone."

Her eyes drooped at the corners. "Really, Ty? It sounds like you don't care about me at all."

"I do care. I wish you the best. Really, I do. I just . . ."

"Don't love me anymore." Her plush lips turned down in a pout.

"No, I don't. I'm sorry if that sounds harsh, but I believe our relationship has run its course. And for what it's worth, I don't think you're in love with me either. Maybe you're just at loose ends and looking for something or someone to make you happy. But we've been down this road before, and it didn't end well."

She blinked away the tears that had gathered in her eyes.

"I'd like to just take the good memories we had and leave the rest behind."

She dashed away a tear. "Maybe you're right."

"I'm sure you have good things going on in your life. You said your job's going well." She was a residential interior designer with a prominent group.

A light shimmered in her eyes. "I'm up for a promotion soon. I'm pretty excited about that . . ."

"There you go. I bet you'll get it."

"I think I will. Yeah. That'll feel pretty good, being head of all the other designers."

"You're very good at what you do."

Britt finished her drink and offered him a hopeful smile. "Thanks, Tyson. You always know just what to say." She checked the time. "I should probably go. Mom and Dad are expecting me."

As they scooted from the booth, she tossed him a wink. "But if you ever change your mind . . ."

He resisted the urge to roll his eyes. "Take care, Britt."

At the door she gave him a brief hug. "See ya, Ty." Without a backward glance she sashayed from the shop, her little skirt swishing behind her.

Ty shook his head as he headed toward the restroom. He was glad to have that conversation over with. Just needed to splash some cold water on his face. Was it eighty degrees in here or was it just him?

When he left the restroom he exited the building and headed down the gravel lane to the parking lot in the back. He was glad there was no sign of Britt. He hoped he wouldn't run into her again while she was on the island. But if he did, maybe they could just be casual. Exchange a friendly hello and let it go at that. Maybe today's conversation had offered her some closure.

The thought had no sooner occurred than Marissa stepped around her car on her way to the coffee shop's entrance. It was impossible to miss her as their cars were the only two in the lot. She wore her paramedic uniform as she'd just come off shift.

Must be his lucky day. "Afternoon."

Something flashed in her eyes. "What, are you stalking me now?"

"I was here before you, Marissa."

"Yeah, but I come here every Sunday afternoon . . ."

She was deluded. “Well, enjoy your drink.” He moved toward his truck.

“Wait. What were you doing here then?”

He spoke slowly. “Getting coffee.”

“Where is it?”

Something was seriously wrong with this woman. “I drank it inside. Have a nice afternoon.” He turned back toward his truck, trying to shake off the encounter.

“You probably think you’re hot stuff, don’t you? Being written up in the paper like you’re some kind of hero.”

He was done with this. He shook his head as he slipped inside his truck and closed the door.

Chapter 44

Cool air washed over Jenna's skin as she entered her apartment, a welcome relief from the July heat. After being relatively sedentary all week, she'd had the bright idea of going for a three-mile jog. But the eighty-five-degree evening had whipped her butt.

She dropped onto her sofa, sweat and all. She'd rehydrate, then shower. But at the moment she was too exhausted to even kick off her tennis shoes. Perhaps she'd overdone it. But the Oreos had been a regular companion this week. Last night had been a full-sleeve night. Not good.

She'd gone for a jog because she'd been desperate to escape her thoughts, which tended to hover around two subjects. Her mother's love life being one. It had been more than twenty-four hours since Jenna visited Gordon. She'd hoped her mom would've called by now with good news. Jenna put it all out there, but it was in his hands now. With each hour that ticked by, her hopes sank inch by inch.

The other intrusive subject was, of course, Tyson. Even the jog couldn't distract her from missing him. She wished she could just call him to chat—even as a friend.

But that was absurd. She couldn't think of him that way now. Not when they'd been so much more. Not when her heart ached for want of him.

She rolled her eyes at the melodramatic thought. Cheesy as it might sound, it was true. She took a long drink from her water bottle and was setting it back on the end table when her phone buzzed with an incoming call.

Tyson?

Her heart rate jacked right back up. Or maybe her mom.

A peek at the screen revealed the caller was neither. The spurt of adrenaline fizzled as she answered the phone. "Hey, Sofia. How's it going?" They'd talked earlier in the week, mostly just a postmortem on Tyson and Jenna's relationship. Sofia had been a sympathetic ear.

"Pretty good. I was wondering how your first week went. I know you were feeling a little overloaded the other day."

"There's a lot to learn, but I'll get on top of it." She'd actually been in her office a lot more than she'd anticipated. Hopefully that would change once she stepped fully into her role.

"You'll be amazing. I just wish you could be amazing a little closer to the island."

"Me too. It's a shame the cost of living has increased so much there."

"It's made things difficult for a lot of residents. So tell me how your talk with Gordon went yesterday."

Jenna filled her in on the visit from start to finish while Sofia listened patiently. "I'd hoped to hear something from my mom by now."

"Maybe he needs a little time to process. You did all you could—and it was very courageous of you to hunt him down and confess what you did."

"It was the least I could do."

"It's in God's hands now. Try to have a little faith."

Sofia was always quick to remind her that just because something was out of *Jenna's* control didn't mean it was out of God's control. A male voice sounded in the background.

"Is that Jack?" Jenna asked.

"He's fixing the dishwasher."

"Oh, I didn't know he was a handyman."

Sofia lowered her voice. "He's not. He'll try to fix the dishwasher, get frustrated, then give up and call the plumber. I already have the number ready."

Jenna chuckled. But inside she longed to have that in her life—someone she knew so well, someone who knew her too, and loved her anyway. It had been pretty stellar for a while.

"How are you doing otherwise?" Sofia asked.

She meant in regard to Ty, of course. "I'm okay."

"That wasn't very convincing."

Jenna sighed. "I try to stay busy. I just returned from a three-mile jog, which goes to show you exactly how desperate I am. I love him so much, Sofia. I don't know how it happened so quickly or so thoroughly."

"Oh, Jenna . . ." Something foreboding vibrated in her tone.

It sent a jolt of dread through Jenna. Her heart beat out a heavy tattoo while she waited for Sofia to continue. When she didn't, Jenna said, "What's wrong? Is Tyson okay?"

"He's fine. I was just weighing if I should tell you something."

"Well, you have to tell me now." Jenna clutched a pillow to her chest as if it could serve as a barrier against whatever Sofia was about to say.

"I stopped in AmaRin this afternoon and Ty was there." The pause seemed to last eons. "He was in a corner booth—with Britt."

Jenna hadn't even realized his ex-wife was on the island. "Oh."

The thought of Ty with *any* other woman, much less Britt, made Jenna's heart hurt. But meeting up with Britt didn't mean anything. "I'm sure he was just getting closure or something. The relationship ended pretty suddenly. He kind of spun out."

"That's true. That's completely possible."

She knew Sofia too well. "What aren't you saying?"

"I was in the lobby and I didn't have a great view of them. But they were holding hands across the table, Jenna. And the way she was gazing at him, all moony eyed . . . it didn't look good."

It was impossible to believe Ty could've moved on that fast. "I don't know what you saw, but I know Ty. He would never go back to Britt. Certainly not one week after our breakup."

"I didn't think so. But I thought you deserved to know what I saw. You're probably right. It was just closure, I'm sure."

It was all innocent, no doubt. But eventually Tyson would find someone else. The thought of him moving on made her feel sick. She'd finally fallen in love with the right person. But it hadn't been enough.

"You okay?" Sofia asked.

"Yeah." Her voice wobbled on the lie.

"Can I be honest, Jen?"

"Therapist honest or best-friend honest?"

"A little of both, I guess."

What did Jenna have to lose? She was already miserable. "Lay it on me."

"A while back you mentioned some counseling for those grief issues. Have you given that any more thought?"

"I assume you think I need it."

"It wouldn't hurt, would it? You and Tyson were so good together. I hate that you gave up something that made you so happy."

"I didn't even have to give it up—Ty just knew what was going on inside me. He practically read my mind." She remembered Jason's reason for proposing—because she just "needed a little push." What a contrast.

"He knows you so well."

"Being with him was everything I dreamed. It felt like I was exactly where I was supposed to be. But when he had that accident, I realized it wasn't enough."

"What do you mean by that?"

"It scared me so badly. I don't want to give someone my whole heart only to lose him."

"Like you lost your dad?"

"Yes!" It was hard to admit out loud. She didn't want to believe she was such a coward. "My stupid fears got in the way, and I let go of the man who was meant for me in every way."

"Jen, this isn't an irrevocable problem. Fear can be overcome. It might take time, but you're strong enough to fight through it and reach the other side."

Was she? It sure didn't feel like it.

"You can do this, Jen. Trust me on that."

Jenna wiped a tear from her cheek. "Well, you are an expert."

"I am, aren't I?"

Maybe it was time. After all, if she didn't overcome this fear, how would she ever have a healthy relationship? And if anyone was worth the effort, it was Tyson. "All right. I'll look into it."

Her phone vibrated and she checked the screen. *Mom.* Had Gordon called her at last? "Hey, my mom's calling."

"Okay, I'll let you go. Check back in later, all right?"

"Will do. Thank you, Sofia. I appreciate your help."

"Anytime, friend."

Jenna ended the call and accepted her mother's, hope lilting her tone. "Hey, Mom. What's up?"

"Hi, honey. You'll never guess who's here." The smile in Mom's tone said everything Jenna needed to know.

A grin spread across Jenna's face as her mom told her about Gordon showing up on her doorstep this afternoon with an armful of red roses. He'd told her about Jenna's visit and confession and asked her mom for another chance. As the story unfolded, Gordon chimed in with charming little snippets that made her mom giggle.

They both sounded so blissful, Jenna felt her heart squeeze tight.

And if, twenty minutes later when they got off the phone, a tear or two trickled down Jenna's face . . . well, they were just tears of happiness.

Chapter 45

Ty wasn't too worried as he pulled into the fire station the next day. Chief Jones had called this morning to set up the meeting. Ty had known this was coming. Nine days ago he'd defied the chief's orders at the scene, and it was time to face the consequences. A tongue-lashing at the very least. Ty got it. He couldn't go around defying orders.

He was glad Marissa's car wasn't in the lot. Didn't care to run into her after yesterday's weird encounter. The building was cool and quiet, with just the hum of the air-conditioning filling the space.

He headed to the chief's office and found him frowning at some papers on his desk. "Hey, Chief."

The man stood to his full six-foot-four-inch height, offering a grim smile. "Parker. Come on in. Have a seat."

Ty's stomach sank at his demeanor as he followed orders. Best to get out in front of this. "I know I was wrong to defy your orders at the scene, Chief. I handled the situation badly. And even though it turned out well, I know it could've gone very differently. Very badly."

"It was unlike you to go rogue like that. Not the kind of conduct I expect from a captain."

Ty gave a nod. "Understood."

"We'll need to talk more about that. But that's not why I called you in today."

Oh. Well, if it wasn't about that, then what?

His boss leaned back in his chair, studying him. "How've you been feeling? Your throat sounds better."

"Headache's gone and my doctor's appointment is tomorrow. I expect to get the all clear." Thank God he wouldn't miss Pony Penning Days. He could hardly wait. In less than two weeks they'd round up the southern herd, then the northern. Then Ty and the other saltwater cowboys would lead the northern herd down the beach to join up with the southern herd for vet checkups before the famed Pony Swim.

The chief hadn't yet responded to Ty's answer. The man's gray brows pulled together and a ridge of lines rippled across his forehead—never a good sign.

"I promise I'm fine. No headaches or nausea, and I've been back to work for almost a week."

The chief leaned his elbows on his desk. "I don't doubt that. This is actually about Marissa Moran. She came to see Geena and me this morning, told us about an encounter the two of you had yesterday in a parking lot."

Tyson blinked. "We ran into each other, if that's what you mean. She said some weird things. Acted like I was stalking her or something. I tried to be polite." What was going on here? "Listen, I don't like to make accusations, but I think there might be something off about her."

Chief Jones nodded thoughtfully. "Tell me about the encounter."

Dread inched up Ty's throat. But he told the man everything he remembered about the brief conversation. "It was very strange. I'm not sure if you've heard about our history—if you can call it that."

"I've heard a few rumors. I'd like to hear it from you."

Ty started at the beginning with what was supposed to have been a couple of casual dates but quickly escalated when Marissa had run into him and his date at The Pearl. He noted the false rumors afterward that Ty had slept with her and the way he'd tried to apologize to her several times only to be rebuffed. When he was finished, the chief's expression warned him there was something he wasn't saying. "What's this all about, Chief?"

The man heaved a weary sigh and met Tyson's gaze. "Marissa's version of your encounter yesterday is quite different from yours. She said she arrived first and you followed her into the parking lot."

Tyson frowned. "That's not true."

Chief held up a hand. "Furthermore, she said you accosted her about wanting her back. That you put hands on her."

"*What?* That's a lie! I never touched her. And I sure don't want to be with her."

"Was anyone else there in the parking lot? Someone who might've seen what happened?"

"No, we were alone. Our cars were the only ones in the lot."

"That's too bad." The chief held his gaze, his eyes drooping at the corners. "She had bruises, Tyson."

"Well, they weren't from me!" He resisted the urge to shoot to his feet. What was going on here? What kind of woman made up these kinds of allegations?

"The company shouldn't really even be involved in this. It happened off the job, in a public location. But she came to us as a 'courtesy.' She intimated that if we don't address the situation in a satisfactory manner, she'll go to the police."

Ty gripped the chair's armrests. "Well, let her. I didn't do anything wrong."

"Not so fast there. If we can keep this from escalating, we should."

"I know most of the officers at the CPD. They know me too—and they know I'd never lay hands on a woman." Ty was starting to wonder if his chief felt the same.

"Maybe you're not aware, but Marissa's dad used to be on the CPD. He's a deputy for the county now."

The news stopped Ty cold. What kind of influence would her dad have here? Ty couldn't believe this was happening. "So it's a he-said, she-said situation? Can I be punished for something I didn't even do? Did she say I hit her or something?"

"She has bruising on her arm. Fingerprints, looked like."

Tyson shook his head. "I didn't touch her. I would never do that."

"She also reminded me that a concussion is a traumatic brain injury that can cause mood swings."

Ty gritted his teeth. "I haven't experienced any mood swings." Until now. "*I didn't do this.*"

"I believe you, Tyson, I do. And I agree that there's something off about her. But I also think it's in your best interest to avoid a formal charge here. I was thinking you could just lay low for a while. Let the dust settle a bit."

"Lay low as in stop running calls?" A new thought occurred—the pony penning and Pony Swim. "How long are you talking about here?"

"I don't know exactly. I can talk to Geena about it. Marissa seemed pretty . . . affected. A short hiatus might appease her."

Appease her? He hadn't done anything to her!

"Perhaps a month from now—"

"A month? I'm not missing the Pony Swim. I've been part of it since I can remember." Dad had brought him to the pennings since he was a kid. Trained him until he was old enough to manage a horse on his own.

"Ultimately, it's up to you. But I highly advise you to put some thought into this. We could call it a medical leave. No one else would be any the wiser. And in the meantime you might consider getting legal counsel."

At the thought of attorneys and courtrooms, panic flooded Tyson's veins. Why was this happening? And more importantly, how could he prove that he'd done nothing wrong?

Chapter 46

Jenna disconnected the call and glanced out her solitary office window. The sun was shining and the sky was clear blue. It was another beautiful summer day. Too bad she was stuck in her office.

The gym where they hosted the MWF basketball program for elementary kids had a plumbing issue. There was an inch of water in the gym, which meant she spent all afternoon trying to locate another venue. Finally she'd found one.

Before that she'd had to deal with two minor injuries that had happened during their programs this week—and all the insurance paperwork that went along with them. Nancy had been a great help guiding her through the process. She'd known her job would entail this kind of work; she just hadn't known it would absorb her entire day.

Hopefully this week was just an aberration. Nancy had told her that once she finished the necessary office work during the week, she would go to the activity sites and oversee the sports programs and their coaches.

But it seemed as though there was no time for that unless she worked beyond the forty-hour workweek. And since she was on salary, that hardly made sense. Despite that, she'd stopped by various activity sites each evening this week to get the lay of the land. And also to eke a little enjoyment out of her job.

It was already nearly six o'clock and she'd just finished the office work. She'd planned to stop and observe the adult volleyball league tonight, but her brain was fried. She'd been under fluorescent lights all week. Her stomach gave a hard rumble. She'd brought in food, thinking she could work through lunch and free up some time to catch the afternoon senior yoga session. So much for that.

The office was quiet as she exited the building. Nancy and her assistant had already left for the day. Jenna locked up and headed to her car. On her way home she stopped at a drive-thru because she hadn't had time to shop for groceries this week.

After parking her car she made her way to her apartment, breathing in the scent of hot pavement as the sounds of passing traffic filled her ears. She missed the smell of the ocean and the sounds of the breeze rustling the tree leaves. She missed the local restaurants where she could pop in and spot a friend or neighbor. She missed the glorious sunrises, the windswept beaches, the shimmering bays. She missed the sight of wild ponies grazing in the salt marshes and the familiar rock of her kayak.

Jenna shook the thoughts away. She'd made her choice. She had to make the best of this.

Once inside her apartment she devoured a salad with cold chicken while she caught up on sports. When the Braves recap came on, she turned it up. They'd just swept the Phillies in a three-game series. She grabbed her phone to text Tyson, a ready smile on her lips.

Then her smile wilted. She kept forgetting they were taking space from each other. She put down her phone, that familiar sinking sensation weighting her stomach.

She hated this. She missed him so much. He was the one she talked sports with. This summer he'd become the one she talked to about everything. And now she was just supposed to quit him cold turkey?

Her insides ached. She wanted to tell him about her disappointment with her job and hear his encouragement. She wanted to share about her visit with Gordon and the way he and her mother had patched things up. There were a dozen things that happened on any given day that she wanted to tell him. And that didn't even touch on how much she missed being held in the safety of his arms.

She hated not knowing what was going on in his life. Was his health back to normal? Was he running calls again? What had become of the bet with his brothers? Of the situation with Marissa?

Did Tyson miss Jenna as much as she missed him? Or was he hanging out with Britt here and there? Possibly testing out the idea of a reconciliation?

No. She would not go there.

She scrapped the rest of her salad, then put this morning's dishes in the dishwasher. This week she'd taken Sofia's advice and made an appointment with an online counselor. It wouldn't be easy, but she had to work through her fear. Trust that she was strong enough to get through it. Sofia's belief in her buoyed Jenna's spirits. She was already getting glimpses of the truth: Tyson was the right person—but she had to deal with her own issues to make it the right time.

Her phone buzzed in her pocket. She dried her hands and told herself it wasn't Tyson. But her heart didn't listen. It thrashed around as she checked the screen.

Disappointment swept through her at the sight of Miss Molly's name. Even so, Jenna managed a small smile as she greeted the woman. "Well, hello, Miss Molly. How are you?"

"I'm doing all right, I suppose. And how are you doing, dear? All settled into your apartment and new job?"

"I guess you could say that. Although it might take a little more time to get my feet under me."

"Well, there's a learning curve with every new job. I'm sure you're doing great."

"I haven't had any complaints yet at least." She pictured Miss Molly pushing her glasses up with a slender finger and suddenly missed her and everything about her old job. She could almost hear the water rippling against the pilings and the flag pole's hardware pinging in the breeze. "How's the business going? How's Mr. Paul? Catch me up on everything."

"The business is doing great. You know how it is in July."

"I remember. Your busiest week is yet to come." Pony Penning Days was absolutely crazy. Everyone wanted a peek of those beautiful wild ponies emerging from the water in glorious fashion, and the channel view was unbeatable.

"We're gearing up for it. Paul's helping out where he can, but he's got that bad back, and as you know he's not so great with customers."

"He can spray down the kayaks like a pro, though."

"That he can." Miss Molly cleared her throat. "Listen, honey, I don't want to take up too much of your time. But there've been some recent developments with my daughter Lisette." Her tone was sullen.

"Oh no. What's wrong?"

"That surgery she had didn't take well. She's going to need permanent help with the children."

"Oh, Miss Molly, I'm so sorry. Will she be okay?"

"She'll be all right, but she won't be able to manage on her own while David's at work. So Paul and I will be moving to Asheville as soon as possible."

"Of course. I'm sure Lisette will be so glad to have your help."

"We're sad to leave the island, but this is the right thing to do. The hardest thing is . . . I have to sell my business. This will be a permanent situation, and I can't see running it from afar."

Jenna winced. "I know that must be very hard for you. It's your baby."

"Well, I suppose it had to happen sometime. I'm no spring chicken, but I'd planned to put in a few more years at least. Thing is, Jenna . . . I wondered if you might be interested in buying it."

Jenna froze. Blinked.

"I know you just started a new job and the timing isn't ideal. I'm not sure of your financial position, but I'd be willing to work with you on that if you're interested. I can't think of anyone I'd rather take the reins than you."

"Miss Molly. I'm so honored you thought of me."

"Of course I'd think of you. No one else has the kind of passion you do for sharing our island's history. You know the business—you've worked it from the bottom up, and you've got a business degree to boot. You're ideally suited for this, Jenna."

She was. She absolutely was. Her pulse raced now, but for a much better reason. She could run Coastal Currents. But could she earn enough to afford island life? Mr. Paul and Miss Molly had a nice life and a beautiful little inland home. But they'd been a dual-income family, so it was hard to know how profitable the kayak company was.

"I've caught you unaware. I understand this is a big decision with a lot of moving pieces. If you're interested at all, I'll send you the financials, and we'll talk about what I'm looking to get out of the business. I'm flexible with the buyout. Paul and I don't need to be paid out all at once. But all of this is irrelevant if you have no interest."

"No, I'm interested," she blurted.

Miss Molly chuckled. "Well, I always knew you were a bright girl.

I can send you the financials tomorrow and you can look them over. How does that sound?"

"It sounds great, Miss Molly. I—I can't even wrap my mind around this. Thank you for thinking of me."

"Oh, honey, who else would I think of?"

The woman's teasing voice echoed in Jenna's head as she set her phone down in a daze. Could this really work? Buying her out might not be as difficult and lengthy a process as Miss Molly thought since Jenna had her grandma's trust.

If the financials looked good, it wouldn't be money holding Jenna back from grabbing the opportunity. It would be the thought of sharing the tiny island with the man she loved.

Chapter 47

Tyson's heart was heavy as he navigated the Friday night traffic on his way to the coffee shop.

From the passenger seat, Seth jacked up the air-conditioning. "I hope the heat lets up soon."

It had been in the high nineties most of the week. Pony penning started a week from tomorrow, and it would be better for the ponies, spectators, and saltwater cowboys if the weather cooled a bit. Not that Ty would be sitting horseback at this rate.

He'd been cleared by his doctor on Tuesday, but he was still lying low around the fire station. He hadn't spoken to Marissa a single time since her ridiculous allegations, but he'd sure thought about it. His family had convinced him it would be unwise.

But that didn't stop him from trying to figure out how to prove himself innocent. A call to the coffee shop had relieved him of the hope that they might've caught the interaction on camera. They didn't have security cameras, and none of the employees had been watching out the window—why would they?

He wasn't sure why he'd thought coming down here again might help. Maybe reenacting the encounter might bring something helpful to mind.

As he pulled into the lot, gravel popped under his truck's tires, making Ty remember that ding someone had put in his car door back in May. Could that have been Marissa? He never would've thought it at the time, but now he understood just how vindictive she was.

The coffee shop was closed, which would give them the privacy he preferred. "I was parked here." Tyson pulled into the space. "And Marissa parked over there—two spots closer to the entrance."

Once he shut off the engine, they exited the vehicle.

"You were leaving the shop?"

"Right." Tyson walked toward the entrance and turned. "I was coming out and there were only our two cars. I saw her when she came around her vehicle."

"Like this?"

"Right." Ty retold the conversation as they stood where he and Marissa had five days ago. He'd reviewed it in his mind a hundred times. "Then I started walking away like this and she said I must think I'm hot stuff after being written up like a hero. I ignored the comment. Just went to my truck and got in."

"So you never even got close to her."

"I was a good five feet away at the very closest."

Seth frowned. "I wish someone had seen it."

Ty glanced around the property. Somewhere nearby a car door slammed. He tracked the sound to the motel lot that was adjacent to the coffee shop parking lot. A sparse tree line separated the properties. "I wonder if the motel would have an exterior camera."

"Good question. I know the manager. Did a little marketing for her last summer. Let's head over."

They walked toward the hotel entrance and once inside found a middle-aged brunette working the lobby desk.

"Hi, MaryAnn," Seth said. "How've you been?"

"Seth." She beamed. "Good to see you. I still tell Mr. Mays all the time that we need to hire you again."

"I'm glad the campaign worked out so well for you. This is my brother Tyson." Seth glanced at his brother. "MaryAnn pretty much runs this hotel single-handedly."

"Oh, I have plenty of help. Nice to meet you, Tyson. Your brother's a marketing genius."

"We try not to butter him up too much. We have to live with him."

She grinned. "Fair enough. What brings you guys by? I can't imagine you need rooms."

Seth leaned on the counter. "Actually we have a weird question for you. Do you happen to have exterior security cameras?"

"As a matter of fact, we do. We had a problem with auto break-ins last summer and Mr. Mays had them installed. Why do you ask?"

Seth went into the story, giving only the pertinent details about Ty's encounter with Marissa and her false allegations, without naming her.

Her gaze swung to Tyson. "Oh my. You were accused of accosting her? When did this supposedly happen?"

"Last Sunday around three fifteen. I'm really hoping you have footage of the event so I can exonerate myself."

She gave a sharp nod. "Well, we're gonna find out right now. Come on back to the office and let's see what we can pull up."

"There she is," Seth said.

Tyson couldn't believe it. The motel's camera view was black and white and focused on their own parking lot, of course. But just through the gap in the bushes, Marissa exited her car. And then there he was at the very top of the screen. They came to a stop and exchanged words. You couldn't really see their expressions or hear what they were saying.

Then Tyson walked away from her, leaving the screen. Marissa headed toward the shop entrance. A moment later the bottom of Ty's truck passed by as he exited the lot. He had everything he needed right here. Relief flooded through him, nearly wilting him.

"Bingo!" Seth said.

"Wow, you didn't even go near her." MaryAnn pecked a few keys on the computer. "She won't get away with this. What's your email? I'll send you the file."

Tyson rattled it off, his mind still whirling. He couldn't wait to send that footage to Chief Jones.

Seth clapped him on the back. "It's over, buddy. Marissa's been caught in her lies red-handed."

As soon as Tyson got back to his house, he forwarded the video to the chief with a message explaining where he'd gotten it and including MaryAnn's number. A few minutes later his phone rang.

"I just saw the footage," Chief Jones said. "Sure seems indisputable to me. I'm going to call Geena into my office, and I'll let you know how it goes from there. Great job on this, Parker. I'll get back with you soon."

After Ty disconnected the call, he heated up some leftover pizza, but he hardly tasted it as he ate. Surely the EMS director would see he was innocent of Marissa's accusations. When she'd made her allegations she'd given the day and time of the encounter, which were time-stamped on the footage.

For the hundredth time this week he wished he could call Jenna and talk to her. It had been lonely going through this without her—even though Luke's and Ty's families had been supportive. He'd been at loose ends without the fire company, wondering about the new rumors Marissa might've started or what other drama she might be stirring up.

Jenna.

How long was this time-and-space thing supposed to last? Until his feelings were gone? He gave a wry laugh. At this rate that might be never.

It was your bright idea, genius.

Yeah, well, it wasn't working so well—at least not for him. There was an empty, Jenna-shaped hole in his heart that seemed like it would never be filled. How was he supposed to live like this?

The phone buzzed, claiming his attention. Nerves clamoring, he snapped it up.

"She's history," the chief announced with no preamble. "Geena's giving Marissa her walking papers as we speak."

Tyson blew out a deep breath. "That's great news. I'm so relieved to hear it."

"Geena also called Marissa's former employer over in Wattsville and discovered they had trouble with her there too. Her previous boss suspects Marissa is a narcissist. Said she wouldn't be surprised if Marissa put those bruises there herself."

"Wow."

"Geena's kicking herself for not checking her references, but she was desperate to fill that spot. I'm sorry this happened, son. But boy, it sure is good when the truth prevails, isn't it?"

"You can say that again."

Marissa's downfall was the main topic the next Wednesday at Ty's parents' house. Ty loved recounting Luke's story about the paramedic storming out of the fire station. How fortuitous that he'd been present for the moment. It gave Ty plenty of satisfaction to see justice carried out.

His parents had invited Ty and his brothers for supper—Alex had picked up Cosa's pizza on the way, and Ty was currently regretting that sixth slice. He wiped the grease from his fingers and leaned back in his chair, holding back a moan of misery.

Mom, sitting between Ty and Seth, removed the last slice from the box and set it on Seth's plate.

"Thanks, Mom. Don't mind if I do." Seth had a bottomless stomach.

"Save some room," Mom said. "Dee brought over brownies this afternoon."

"I'm going to need a little break," Alex said even as he finished chewing a bite. "So, Mom, we're only a week from the pony auction. Have you guys decided if you're bidding on the foal?"

"Oh boy," Dad said. "Here we go."

Seth leaned in. "I got a glimpse of Patches' sibling last week. He's a pretty cute little guy. He might not go for a lot either since he's a bay."

Mom swung her head Ty's way. "And what do you think, Tyson?"

"Um, yeah, Seth's right. That's the way it usually goes." The pintos typically brought a higher bid since they more closely resembled the fabled Misty of Chincoteague.

Mom dropped her napkin on her plate. "Well, I just can't seem to decide."

"What do you think, Dad?" Alex asked.

Dad's gaze sharpened on their mother. "I think your mother has a mind of her own."

Ty traded a grin with Seth over their mom's head. Looked like this bet might go their way after all. And good thing, with five hundred dollars on the line. He could almost see that big-screen TV hanging on his wall.

Mom patted Ty's leg. "Well, all those articles were very helpful, honey. And Seth, those website links you sent me . . . I just couldn't have asked for more timely information."

"Glad we could help." Seth shot Alex a smug look. "So you're leaning toward buying one?"

"Oh, I'm leaning toward buying one all right." Something was off about Mom's tone.

Ty frowned. He glanced her way just as her benign expression flipped to a scowl. "What is wrong with the three of you? Do you think I'm stupid? I'm onto your little bet. You're about as subtle as a flashing neon sign."

Ty's face warmed as he met Alex's "uh-oh" expression across the table.

"She's been onto you since the beginning, guys," Dad said.

Ty darted a look at Seth—just as Mom whacked the back of his head.

"Hey!" Seth said. "What about them?"

"I can't reach Alex," Mom said, "and Ty has a concussion. Really, you three thought you'd play your dad and me? Did I not give birth to each one of you? You should realize by now that I know your every thought before you even think it."

"I don't know about that . . ." Alex pouted.

Dad smirked. "What's that bet up to now, boys?"

What? How'd he know they'd been raising the bet?

Seth frowned, seeming as uncertain as Ty felt. "Five hundred."

Ty could feel five hundred big ones—and that big-screen TV—slipping away.

Now it was Mom who looked smug. "Thank you for accommodating my plans by upping the ante."

Ty shifted uncomfortably. "What plans?"

"I'm so glad you asked," Mom said. "Since you and Seth were so certain I should bid on a pony, you're going to chip in for a buyback next week—that's five hundred from each of you."

Alex cleared his throat. "I wasn't trying to talk you into bidding."

"No, you were too busy trying to manipulate me into doing what your father wanted. So I hope you're not trying to weasel out of paying your dues."

Alex had the grace to look guilty. "No, ma'am."

"I thought not. Fifteen hundred won't be enough for a buyback, but your dad and I agreed to chip in the extra. It's for a good cause after all."

Dad took her hand. "A very good cause. Wouldn't you say, boys?"

"Yes, sir," they said as one.

And just like that, Ty was financing a buyback—and saying goodbye to his big-screen TV.

Chapter 48

It felt even better than usual to sit on horseback this year. And that was saying something. On Saturday of the following week, Ty and his fellow saltwater cowboys rounded up the southern herd. A huge crowd gathered to observe the penning.

Then the next day the cowboys rounded up the northern herd on the refuge's restricted land. While the public wasn't allowed on this part of the refuge, they showed up in full force for Monday's annual beach walk. In an impressive display the cowboys ushered the northern herd along the Atlantic shore toward the southern pen.

The sun was barely over the horizon as they made their journey. A mild breeze carried the scent of salt and horseflesh as foals followed their mothers down the beach. The crowd cheered and took pictures as cowboys herded about fifty ponies and foals in all.

Tyson was relieved when they arrived at the pen without too much trouble. But they had difficulty getting some of the ponies into the corral. A few feisty stallions led the charge. It took a lot of finagling and the wisdom of some old-timers to make it happen. Finally the two herds were safely joined together.

That night Tyson collapsed into bed exhausted. But instead of sleeping, he thought of Jenna. He wished she were here. Even when she'd lived away from the island she'd always returned for Pony

Penning Days. It felt so strange not having her here. Strange peering into the crowd and not seeing her smiling face.

His heart gave a hard crack and he rolled over, seeking a better position. Was it too soon to call her? But he already knew the answer to that. It had barely been three weeks since they'd broken up, and he certainly wasn't over her. He'd promised her time and space. But then again he'd also promised this would get better. And so far he'd been completely wrong about that.

It wasn't the only thing he'd gotten wrong. He'd thought he'd gotten past his dad's abandonment. But Jenna's leaving had helped him see that wasn't entirely true. He understood her reason for leaving, her fears. And he had to accept that when people left, it wasn't necessarily about him.

And most importantly, that the people who loved him would eventually come back.

There would always be things he couldn't control, whether it was someone leaving him or an accident victim's fate. His new therapist was helping him understand that. Like Jenna had told him, he needed to learn to let those things go. He sure shouldn't let them stop him from living his life and loving himself.

He must've fallen asleep at some point because the blaring of his alarm woke him the next morning. He rolled out of bed, trying to hype himself up for today's vet check.

Ty reached the pen at sunrise. He and a few others had the honor of choosing the buybacks that would return to Assateague with their herd after the festivities. Those lucky foals—eleven this year—were chosen based on markings, parentage, and health. Ty had been hoping all along they could choose Dream's foal, and he was relieved when the filly passed the screening with flying colors.

The others agreed she was a good, hardy choice. He only wished Jenna would be here to see the auction that would set Dream's foal free.

The long day passed, followed by a restless night.

And then it was the day of the Pony Swim. Wednesday dawned and about forty-five cowboys arrived at the southern pen, tired from a long, exhausting few days but also exhilarated at the thought of the big event.

There was a lot of stress involved in herding 150 ponies and their foals over two miles of muddy marsh. The journey to the channel was always nerve-racking and somewhat perilous. It was challenging to get the whole herd to the crossing site in one bunch. Furthermore, for the ponies' safety, they had to cross during slack tide—a thirty-minute window between high and low tides when there was no current.

No one wanted any harm to come to the beautiful animals. Not to mention all the media or the tens of thousands of people who waited to experience the famed Pony Swim. It was a lot of pressure.

Tyson pulled his hat low on his head as Joe Barnes, one of the old-timers, opened the pen. "Let's do this!"

Jenna stifled a yawn. She'd been up before the sun and on the road. It was still early when she reached the causeway to the island.

A sense of freedom hit her as she drove over the channel. She was home, this time for good. Her life in Alexandria was over, and the thought didn't even make her sad. That chapter was over, and a new, exciting one was about to begin. Maybe her years away from the island hadn't gone exactly as planned. But she'd learned what she needed to learn. She'd arrived exactly where she was supposed to arrive.

And this chapter—the one that picked up where it had all begun—had been written just for her. The thought made her smile.

She couldn't wait to start her new job. Coastal Currents had always felt like a home away from home, and it would soon be hers. What a dream it would be to wake up every day and run the business she'd always loved. To see her beloved island's history passed on. She was equally confident her grandma would've approved of her use of the trust she'd left Jenna for her dream. She'd never felt so certain of her career's direction.

Even if she was less certain of other things.

Mom's house was a quick ten-minute drive from the bridge. Gordon's car wasn't there, but then Jenna had known it wouldn't be. He'd returned to DC, and the two were courting long-distance with visiting privileges extended both directions. Jenna thought that was wise of them. No reason to rush things.

Not bothering to knock on the front door, Jenna followed the pavers around the house where she found her mom enjoying her coffee and morning devotional on the deck. A cardinal tweeted from the bird feeder hanging nearby.

A pebble scraped the cement under Jenna's foot, alerting her mother to her presence.

Mom's eyes widened, then a smile bloomed across her face. "Jenna! What are you doing here?" She popped to her feet, still wearing her pale pink pajamas, and threw her arms around her daughter.

"You didn't think I'd miss the Pony Swim, did you?"

"Oh, I'm so glad to see you. You didn't tell me you were coming."

"I wanted to surprise you. And well, I hope you meant what you said about me staying awhile. Because it turns out I can't move into my rental until the end of August."

Mom drew back, hope in her eyes. "Your rental?"

"I'm moving back to the island, Mom."

"Oh, honey!" Mom threw her arms around Jenna again.

She laughed. "You're strangling me, Mom."

"Sorry!" She let loose of her iron grip. "You're really moving home? What happened? I thought you liked your new job."

"I liked it okay. It just wasn't what I needed right now. And then a week and a half ago I got a call from Miss Molly. She's selling her business, Mom—to me."

"Oh my gracious!" She clapped her hands in glee. "You love Coastal Currents. That's just perfect."

"Isn't it? I couldn't believe it when she offered it to me. I've been going over the financials for days, and it makes good business sense. The buyout will take place over the next two years—the trust Grandma put in place will be put to good use after all."

Mom gave a mock scowl and swatted her arm. "You could've told me. I've been over here missing you like crazy."

"Again . . ." Jenna waved jazz hands. "Surprise!"

"Oh, you! I suppose I can forgive you since you're moving home and all. Now sit down and tell me everything."

Jenna told her about the cute Cape Cod she'd rented over on Poplar Street. Miss Molly had agreed to pay Jenna a generous salary until the buyout was complete. Eventually she hoped to purchase a home—but that was a ways down the line.

When Jenna finished giving her mother all the details, Mom turned hopeful eyes on her. "And what about you and Ty? Are you back together?"

Jenna's heart sank a bit. She'd been so foolish to let him go. And now there was a possibility he'd decided to move on. She tried for a brave smile and told the truth. "I'm afraid not, Mom."

Chapter 49

Jenna shielded her eyes from the sun. Thousands of spectators waited to catch a glimpse of the saltwater cowboys and the herd of ponies across the channel on Assateague Island. Slack tide was starting, so it wouldn't be long now—if the journey had gone to plan.

The mayor emceed the event, broadcasting updates, her voice ringing loud and clear as the excited crowd watched and waited.

Jenna was on the pier with her mom and the Parkers, who'd come early to save their annual spot for the viewing. There'd been plenty of time for Jenna to catch them up on her good news, and the Parkers seemed thrilled she was moving back to the island.

On a happy note, Jenna finally got to chat with Alex's girlfriend, Suni, who'd come with him today. She seemed as delightful as Jenna remembered with a sunny personality and sparkling eyes that lingered on Alex. It pleased her to see Alex being treated with such affection. His whole family seemed fond of the woman, who'd apparently started coming around over the past couple of weeks.

While they waited for the ponies, Seth caught Jenna and her mom up on the drama at the fire station. Jenna could hardly believe Marissa had falsely accused Tyson of violence. Jenna hated that she hadn't been there for him in his time of need the way he'd always been there for her.

As if by design her eyes fell on a woman just down the shore. Her long blonde hair fluttered in the wind, and she tucked it behind her ear as she said something to her mom.

There was no denying that one-hundred-watt smile and dainty figure. She and her parents had a front-row view of the Pony Swim. A front-row view of the saltwater cowboys, who'd soon appear on horseback to the rousing cheers of the crowd.

Was Tyson thinking of a reconciliation? Had Jenna lost her chance with him?

"And here they come!" the mayor announced over the microphone. "Let 'em hear you!"

The crowd responded with enthusiasm as Jenna shaded her eyes. Sure enough, there were the cowboys, followed by the herd of ponies. They seemed to move as one large entity toward the channel. Whips slapped the air, the noise urging the ponies forward and into the water.

"Let's show 'em some encouragement, folks!" the mayor called.

The crowd cheered once again as the ponies plunged into the water. The older ponies who'd been doing the swim for years knew the drill. They led the way on the mile-and-a-half swim, which typically took only three to five minutes.

"Come on, babies, come on!" the mayor called as the ponies swam their way across the channel.

Minutes later as they neared shore, the sounds of neighing reached Jenna's ears. She skimmed her gaze over the herd for Dream and found the pony toward the front of the pack, her foal swimming at her side. Jenna mentally cheered them on.

Look at them, Dad. So strong and regal. Do you see them?

A moment later the ponies emerged onto the salt marsh and spread throughout the space as the spectators cheered their arrival.

Dream and her foal wandered into the grasses, meeting up with the rest of her band.

As the last of the ponies reached shore, Jenna smiled. Another successful Pony Swim for the books.

She gazed back at Assateague where the saltwater cowboys remained, watching from the shore. She scanned the group and thought she spotted Tyson's familiar silhouette staring her way. She imagined he was looking at her, though she would be impossible to pick out among the crowd. But she knew how he felt in this moment. The wave of relief that washed over him when they'd safely delivered the ponies.

You did it, Ty. Good job. I'm so proud of you. In the space of a few heartbeats, she felt such a connection with him.

But then she remembered how she'd left him, and the moment was gone.

After the swim Jenna and her mom made their way to the carnival grounds on foot. After a forty-five-minute rest the ponies traveled along the crowd-lined streets to the carnival grounds. She didn't have to wait long for their arrival. Led by the cowboys, the ponies appeared down the sandy lane and dispersed into the large pasture.

Ty stood at the corral gate, boot hitched on the low bar, watching the ponies settle. Jenna drank him in. She'd missed him so much. Longed to go right up and wrap her arms around his middle and press her cheek against his muscular shoulders.

But that was no longer her right.

Heart in her throat, she headed toward him, schooling her features into a benign expression. They were back to being just friends, which they'd been most of her life. Surely she could remember how—or at least manage to fake it.

Tyson turned and spotted her.

She froze for an instant. Her breath stuttered to a halt.

Then his lips curled into a surprised smile. "*Jenna.* I didn't know you were coming." He strode her way and gathered her into his arms.

Her soul seemed to relax into the embrace. She squeezed him, taking in the familiar scent and feel of him. She wanted to keep him right here where she could revel in his solid strength.

But he wasn't hers anymore. She forced herself to let go and propped up her smile. "I didn't tell anyone." She cleared the lump from her throat. "The swim went great. Mom and I watched with your family. Did you have any problems along the way?"

"Just the usual. Overall it went pretty smoothly." His gaze drifted over her face, lingering on her eyes for a moment. "I can't believe you're here. It's so good to see you."

The words put a catch in her throat. *Friends. Just friends.* "You too. You're looking well." She hated the formal note to her voice. Striking this balance was harder than she'd feared.

"Got a clean bill of health."

"I heard. Alex told me all about Marissa's shenanigans. How awful. I'm so glad you came out unscathed."

"That was a pretty stressful week. I'm sure glad it's over. But what about you? How's your new job going?"

"Oh, well . . . it was going okay, I guess, but—"

"Was?"

She gave a sheepish grin. "I don't work there anymore. In fact, I'm moving back to the island and I'm buying Coastal Currents."

His head jerked back. "*What?* Are you serious? Jen, that's amazing." He grabbed her up in another hug. "I'm so happy for you."

"Thanks. I'm really excited." Her smile was real this time because running that business would be a dream come true. But also because she was savoring the feel of Ty's strong arms and the familiar weight of his head resting on top of hers. He seemed genuinely happy she was coming back.

But the realization that she'd given all this up wiped the smile from her face. It was time to apologize for her appalling lack of courage. She'd hurt him too, after all.

"How did all this come about?" he asked.

She drew away. Tucked a wayward strand behind her ear. "Listen, Ty . . . I'll tell you all about it. But first I owe you an apology. The day I left I was a wreck. I let my fear take control and all I wanted to do was run."

He took her hand, his eyes softening. "I understand, Jen. I didn't like it, but I did get it."

"But those are *my* issues. I need to deal with them—and I'm doing that. I'm not going to let my fear hold me back anymore."

Something glimmered in his eyes. "That's great, Jenna. I want what's best for you."

Her eyes burned with tears at his selflessness. She squeezed his hand. "I feel the same about you. But I know I blew it when I left. And I wouldn't blame you if you've decided to move on."

"Move on?"

She had to come clean. "I heard you met up with Britt recently. I don't know what happened or is going to happen, and that's really none of my—"

"Jenna, stop." He pinned her with his steady gaze. "Nothing happened. Nothing is going to happen. I ran into her at the coffee shop and she asked me to sit with her. I'll admit she had some ideas about reconciling. But Jenna . . . I don't have feelings for her anymore." He squeezed her hands in his as his eyes grew intense. "Surely you know there's no room in my heart for anyone but you."

A chill swept over her. Her breath whooshed out as the tears overflowed. "Really?"

"How could you think anything else? I love you, Jen. I've missed you like crazy. Every day without you has been a battle. I picked up the phone a hundred times to call you."

"Oh, Ty . . . I've missed you too. I love you so much."

Joy flickered in his eyes and his mouth turned up at the corners just before his hands held her face just so as he brushed her lips with his.

Jenna melted in the wake of his gentle kiss. Was this really happening? She hadn't ruined things after all? She drew back, needing to see the answer in his eyes.

It was there, shining back at her in the steady affection in his eyes. In the soft tug of his grin. And then it was there in the form of his wonderful words.

"Welcome home, Greene. Don't you ever leave again."

Epilogue

It seemed spring had arrived early this year. The sun glimmered on the water as Jenna and Tyson guided their kayaks across the channel. Their paddles sluiced quietly through the water, propelling them toward Assateague. She relished the delicious warmth on her skin after the long, cold winter—their second together.

Three months after she'd returned to the island, Tyson proposed. Why wait when they'd already known each other for years? He popped the question as they sat cuddled on the beach, enjoying a magnificent sunrise. They had the moment all to themselves. His words sank soul-deep, the ring was just to her taste, and the look in his eyes was everything a woman could dream of. When it was the right man, the right moment, there was no doubt. No confusion. No panic. Just perfect peace and a beautiful, buoyant hope for the future.

They'd married last year, right before the season kicked off, in a small beach ceremony. It was a perfect May evening, mild temperatures with a gentle breeze coming off the water. Ty was so handsome in his suit. In front of the small gathering he held her hands and recited his vows, his eyes only for her. She reflected on that day often. On their amazing connection and their beautiful love born of friendship.

She was grateful for it every day. She'd moved into his place and was content in their comfy little nest—for now. But they'd recently begun talking about finding a new home—something with more space.

They'd settled into new routines. Tyson worked long hours at the B and B during the season. When tourism slowed down he took more calls from the fire company. Jenna's counselor had helped her work through her fears. She still got nervous when Ty was called out on a fire. But she was able to manage her anxiety, and Ty was so patient with her.

As for Jenna's business, Coastal Currents kept her very busy during tourist season. She loved the work. And while some days kept her tied up in the office, she made sure she spent the majority of her time doing what she loved—sharing the story of her beloved island and its wild ponies. She was currently anticipating the end of the year when the business would be all hers.

Winters on the island were slow, but she'd started a community volleyball league last year, which was already quite popular. Her mom and Gordon had even joined—they'd gotten married five months after Ty and Jenna. Gordon had sold his DC home to his sister and become a full-time islander. Jenna was thrilled to see her mom happily settled again.

As Ty and Jenna neared the shore, she swept her gaze over the salt marsh. Back in the trees she spotted two ponies from Dream's band.

"There's Dream," Ty said.

The white pony emerged from the woods, her tail almost glowing as the sun shone through it. The sight of her never failed to take Jenna's breath away. Never failed to make her think fondly of her father and remember his love for these ponies—and for her.

"Angel has to be around here somewhere," Ty said.

Two years ago when the Parkers realized Dream's foal had been selected as a buyback pony, they set their hearts on the filly. The brothers' bet money was put to good use. The foal went for almost five thousand dollars—but Jenna, her mom, and Gordon were happy to chip in. And Jenna was touched when the Parkers wanted to name the pony for her dad—Allen's Angel.

Angel recently gave birth to her first foal—a real surprise since the Chincoteague fillies didn't typically foal until their third or fourth year. Ty and Jenna had been driving to the island each day for a few weeks, hoping to catch a glimpse of the foal. They didn't always find the band, but they'd had pretty good luck recently.

As they reached the shore, Jenna let her kayak drift into the marsh and Ty came to a stop beside her. She whipped out the binoculars, adjusted the focus, and scanned the area around Dream. She spotted the band's stallion and another mare farther off. But no sign of—

"Jenna, look."

At his eager tone she lowered the binoculars and followed his gaze to a copse of trees less than fifty yards away. Angel emerged from the grove—and right behind her, a spindly-legged foal. Jenna sucked in her breath at the sight of the adorable pinto. "Aw, Ty, look at her."

"She's a beauty. Got her mama's markings and her grandma's mane and tail."

Jenna grinned from ear to ear as Dream made her way over to the pair. The foal tottered around its mama, short tail flicking. She and Ty watched the three generations in silence as the foal approached Angel and began nursing. Dream grazed contentedly nearby.

Of its own volition, Jenna's hand went to her tummy. She'd planned on telling Tyson tonight after his favorite meal. But this seemed like the perfect moment. She grabbed his hand and pulled his kayak closer.

His gaze sharpened on her face. "What is it?"

She paused a beat. "Angel isn't the only one having a baby."

Surprise flashed in his eyes just before a smile split his face. "Really? You're pregnant? Are you sure?"

Her laughter resulted from pure joy. "I'm sure. We *have* been trying—quite diligently, I might add—for a few months now."

"Oh, honey." He grabbed her face and kissed her sweetly. Then he stared into her eyes, remnants of shock and awe lingering there. "You're pregnant. We're gonna have a baby."

"That's generally what that means."

"Jenna . . . It's just . . . you've made me so happy." He breathed a laugh. "I didn't think I could be any happier, but I actually am."

She took in his big grin and the adoring way he looked at her. "Me too. We're due mid-December—during the slow season, just like we hoped." Jenna would stay home with the baby in the offseason, then her mom would retire to take care of the baby while Jenna worked.

"Best Christmas gift ever." Tyson set his hand on her still-flat tummy, staring at her in wonder. "I can't wait to meet our baby. You're going to be a wonderful mom, Jen." His lips tipped up in a dreamy smile. "I hope it's a little girl with her mama's brown eyes. Fair warning: I plan to spoil her rotten."

"Hmm. Maybe we should root for a boy."

"Honestly, I don't care which it is—so long as we're in this together." His expression sobered as his eyes grew intense. "I keep thinking back to that summer. I thought becoming more than friends was such a big risk. But falling in love with you was the best thing I ever did."

Jenna melted at his words as she cupped his face. "Oh, Ty. I love you." And then, right there in the sun-dappled water, saltwater breezes skating across her skin, she gave him a kiss that showed him just how much.

Acknowledgments

Bringing a book to market takes a lot of effort from many different people. I'm so incredibly blessed to partner with the fabulous team at HarperCollins Christian Fiction, led by publisher Amanda Bostic: Kimberly Carlton, Caitlin Halstead, Laura Wheeler, Becky Monds, Savannah Breedlove, Kerri Potts, Nekasha Pratt, Margaret Kercher, Taylor Ward, Colleen Lacey, Ellie Long, and Fred Sakai.

Not to mention all the wonderful sales reps and amazing people in the Rights Department—special shout-out to Robert Downs!

Thanks especially to my editor, Kimberly Carlton. It's hard to believe this is our last book together. Over the years her incredible insight has helped me take my stories deeper, and for that I am so grateful! I have learned so much from her and will carry those things forward into every story I write.

Thanks to my line editor, Julee Schwarzburg, whose attention to detail makes me look like a better writer than I really am.

Thank you to Hunter Leonard, fourth-generation saltwater cowboy, captain of the Chincoteague Volunteer Fire Company, owner of the Cowboy Cruise Company, and busy husband and father! He wears many hats but still made the time to answer my questions about the island, the fire company, and Chincoteague's beautiful wild ponies. Any mistakes are mine alone.

Author Colleen Coble is my first reader and sister of my heart.

Thank you, friend! This writing journey has been ever so much more fun because of you.

I'm grateful to my agent, Ami McConnell, who's with me every step of the way, cheering me on. What a blessing to have you in my corner.

To my husband, Kevin, who has supported my dreams in every way possible—I'm so grateful! To all our kiddos: Justin, Chad and Taylor, Trevor and Babette, and our four beautiful grandchildren. Every stage of parenthood has been a grand adventure, and I look forward to all the wonderful memories we have yet to make!

A hearty thank-you to all the booksellers who make room on their shelves for my books—I'm deeply indebted! And to all the book bloggers and reviewers whose passion for fiction is contagious—thank you!

Lastly, thank you, friends, for letting me share this story with you. I wouldn't be doing this without you. Your notes, posts, and reviews keep me going on the days when writing doesn't flow so easily. I appreciate your support more than you know.

I enjoy connecting with friends on my Facebook page: www.facebook.com/authordenisehunter. Please pop over and say hello. Visit my website at www.DeniseHunterBooks.com or just drop me a note at Deniseahunter@comcast.net. I'd love to hear from you!

Discussion Questions

1. Who is your favorite character from this story? Why?
2. How did you feel about the opening proposal scene? Did you identify with Jenna's need for escape, or did you feel sorry for Jason? What would you have done in the same situation?
3. Before this story had you ever heard of the wild Chincoteague ponies? Discuss the setting. Is this a place you'd like to live or visit?
4. Jenna and Tyson have been friends for years, through thick and thin. Discuss a similar friendship in your own life and what role it has played.
5. Jenna is suspicious of Gordon early on. Do you feel she had reason? How did her own fears escalate those concerns?
6. Tyson and Jenna are both pivoting from what they expected from their futures. Jenna is returning to the island jobless and boyfriend-free. Tyson expected to be married to Britt forever. Have you ever had to make a similar pivot? How did it feel? What were the results?
7. Tyson is dealing with guilt over losing an accident victim. Have you ever struggled with irrational guilt? What advice would you give him?
8. When romantic feelings develop between Ty and Jenna, they each struggle with the risks involved. Discuss those concerns.

How did you feel about their hesitation? Have you ever had to make a similar decision?

9. Jenna bears scars from losing her firefighter father. How did that trauma affect her life and the decisions she made?
10. In the story Tyson learns there are things he can't control and that he needs to let go of the things holding him back. Discuss the last time you let go of something unhealthy in your life. What was the result?

About the Author

Photo by Salve Ragonton

Denise Hunter is the internationally published, bestselling author of more than forty books, three of which have been adapted into original Hallmark Channel movies. She has won the Holt Medallion Award, the Reader's Choice Award, the Carol Award, and the Foreword Book of the Year Award and is also a RITA finalist. When Denise isn't orchestrating love lives on the written page, she enjoys traveling with her family, drinking chai lattes, and playing drums. Denise makes her home in Indiana, where she and her husband raised three boys and are now enjoying an empty nest and four beautiful grandchildren.

DeniseHunterBooks.com
Facebook: @AuthorDeniseHunter
X: @DeniseAHunter
Instagram: @deniseahunter